THE
PACT
WE
MADE

LAYLA ALAMMAR grew up in Kuwait with an American mother and a Kuwaiti father. She has a Masters in Creative Writing from the University of Edinburgh. Her work has appeared in the *Evening Standard, Quail Bell* Magazine and *Aesthetica* Magazine, where she was a finalist for the Creative Writing Award 2015. *The Pact We Made* is her debut novel.

THE
PACT

LAYLA ALAMMAR

WE
MADE

b

THE BOROUGH PRESS

The Borough Press
An imprint of HarperCollins*Publishers* Ltd
1 London Bridge Street
London SE1 9GF

www.harpercollins.co.uk

Published by HarperCollins*Publishers* 2019
1

A catalogue record for this book is available from the British Library

HB ISBN: 978-0-00-828444-2

Set in Adobe Garamond by Palimpsest Book Production Limited,
Falkirk, Stirlingshire

Printed and bound in the UK by CPI Group (UK) Ltd, Croydon CR0 4YY

MIX
Paper from
responsible sources
FSC™ C007454
www.fsc.org

To Mom, my first reader, for handing me a book all those years ago.

'At a very early period she had apprehended instinctively the dual life – that outward existence which conforms, the inward life which questions.'

Kate Chopin, *The Awakening*

'No man, for any considerable period, can wear one face to himself and another to the multitude, without finally getting bewildered as to which may be the true.'

Nathaniel Hawthorne

1

The Marriage Pact

We were eight years old in my first memory of the marriage pact. Mona and I were at Zaina's house. Her oldest sister had just gotten married, and we were bursting with talk of all that we'd seen and heard at the wedding. We looked like mummy brides, wrapped in her mother's headscarves. Mona had found ribbons and flowers which she'd braided and pinned into our hair. We took turns being the bride while the other two played the parts of sisters, supporting the train, giving admonishing smiles during the *Yelwa*, and bobbing up and down in exultant dances.

'When she came through the door, everyone was so quiet,' Zaina said, standing at the door to her room, holding a bouquet of fake roses. 'All the lights went out and there was just a spotlight on her, and then "Heb AlSa'ada" came on and she started walking. Like this.' She took solemn steps forward, her feet drowning in the heels we'd pilfered. Mona held and re-draped

1

her train as she walked. I was supposed to sing the song, but I was imagining walking down a long aisle with a spotlight on me while everyone stared. It wouldn't be like weddings we saw on television where the man stood at the end. It would just be me and a never-ending aisle leading to an empty settee. I could trip and fall, walk too slow or too fast, forget to smile at the photographer or drop my bouquet. Anything could happen.

'Dahlia!' Mona whined, drawing out all the syllables in my name. I started singing, but Zaina had already reached the desk chair we were using as a *kosha*. She turned to look over her shoulder while Mona metamorphosed into photographer, snapping shots of Zaina smiling, laughing, and looking coy. I knew what was coming next; I always got the groom's role.

'*Yella ya mi'ris*,' Mona hissed, waving me back towards the door.

I obeyed, hurrying down our makeshift aisle. Mona immediately sprang into action, chanting the groom's song as I walked back towards them. The man had it easier; he didn't have to milk the moment. He was encouraged to walk as quickly as possible to his bride. I got to Zaina and gave her a kiss on the forehead before taking the chair beside her. Mona re-draped the train and continued to snap fake photos as we interlocked our arms and mimed sipping juice from tall, flutey glasses.

'We should get married together,' Zaina said, sighing up to the ceiling. 'All three of us, on the same day.'

'Yeah!' Mona cried, clapping her hands together. 'And we can have one big party!'

'We could all walk down the aisle together,' I offered.

'No!' Mona and Zaina shouted, frowning at me. 'We'll take turns,' Zaina said with a nod.

'Who goes first?' Mona asked.

Zaina chewed her lip and picked at a scab from where she'd scraped her elbow. 'We'll go by the alphabet.'

'Yeah!' Mona exclaimed, linking fingers with Zaina and waiting for me to join.

My stomach clenched into something hard and tight and unfamiliar, but I added my fingers to our 'promise' link and we shook on it.

We were terribly young then, and they were only words.

The pact changed, evolving as we matured: at ten, we dismissed the alphabet idea as stupid and decided the eldest should go first; a few years later we would sometimes draw straws or have a competition to see who could flick their marble the furthest. We chose arbitrary ages that seemed far off in some unseeable future—twenty, twenty-two, twenty-seven. By fifteen I wanted out of the pact, but was kept in by Mona and Zaina's unwavering enthusiasm. At nineteen, Mona decided the pact wasn't cool and joined me, but in our early twenties the two of them were back in competition.

Our families thought the pact was charming at first, some adorable little fancy for little girls. They saw it as early confirmation that life would turn out like they expected it to, that their daughters would turn out as planned. Later, it became funny, an amusing anecdote to share at gatherings, something to laugh about with friends and aunties. Finally, it became tiresome, just one more thing for our mothers to worry about in their efforts to see us settled in happy marriages. Whose daughter would go first? Even then, there were comparisons. Mama wanted to beat the record she'd set with my sister Nadia, who was married at twenty-three. When Mona got rowdy, her mother would say she needed to set a good example for her younger sister, but what she really meant was 'Don't do anything to lower your chances.' And Zaina's parents were forever reminding her how small the country was, and how everyone knew everything about everyone and she should never forget that.

I've often wondered whether it might not be better to eradicate the nuclear family altogether, to just let us disperse like loose seeds, striking our roots into some foreign earth, unfettered by customs and bonds and the burden of ancestry. How much damage do parents do, unintentional though it may be? A word that cleaves the psyche, a withheld embrace that ripples through generations, an episode that festers like an open wound. Might these things not be so easily avoided if we all just scattered ourselves to the wind?

There was a lot of weeping in our house, mostly by me, but my mother did her fair share. There were times, when I wasn't speaking and spent my days locked in the bathroom, that I would wander the house at all hours of the night. Gliding down the halls and up the stairs like some restless spirit, I would pass my parents' room, and from within I would hear her sobs – like something was desperate to break free of her – and Baba's quiet, comforting nonsense. I never knew exactly what her tears were for – love, grief . . . despair. With my mother, it was like my little cousin Bader, who could never tell if the face you were giving him was a happy or sad one. I couldn't decipher her tears, and for the longest time I wasn't even sure she was on my side.

Our lives are sustained by rituals. Up in the morning, shuffle to the bathroom, pick out an outfit, coffee run, and head to work. Family lunches on the weekend and rushing outside when the first rain of the year comes. Gathering around the table for *futoor* during Ramadan and buying new clothes for Eid. Compulsory calls to relatives just back from vacation, three days of funerals for those that have died.

A man comes to see you, and it's a whole other set of rituals. You wait at the top of the stairs, never greeting him at the door – that's for your chaperones to do. When your mother and sister and aunts have ushered him into the fancy sitting room, you still wait five minutes or so. You stand on the stairs, and maybe your nerves die away or maybe they gather strength like a western dust storm, obliterating everything in its path. Finally you come down, you kiss his mother's cheeks and nod politely at him. Don't smile too much, that reeks of desperation. Let the chaperones do most of the talking; let him lead the discussion. He speaks English to impress you. Try not to spill the tea when you pour it for him.

'So, I'll be working at St Thomas,' he said, plopping two sugars in the hot liquid, 'but I'm also giving a lecture at Oxford while I'm there.' The stirring spoon looked tiny in his hand, like something from a dollhouse.

'But you're so young,' Mama exclaimed, nudging another slice of pound cake his way.

He shrugged with a smile that was meant to be modest, but I could see he was pleased with her comment. By midnight I would have forgotten what he looked like. 'Yes, well, I worked hard at school.'

'Dahlia always got by well at school,' she said, patting me on the knee. 'Decent grades, but I thank Allah every day she didn't get it in her head to be a doctor or some such.'

'It's difficult work.' He nodded. 'Long hours.'

'Yes, and a woman's hours shouldn't be spent on other women's husbands and children at the expense of her own,' added Mama.

'True,' his mother said, smiling at me like she was proud of the choices I'd made.

I didn't make many choices. It wasn't my choice that they should come over that night, or that I should participate in this ritual. The only thing I had chosen was my dress. It was my go-to number. Black. Simple – 'Boring,' Mama said – and straightforward. I'd worn it so many times that the buttons down the front had gone a bit loose and the organza layers of the skirt had dulled. It was the polar opposite of the one Mama had laid out on the bed. That one was colorful and frilly and not me. She'd bought it the previous spring because I'd needed to 'get in touch with my roots'. The dress was cocktail length, but designed to resemble a *dara'a*, with multiple layers of cotton and chiffon and thick silver embroidery in the shape of Arabic calligraphy. The fabric was rich, weighty with expectation, and I imagined for a moment that I could read my future in those curling, twisting letters: *noon* for Nasser, the name I'd always assigned to the hypothetical husband I might one day have; *ain* for wedding, the word that would return to everyone's lips over the next few months; *sa'd* for patience, which people always told me would be rewarded.

I'd squashed it into a heavy, loose ball and shoved it deep into a drawer.

'Her father considered medicine long ago, but I confess that I talked him out of it,' Mama continued, shaking her head. 'It was selfish, but I wanted him home at normal hours, not spending his nights with dying people.'

'A natural instinct,' the suitor said, inclining his head like he was at an interview, which I suppose he was.

The *sadu* carpet under the coffee table was woven in thick strands of black and white and bold red. Geometric patterns bordered by thick blocks of color. An Arab's idea of neutral. I picked a thread at random and followed it down through the weave. My eyes tracked it up and over the ziggurats, sliding down the incline of a diamond, hopping across little interruptions of white. The pattern was a choice someone had made, the will of another that the thread was obliged to bend to. If you picked the right thread, you could follow it back to the beginning. Thread Zero, the one that started it all, the one holding it all together, that one element upon which everything was built.

Did my life have one such string? If I pulled at it, would it all come crashing down?

*   *   *

7

Later, when our guests had left with promises of forthcoming calls, I headed to a complex of restaurants by the water. It was a beautiful night, clear and calm, with that sweet, clean scent that was such a rarity. The parking lot was full of Porsches and BMWs growling with impatience; I'd borrowed the Jag, and I handed it over to the valet despite knowing Baba wouldn't like it.

I left the line of rumbling cars behind and walked the long corridor of the open-air compound. There were portable heaters dotted around the outdoor seating areas, their flames high and orange. A Mexican place had tiki torches instead, but they didn't seem to do the trick judging by the people in their coats and wraps. There was barely any conversation to be heard over the clinking and clattering of plates and glasses, the obsequious tones of waiters, and the tinny music dropping from the speakers. Hardly any of the people at the tables were even facing one another; instead their chairs were directed at the aisle I was walking down. They fiddled with their phones and watched the people passing by; sometimes they turned to their companion to comment on something – a skirt too short, a blouse cut too low, or a patently ridiculous choice of footwear. I was wholly unremarkable, I knew, with the boring black dress and my sensible slingbacks that didn't have red soles. I passed unnoticed, eyes barely sweeping my form before moving to the next person.

I moved through the outdoor seating area of the Italian restaurant where I was meeting the girls. The queue was five groups deep at the door, but I spotted Zaina seated at the far end of the area and the hostess waved me through.

She gave me a big hug and said, 'Mona's running late as well.'

I took the seat across from her, facing the water. The restaurant jutted out over the shore, slightly away from the main complex; it was quiet away from the hullabaloo at the start of the compound. For a moment I could almost imagine I wasn't there, but at a café on the South Bank, watching lights play over the Thames. But it was Kuwait, and the moon was out, low and slinky in the sky, trailing a long, blurry milky way in the water. A light breeze played with my hair and ruffled my dress, but it really wasn't too cold.

A waiter materialized at our side seeking a drinks order, his gray and white uniform crisp and glowing in the light. I asked for water. Zaina already had a Coke in front of her, and she barely looked up to tell him we were waiting on a friend when he tried to shift to food orders. She tapped at her phone, and I stared at the water. Minutes passed. I got my water, and our table got a bread basket and a plate of vinegar and olive oil before she put it down.

'So, how'd it go?' she asked, coffee-colored eyes turning to me.

'Same old, same old.'

She scowled and leaned forward, elbow to table, rounded chin in palm – the picture of attentiveness. 'Well, what happened?'

I was too tired to rehash it all, but I knew she wouldn't let up, and it was better to get it out before Mona joined us and spun it into a whole thing. I never knew where to start with such stories, so I just said the first thing that came to mind. 'We talked about . . . scuba diving.'

Her brows rose against her pale forehead. 'Why?'

I shrugged helplessly.

'I mean, what got you there?'

I shrugged again. 'We were talking about that Gutentag Red Bull thing—'

'*Flugtag*,' she corrected with a laugh.

'Whatever, and that led us to talking about extreme sports in general, and that took us to scuba diving.'

She frowned thoughtfully, her fingers playing with the gold hoops in her ears. 'Is scuba diving an extreme sport?'

'In my book, it is.'

'And did you tell him you're scared of open water?'

I shook my head. 'Mama was giving me her agree-with-everything-he-says-or-I'll-kill-you look.'

'Ah,' she said, nodding along with the sympathy of someone who'd been on the receiving end of such a look. 'So, not a love match, then?'

I let out a mirthless laugh, my eyes straying over the water. 'That's not really the point, is it?'

She leaned back in her seat, pulling her olive-green scarf tighter around her. 'I guess not.'

The water rolled in and out. Our eyes met, and I could tell she was about to force this cloud away. It was a familiar routine. 'Well,' she finally said, 'maybe he'll want to see you again, and it'll go better.'

I pulled a slice of bread from the basket and started tearing it into small squares I had no intention of eating. 'You do realize we were talking about this same shit when we were in college? Ten years, Zaina.' She nodded along, eyes glazing over, and I knew she was thinking back to those hours in the cafeteria where all we could talk about was which of our classmates we'd consider marrying. 'I was so naive. I just assumed that by the time I was thirty I'd have those things we went on and on about, like it was a given. But look . . . it's a decade later and nothing is different.'

'I know.'

But she didn't know. Her gold wedding band, tucked under the five-year-old engagement ring, bore silent witness to the fact that she might have understood what I was talking about intellectually, but she didn't really *know*. How could she? I shook my head again and turned back to the water. She was preparing a more elaborate reassurance, I could tell, but Mona showed up before I had to hear it.

'Sorry, sorry, sorry. Traffic was a nightmare,' she said, bustling around the table to drop kisses on our cheeks before taking a seat.

Mona was all flashing lights. If I found solace in blending in, Mona was my opposite. She lived for the flash, loved the spotlight, craved all those appraising eyes, confident they always found her worthy. Everything about her was designed to attract attention, from her Mia Farrow circa *Rosemary's Baby* hair to the outfits and the statement jewels. I often wondered if we'd have been friends had we met later in life, or if she'd known at six how little I'd end up caring about fashion, how utterly drab I'd be capable of looking. Though perhaps that was a positive in her eyes, a contrast designed to highlight her fabulousness, like a matte frame on a glossy photo.

The waiter bustled over as soon as she was settled. Luckily Mona was never one to ponder menus and asked for her standard chicken salad. Zaina opted for a salad as well. I'd planned to console myself with a plate of pasta, but I crumbled under pressure and seconded Mona's order.

'How are the plans coming along?' Zaina asked when he'd noted everything down and left.

'Not bad,' Mona said, running a hand heavy with cocktail and knuckle rings over her smooth, brown hair, and I thought, if I were as small as her I'd cut off all my hair as well.

'Rulla's gone a bit crazy on us,' she continued, 'which is weird timing since all the plans have been finalized.'

Zaina gave her a sympathetic look. 'It's probably just because it's getting so close.'

'Yeah, but she needs to calm down. I was never like that for my wedding. She completely lost it at Mom when we were at the tailor the other day. The florist called to say her bouquet would have ten white roses instead of fifteen, and she lost her mind.'

'Why can't she have fifteen?' I asked.

'The bouquet would be way too big, proportion-wise,' she replied, looking at me like it was obvious. 'Rulla thinks bigger is better, but she doesn't need that many.'

Zaina nodded in agreement. 'So what happened?'

'Nothing,' she said with a shrug. 'Rulla and Mom started

yelling at each other, Mom stormed off, and I gave Rulla a lecture on proportions all the way home,' she finished with a chuckle. 'Oh, yeah, I almost forgot.' She put a hand on my arm to get my attention. 'You're going to be in the *Yelwa*, right?'

I was saved from an immediate answer by the arrival of our food and the resultant shuffling of things on the table to make space, the offers of extra cheese, more bread, fresh pepper and the like.

The last time I participated in a *Yelwa* must have been at Zaina's wedding. That particular tradition is the only one where the bride doesn't really take center stage, despite being perched on her own little makeshift throne. No, the focus isn't on her, but on the ones surrounding her – the unwed girls, family and close friends circled around her chair, holding a large, green and gold embroidered blanket over her head. I remember the feeling, standing there clutching my bit of fabric while all the women watched us flutter and flap the thing over the bride's head. They ought to have been directing good wishes to the bride, and perhaps they were, but everyone knew the women took it as an opportunity to get a good look at the unmarried girls. *'That one in pink might appeal to my son.' 'The one in yellow is too tall.' 'Yes, but prettier than the one in ruffles, don't you think?'* We were presented for quite a long time: at least fifteen minutes, or three songs, whichever finished first. Standing there, flapping and fluttering the fabric, trying to keep in time with the music and the chants of blessing. Flapping and fluttering, until our elbows locked and our arms threatened to fall off.

'Hey,' Mona said, drawing my attention back to her. 'You'll do it, right?'

I puffed out a breath, pushing my fork through the salad. 'I don't know.'

'What do you mean, you don't know?' she said, frowning. 'She's my sister.'

'I'll be the oldest one doing it.'

She smiled, and though it was full of sympathy, it wasn't lacking in resolve. 'All the more reason not to say no.'

I looked from her to Zaina. She was holding her breath, forever fearful of confrontation. But it was such a little thing, and Mona and I had been friends for a long time. I nodded my assent.

'Excellent,' Mona said, attacking her salad with relish now that things had been sorted. 'It'll be fun.' I scoffed at her attempt to console me. We'd been to a lot of weddings; she wasn't fooling anyone. 'Okay,' she continued, black eyes drifting up to the sky in thought for a moment. 'You, Heba, Eman, and Fatima makes four from our side. The groom's family can get the rest from their end. Did I tell you how my aunt called to remind me about it?' Zaina and I shook our heads. 'She calls and goes, "Mona, how many virgins have you found for the *Yelwa*?"'

Zaina nearly choked on her chicken, and my laugh caught the attention of the guys at the neighboring table. Mona leaned forward, and we followed suit. 'I said to her, "I can find unmarried girls, but beyond that I make no promises."'

The boys shifted their torsos towards us, leaning forward and back around each other for a better view at what had us laughing so hard. We pulled in even closer to one another, Zaina's hand covering her mouth as she giggled uncontrollably. I shook my head at the nonsense our aunties were capable of speaking. Finally, we composed ourselves, calm and quiet in a moment, reduced to a dome of decorum, and Zaina asked Mona about her job. I wasn't listening though; I kept thinking about what Mona's aunt had said. I wondered what it would be like if the *Yelwa* cloth could somehow detect non-virgins, like if the fabric started to smoke when I held it. I imagined the pointing, the gasping, the shaking of heads as the fabric burned my fingers. I wondered how many girls it would smoke for; would I really be the only one?

Later that night I lay panting in my bed. There was a vise around my lungs, squeezing tight. It burned. I sucked in air through my nose and mouth, great big gulps, but it didn't help. My lungs continued to sting like acid. I flicked on the lights, turned on some music, needing as much stimulation as possible. Maybe it would distract me from the sensations, from the certainty that I was, at that moment, dying.

There's this lore, or perhaps it's superstition. It's about a demon called a *yathoom* who comes to you in the night. He sits on your chest, feet splayed in a squat, growing heavier and heavier until you wake because you can no longer breathe. Even waking will not save you; he'll cling while you gasp and scratch at your breasts. When you feel on the brink, like you can't take it anymore, the *yathoom* rolls off and back down to hell. He's only supposed to visit on Thursdays, which is both arbitrary and unexplained.

I've had one for years. He adheres to no schedule and cannot distinguish day from night. His splayed feet bear claws, sunk into my chest beneath my armpits. He is a compression on my lungs that I can't shake. Some days he gives me respite, curling on my diaphragm so I'm hardly aware of his presence, but it's never long before he's back, slathering my lungs with his black cement tongue. I tip my head back every so often, mouth open in a silent scream, but nothing startles him. He just hugs me tighter.

Sometimes I think my *yathoom* is my loneliness in form and function. Something my subconscious has obsessed over so much, it's been made real, like that mythological monster who only exists because you believe in him. Maybe that's true of all monsters, I'm not sure.

2

Hush

'So I'm going to start a film club,' Yousef said, plopping himself down on the corner of my desk and sending documents drifting to the floor.

I scowled and bent to retrieve them. 'Like a movie club but pretentious?'

'Ha ha,' he replied. 'No, seriously. I want to start a club and every month we'll screen a film and discuss it. And it won't be blockbusters or even festival darlings, it'll be little-known movies and adaptations . . . like that *Tempest* film we watched. That was fun, right?'

I nodded. 'Sure.'

It had been fun. He'd set up a projector in the apartment he had created for himself by converting the basement of his parents' house. He had low, squishy sofas that swallowed you when you sat in them and a large blank wall onto which he projected movies. The copy had been of poor quality; he'd said it was from the 60s and had been meant for television.

Less fun had been the discussion, though it was more of a lecture, that had followed the film. We'd both read the play in our respective schools, but he maintained that sixteen-year-old me couldn't have hoped to contemplate something so complex. I couldn't say twenty-nine-year-old me fared any better, but I could see how into it he was. He spoke of how the sprite Ariel and the monster Caliban were facets of Prospero's identity – how Prospero wanted to protect his daughter, Miranda, while also lusting after her in some subconscious beastly manner. Putting his psychology degree to some use, Yousef went on about ids and super-egos and the renunciation of power and dominance.

It was all well and good, but such concepts flew right over my head. All I'd gotten from the film was a strange crush on the actor playing Ariel, captivated by the shapes his body made as he flung himself around the rudimentary set. I was left with a desire to sketch him – the pointy ears and sharp features and wiry hairs sprouting from his blue-silver head.

'So, yeah, I'm going to start one out of my house. Spread the word,' Yousef said, twisting his torso so he could see his reflection in the window of my cubicle. He wore fancy shirts to work, with slim-fitted jackets and pocket squares and tapered pants, instead of the standard *dishdasha*. In all the years I'd known him, I'd never seen him in one, and I always suspected it was more to do with not wanting to wear the *ghutra*, which was notorious for causing premature baldness, in order to preserve the thick, black hair he kept gelled in a perfect wave rising up and away from his forehead.

We left my cubicle and headed for the staff room. Yousef busied himself making a pot of coffee while I dug around in the cabinets. As the coffee started brewing, Yousef lit a cigarette and started smoking out the open window, trying not to set off the smoke alarms.

'You're going to get in so much trouble one day,' I said, shaking my head.

He shrugged like trouble was inevitable. 'I forgot to ask,' he said, tapping the cigarette against the window sill, 'did your mom bring that guy over to see you?'

'Yeah,' I replied with a grimace.

'And?'

'Disaster.'

He chuckled. 'As expected then?'

'Yeah,' I said with a little laugh.

He nodded and poured out half a cup of coffee. Taking several puffs from the cigarette, he put it out on the sill and tossed it in the trash. He held out the pot of coffee, but I shook my head. 'Well, I wouldn't worry about it.'

'Why would I worry?' I asked with a frown.

'Just because . . .' We made our way back towards the office, and he paused at the elevator. I was going up two floors to a meeting. 'You know . . .' I did know. I adored Yousef, but I felt like stabbing him with a pen. Forcing a smile and a nod, I waved him away.

Yousef, like everyone else, it seemed, was tremendously worried about my next birthday. Still months away, and its significance had already grown to mythic proportions. If I remained prospectless at thirty, I may as well give up on life entirely; the pool of acceptable men, already quite small, would shrink further as they set their sights on younger and younger girls. My aunts would start calling with questions like, 'Is it okay if he's a divorcé?' and 'How do you feel about raising another woman's children?' As though these were questions with clear-cut answers.

With arranged marriages you're asked to pass judgment on people you don't know and on situations you don't fully understand. Those initial queries of interest have nothing to do with personal compatibility. They're as impersonal as questionnaires. I wondered what potential men were told about me . . . *'Well, she doesn't wear the* hijab – *is that okay?' 'She's a bit tall for a Kuwaiti girl.' 'No, I don't know how much she weighs, but I'll ask.'*

Bu Faisal was there when I arrived, sipping at a Turkish coffee and reading the front page of the paper. He rose to greet me with a smile and firm handshake, purple prose spilling from his lips like it always did. There were at least fifteen minutes of embarrassed laughter as he ran through his 'There's my favorite account manager' and 'They should put your picture up in reception: boost business!' routine. He was of my father's generation; they'd gone through the same bureaucratic training ground before heading off to their careers. Our families had been quite close once upon a time, spending weekends at each other's beach houses and meeting up on summer trips to London or Paris. His dark eyes were kind, but practically disappeared beneath low lids when he smiled, the crow's feet extending far and deep. He had a generous mouth and thin black hair that was salted at the temples.

Our ceremony done, he tugged at his pants' legs and took a seat. Bu Faisal with his three-piece suits, always the same design, whether it was blue or black or gray or brown. He must have had a dozen of them made – all of them expertly stitched in heavy fabrics, twills and sharkskin wools, with Thomas Pink shirts peeking out at the collar and sleeves, and color-coordinated silk pocket squares. Like Yousef, I'd never seen him in a *dishdasha*.

'How are you, my dear?'

'I'm good,' I replied, settling into my seat across from his at the small meeting table. 'How was Tokyo?'

'Oh, you know the Japanese,' he said with a wave of his hand.

I shrugged and chuckled. 'I don't actually.'

'Everything's so small there. Makes me feel like a bear blundering through a museum gift shop. I did find this for you though.' He reached under the table for a black gift bag.

'You shouldn't have,' I said with a small frown. Bu Faisal had a habit, which I could not break, of bringing me little things from his business trips. Chocolates, perfume, scarves and trinkets. I tried to hint that it was inappropriate to accept gifts from clients, but he never got it, or more likely chose to ignore it.

'It's nothing at all,' he said, waving his hands as I peered into the bag. 'Just a little thing I saw that made me think of the flowers you draw everywhere.'

I pulled out the item nestled among the white and pale pink gift paper. A Japanese folding fan. It was made of light-colored bamboo, overlaid with scallop-edged ivory silk. The design on it looked hand-painted and very old: a winter landscape, all white fields, black trees, gray skies and crystal blue ice. Snowflakes fell from the sky, looking like cherry blossoms coming to earth. There were ladies walking through the scene, ducking beneath parasols, the reds and oranges of their kimonos like red-breasted robins streaking across the snow. The trees were black and bare and laden with powdery white; bent with hunchbacked heights, they made me think of this ukiyo-e art I saw in a book, floating worlds, like Hokusai's *The Great Wave off Kanagawa.*

I turned it over, gently running my hand over the delicate silk. 'Is this an antique?'

'I don't know,' he replied. 'I found it in a shop and thought you'd like it.'

I shook my head, trying to think how much it might have cost him. 'I can't accept this.'

He pulled back with a look of mock horror. 'Don't be silly! What will I do with it if you don't take it? Keep it. It's nothing, I promise you.' I was of a mind to protest further, but he changed the subject. 'My accountant still needs to send you some documents, but you should have them within the week. How's work anyway?'

I shrugged, returning the gift to the bag and laying it on the table. '*Hamdilla*. Work is good.'

'And our boy, Yousef?'

'Really good. We can stop by and see him after the meeting if you like.'

'Yes, yes, after the meeting,' he repeated with an officious nod and a grin. 'Let's talk risk, shall we?'

And we did. We talked risk and premiums and protections. We went through all the accounts, for all the many holdings across all his many businesses, all of them insured by our little firm because our chairman was an old squash buddy of his. I didn't know exactly how insurance schemes worked, and he had so much money that at times I felt like he must have been insuring himself as well as all our other clients in some round-about manner. I was not qualified when I took over his accounts a couple of years ago. Bu Faisal and I had run into each other by chance when he came by to say hello to the chairman. After asking how the family was getting on, he'd asked Bu Mohammad if I could handle his accounts. I was given some of his smaller holdings to start with, but he preferred dealing with me rather than Old Haithum, who'd been with the company thirty years and always smelled like cardamom and paprika, so after a while I was given all of his accounts to manage. For the most part, the work took care of itself, and when it didn't, he usually knew what I needed to do to fix it.

Bu Faisal was married to an old friend of my mother. Despite how close they used to be, I only saw his wife every once in a while, at a wedding or reception of some sort. She looked how most Kuwaiti women of her generation would like to look: hair long and thick, with highlights that looked natural; a face kept young with regular injections of Botox and collagen; a body

23

that didn't bear witness to the four children she'd had. She would get up and dance with the younger girls at weddings, tying a scarf around her hips when the belly-dancing numbers came on. She wore the outrageous jewels and big-name brands that she told you were from Paris or Milan, even though they all had branches at the local mall.

When I was younger, when our families used to spend time together, Mama would bring up their marriage a lot. 'Look at how Bu Faisal treats her,' she would say, pointing at him serving his wife tea, so unlike my father and uncles, who expected their wives to do that sort of thing. Or when his wife would show off a ring or necklace he'd bought her, and Mama would turn to me and my sister and say, 'That's the sort of man we want for you,' as though lavishing someone with gifts made for a perfect marriage. She painted him as the ideal man, and my sister gobbled it up, but I wasn't so easily convinced. At an early age I'd learned about men and the masks they wore.

Evening fell and with it the temperature. There was a definite chill in the air: on the tip of your nose; in the soles of your feet; across your shoulders. I sat in the garden, giving in to my desire to sketch Ariel from the film I'd seen with Yousef. I was attempting to duplicate those delicate features and lithe form, but my sprite was looking nothing like the actor.

It was something I often did, try and replicate things I'd seen in films or famous paintings in galleries I visited on vacation. Usually I would alter the paintings in some way, twist them into something relevant to my own time and place; I'd add

Bedouin tents to a background or turn an English nose into one more reminiscent of a Saluki. Less often an image would come to me, fresh and original, and I would rush to transfer it to a sketchbook, but I was, for the most part, powerless to execute these things my mind conjured. I found more success with paintings and illustrations that were already created. When I was younger, I'd dreamed of going to art school, of becoming an artist, but Baba maintained that art was a hobby and not a career and besides, copying work rather than creating it probably wasn't what art schools looked for. I'd done business at university because I was 'meant to', and I subsequently took a job in the finance industry because I was 'meant to'. It was expected of me, like it's expected of most of us.

I abandoned Ariel and started doodling my namesake in a halo around his head, petals curling around his pointy ears. I'd been drawing dahlias since I found out my name was a flower. My father had come back from a business trip once and brought me a coloring book of different flowers. When I'd colored them all, I tried drawing them from scratch. He bought tracing paper and taught me how to secure it with paper clips, then, his hand over mine, he showed me how much pressure to put on the pencil as I followed the lines and curves. Over and over, until I could do it with my eyes closed.

My dahlias were everywhere: on old schoolbooks; on the knees of the faded jeans I ran around in; along the borders of other illustrations I attempted; on steamed-up car windows, notepads at work and paper place mats at restaurants.

Raju, the houseboy, startled me, wheeling out the *duwa* – the

25

tea trolley with built-in charcoal pit. It was brass and silver with shiny black wheels. A tea set was loaded on the bottom shelf: little glass cups; sturdy metal teapot from the old *souq*; mini-cans of condensed, tooth-rotting milk. He set it before me like I'd asked for it and went about lighting the charcoal cubes. Baba stepped out the front door with a 'Ha!' when he saw me curled up in the wicker chair. He swung his arms to the front and side, an akimbo Macarena, a bastardized version of the routine we'd all done during morning assemblies at school.

He stepped off the porch and into the yard, surveying the grass for bald spots and inspecting the date trees. It's a barren land, but you wouldn't know it looking at our garden. The proper names of trees and vegetation aren't common knowledge in Kuwait, at least not among the younger generations. If pressed I could possibly have identified an orange tree, but only if it were blossoming. Baba wandered over to his herb corner as Raju finally got a proper fire going and left the *duwa* in my care. My father squatted down on his chicken legs to check the nets protecting his rosemary and mint. He was happy, enor-mously happy, his only concern whether the street cats were messing with the herbs again. There was a particularly fierce tom, a wall-prowling howler with a personal vendetta against mint, who tore through the nets Baba set up and gnawed at the baby stems and leaflings. This infuriated him. I'd suggested, more than once, that he move his herbs inside, but he said they would taste different if they were grown through glass.

The front gate opened, and Nadia and her brood spilled into the yard. First came the twin boys, tearing across the grass to the trampoline Baba had set up for them in the corner. 'Shoes off!' I called as they hoisted themselves over the bar, a directive that was ignored until their grandfather sent over a quelling look.

Then came the little one, Sarah, tiny hand clutched by Nadia as she had a distressing tendency to sprint towards the street. She tugged and tugged, but only when the gate was firmly shut behind them was she released and allowed to fly through the yard and jump in my lap. Nadia couldn't get so much as a greeting in until Sarah was done telling me about her day: there was the spring show rehearsal and the girl next to her who didn't know any of the words; there was the PE class where she wasn't chosen in Duck, Duck, Goose; there was the teacher who was having a baby, and why couldn't Mommy have one too?

I laughed over at Nadia, who had a horrified expression on her face. 'Maybe in a few years, baby,' I consoled Sarah, running my hand over her curly hair, so much like mine when I was her age.

'But I want one now,' she whined into my neck.

'I'd sooner shoot myself,' Nadia mumbled, jerking her chin towards the boys, who were half jumping, half wrestling on the trampoline.

I cuddled the little one tighter in my lap. 'It'd be okay if you had another girl.'

'Can I get a guarantee?'

Mama came out to join us, and Nadia rose to greet her. Sarah wanted to stay put, but I nudged her to her feet and over to her grandma.

'*Hayati!*' Mama lifted a wriggling Sarah up into her arms for a hug and a smattering of kisses. When she put her down, she scurried back and climbed into my lap. 'Go play with your brothers.'

'*La Yumma*,' Nadia said with a shake of her head. 'They're too rough with her on there.'

Sarah didn't seem inclined to move anyway, snuggling up to me while we talked over her head. Eventually Baba abandoned his garden to come get her; he pushed her on the swing set, trying to teach her to propel herself. I'd forgotten about the *duwa*, but Nadia always had impeccable manners, and she got up to serve Mama. The tea might have been too strong at that point, but she tipped the pot over a cup so it came out in a steaming, perfect arc. She filled the cup almost to the brim, knowing how our mother liked it, then cracked open a can of condensed milk and filled the remaining space with the white, syrupy liquid before handing it over.

I was a mistake. Various members of my family, at various times, have said it. Always with a smile or a wink, but the words don't change. My parents, though they married young, had problems conceiving. Mistrustful of Western medicine, my mother watched the moon instead, counting her cycles, frequenting the lesser pilgrimage, and drinking teas of sage and fenugreek and anise. After six years, when the dismay was so entrenched that Mama had broached the topic of my father taking a second wife to give him children, she finally conceived. Nadia was received like an heir to something greater than what my parents had to offer. They took their miracle baby and wished for nothing more. Eight years later, I announced myself when Mama vomited at a table laden with four types of fish.

'Oh,' my sister said, turning to me, 'I forgot to ask how it went the other night.'

I winced. Mama frowned, but I couldn't tell if it was because of the topic or because the tea was too hot. 'No effort from this one, as usual.'

'*Yumma*, don't start,' I said, shaking my head.

'What? She should know what I go through with you. I set out a beautiful *dara'a*, blue and silver and bright, and she wears black like she's going to a funeral. He's a wonderful man. Tall, smart, lovely eyes, and she stares at her knees all evening.'

'I was being demure.'

'Ekh!' Mama said, flicking her hand at me like I was a fly that required swatting. 'Allah forgive me, it's almost like you don't want to get married.' She shook her head, giving off an impression that was equal parts martyrdom and disappointment. If she were Catholic, she'd have been crossing herself. Turning to Nadia, she added, 'Talk to your sister before she becomes a spinster and—'

'Dies,' I finished, making Ariel's wiry hair a bit too dark.

'Allah forgive you,' she hissed, smacking my thigh. 'Don't say such things.'

'You're the one talking about spinsters,' Nadia retorted in my defense.

'Well, we're getting there.' She sighed like she was carrying an impossible burden and folded her arms over her stomach.

I dropped the sketchpad and pencil on the floor and went

to join the kids. The boys were running screaming circles around Baba. They would never have to concern themselves with this. Their lives would be so easy. They would have freedoms my sister and I never contemplated: the freedom to study anywhere in the world; the freedom to live their lives without constant scrutiny, where society responded to their mistakes with 'boys will be boys' instead of 'you bear the family's honor'; and, perhaps most meaningful of all, the freedom to *not* marry without shame or guilt. My heart slumped at what was in store for Sarah. She was still in the swing, whining about not being strong enough to propel herself yet, so I obliged her. Nadia and Mama continued to talk, my sister tossing out gentle reprimands that my mother deflected like a ninja.

Let them talk. It was all just words.

3

A Grotesque Pandemonium

Did I have a happy childhood? It's hard to say. I suspect many of my memories are compiled from the stories of others. That if I peeled back Nadia's hand gestures, tossed out Mama's commentary, and blacked out Baba's impressions, I would be left with no memory at all save for perhaps some flashes of light or lingering scents. As a result, I put very little faith in my recollections. I'm unattached to them, can go over them with all the emotional connection of someone flicking through a waiting-room magazine. Mona and Zaina would argue about things in our past, each passionately denying or affirming what had or hadn't happened and in what sequence. And when my vote was sought, they'd huff when I insisted I didn't remember.

I was rarely lying when I said that.

There are flashes, though; scenes I remember with eye-watering clarity. One vacation in London where Baba took us to a museum because, 'You need culture. Not just games and fun and shopping.' I was twelve, and Nadia and I rolled our eyes all the way to Bloomsbury; even Mama huffed when the taxi drove down Oxford Street. Once there, Baba hustled us through the courtyard, not allowing us to pose for the obligatory gate shot: 'Later, when the rain stops.' It was before the renovation, before that geometric-patterned, glass monstrosity was installed overhead. He pushed us past Ancient Egypt, past the idols and the hybrid gods with their perfect posture. He allowed no more than a pause before the hieroglyphs. On through to the Assyrians, to something we could claim, as though our family roots were in Iraq and not central Saudi Arabia. We stood before reliefs of military campaigns, of hunting with chariots, of demons and human-headed bulls, while Baba talked about what he knew of Mesopotamia. Nadia got into it; she had wanted to study history at university, and she started arguing with him about the city of Ur, only for him to spin it into a discussion of Ibrahim and Nimrod and a fire that didn't burn.

Mama and I left them there and meandered through Greece and Rome, past the amputated statues and more white reliefs showing battles and processions. Mama admired the drapes and folds wrapped around the sculptures, the way they looked like real fabric, and I stood over the shoulder of a girl as she sketched what she saw before her – hands and arms, tilting heads, and warrior poses. I watched her hand, the deft and sure movements, and the way she looked up, then down, then up again – drawing as she watched, and watching as she drew. It was mesmerizing, like a pendulum swinging back and forth. Mama took my hand and we stepped into the Parthenon, our footsteps loud in an otherwise hushed room. We went down the line quickly, hardly stopping to look at the chariots or centaurs or horses. 'They all look the same,' she said. I allowed her to pull me along; those headless figures didn't interest me. And then we reached the end of the room and came face-to-groin with a statue of a man, his privates on display, hanging there like forgotten fruit. My eyes went wide, and my mouth fell open at the sight. Mama gasped, this choked sound that seemed to bounce off the marble and multiply. She clapped her hand over my eyes as she urged me to the door, but my hearing was heightened and all the way back to Baba and Nadia, I heard her stifling her laughter.

For the remainder of the day, every time I caught her eye or she mine, we would giggle behind our palms like schoolgirls.

Mona's husband, Rashid, joined us at the mall for lunch on Saturday. Architect by day, sculptor by night, I liked him from the first time I met him. I hid it well, my affection for him. Even Mona, with all the years she'd known me, with the very way in which they'd met, had never realized it. And on the occasions when he joined our outings, or nights in, or the odd time – like that Saturday, when I became a third wheel – I was careful to remain distant so as not to sound any alarms.

After lunch we went our separate ways, Rashid to the furniture stores while Mona dragged me around the shops. She tried on outfits while I oohed and aahed on cue. I tried on shoes while she thumbed-up or thumbed-down. I endured a makeover at the makeup counter, docilely accepting lipstick and mascara while trying not to think about communicable diseases and whether there was such a thing as eye herpes.

The mall was a series of shop-lined walkways that fed into wide, octagonal spaces where you could pretend it wasn't as claustrophobic as it seemed. You could imagine you didn't feel the need to curl into yourself, smaller and tighter, until you were a ball of no consequence. On weekends the malls were packed: high school and college kids in their designer clothes loping from one end to the other; girls in their sky-high heels pouting their lips and flipping their hair; the brunch groups taking pictures of their food and asking the waiter to take one more shot of them. For each group like these you'd find one of the more traditional sort, women in full *niqab* with their little girls covered up in the *hijab* and their husbands with the long beards and short robes moving from one end of the mall to the other like it was another kind of pilgrimage.

There was so much there, stimulants bombarding you from all sides: bright lights bouncing off gleaming floors; neon in all the windows, on the people; shouting and laughing and music and shopkeepers asking 'Can I help you?' over and over. Try the new fragrance from so-and-so, the new moisturizer from this-and-that. Buy, buy, buy. Maybe if you consume enough, you can fill all those holes in your heart and head and soul.

Too much. It was too much. It attacked me from all angles until a circuit tripped in my brain. And then, a fog would descend and I could pretend, for just a moment, that I was like all the others. Normal and in desperate need of an edible food basket for a friend's birthday.

They didn't often believe me, on those rare occasions when I divulged my anxiety; people sought justification, saying it was impossible to feel panic on, say, a lazy Saturday at the mall. 'Besides, you don't look like you're having any kind of attack,' they'd say, gesturing at how still I was when inside I was malfunctioning. They didn't understand how, at those times, it wasn't so much that the panic was taking over as that the calm was evaporating. And I had to reach and grab for it like the string of an escaping balloon. Sometimes I'd catch it; I could bring it back down and hug it to my chest. Other times, it just floated away.

In any case, I had a firm grip on it that day as we walked through the crowds. Past the perfume corridors and café eyes, we wound up at a fro-yo place. Mona took a seat, giving her shopping bags over to the empty chair beside her, and turned to face the people walking by. She liked to be prepared. We'd already run into two former colleagues of hers and a girl we'd gone to university with. Saturday at the mall, it was unavoidable, and Mona liked to see before she was seen.

It was my turn to choose, so I stood in line, looking over the options, while she scanned the faces in the crowd. By the time I'd picked our toppings, she was on the phone. I shoved two spoons in the swirled yoghurt and fruit and headed back to the table. As I slid into the seat on her other side, she mouthed 'Rashid' while pointing at the phone and rolling her eyes. I smirked, imagining he was trying to convince her they needed a new coffee table or corner piece. She listened mainly, saying 'yes' or 'no' but not much more.

35

And then it happened. Just like in the movies. My spoon even froze halfway to my mouth and my brain stuttered like it had hit a speed bump. Rashid walked by, with that purposeful New York City stride he'd never lost, head down and eyes on the store catalog in his hands. Mona turned to see what I was looking at, her mouth dropping open then sucking her bottom lip between her perfect white teeth. I could still hear a male voice, tinny and far away, yammering into her ear. But it was not him.

It was not him.

Rashid didn't see us and kept walking. I returned my spoon to the bowl and stared into the crowd. Mona hissed and snapped into the phone before hanging up and dropping it into her open purse. She steepled her fingers, a ring on every one so you could hardly see the wedding band, and met my eye.

It was a long silence. Her soda fizzled and snapped. The fro-yo started to melt. My heart pounded, and I had trouble thinking. Her foot jiggled under the table, tapping mine with every other beat, but she must have thought it was the table leg. The people were loud; they passed in front, behind, and around us. They yelled out orders to friends heading to the counter. They laughed about things we couldn't hear. They scraped back chairs and rapped knuckles on tables.

'If that was a colleague or friend, you would have said so,' I finally managed, but my voice felt like it wasn't mine, and I didn't know where the words came from.

'Dahlia . . .'

'Why didn't you just say that?' I asked, shaking my head 'Why didn't you just say *that*?'

She mirrored the shaking, her eyes going shiny, and I thought to myself she'd better not cry. 'I wasn't thinking.'

'What?'

She repeated herself, but it didn't get through. I leaned towards her. 'Are you sleeping with him, whoever he is?'

The look she gave me was very close to pity. 'Dahlia . . .'

I nodded, feeling foolish. 'How long?'

'Please—'

'How long?!' I tried to keep my voice down, but there was adrenaline and my fingers trembled.

She shook her head down at the table. 'A couple of months.'

My brain stuttered again. I leaned back in my seat, crossed my arms and covered my mouth with my hand. It was not possible. This was some bizarre dream. My best friend couldn't be one of those people, the kind we heard about all the time and shook our heads at. Mona put her elbows on the table and pressed her palms to her ears, like she was trying to block out the noise around us or contain her thoughts.

'You don't understand.'

'What's there to understand? Rashid is perfect.'

She flopped both arms to the table and scoffed. 'Nobody's perfect.'

'Clearly,' I sneered. 'I can't believe you would do this. I honestly can't believe this.'

She reached forward to grip my hands, but I recoiled. 'You can't tell anyone.'

'Are you even listening to yourself?' I barked. 'What is wrong with you?'

'Look.' And now she had her 'be reasonable' face on, the face that managed to convince anyone of anything, and I turned my head to avoid it. 'I made a mistake, okay? An awful mistake.' I snorted, but she continued. 'Things have been rough with me and Rashid these last few months and I made a mistake. But I'm going to end it, okay?' I looked at her. She looked sincere. I wanted to believe her, but she felt like a stranger. 'Just don't tell Zaina, please. I'd die if she knew about this. I'm going to end it.'

'If you don't want to be married, tell Rashid you want a divorce.'

'I love him.'

'Give me a break,' I replied, shaking my head again. 'You wouldn't treat him like this if you loved him.'

She leaned forward, eyes darkening. 'You don't know anything about marriage, Dahlia, even less about love. You don't know what my relationship with him is like, so don't sit here lecturing me about what love means.'

I sat back and crossed my arms, averting my gaze. 'I've been in relationships.' She made a sort of mocking sound. 'I have,' I insisted.

'Who?' she replied. 'That Fahad guy? That lasted like two seconds.'

'Not Fahad,' I said, my voice low, my eyes on the strangers passing by, on their way to regular lunches on a regular Saturday at their regular mall.

She followed my gaze, chastened. 'Hamad.' She nodded. 'That was real.'

It had been real. My first boyfriend: we'd met at my first job when he spent a few months interning there. He'd reminded me of Rashid in a lot of ways, and perhaps that was why I'd said yes to him when I'd never so much as entertained the thought of anyone before. He had the same prominent nose, kind, sleepy eyes, and a full mouth that was always smiling. Only his build was different – slighter than Rashid's tall, broad frame. He was patient and gentle, eager to please and reassure.

Slowly, so slowly, he coaxed me out. His kisses were praising and yielding. His hands the hands of a follower, a supplicant, never demanding more than I would give.

We spent hours in his green jeep, parked in dark, empty lots, at the beach, or on empty side streets. We would talk about life, about leaving Kuwait, about religion and Ancient Egypt. He told me about Istanbul, the only place outside of the Middle East he'd ever been, and I told him about our family trips to anywhere Baba could think of. We sang along to the radio and played thumb-war and tic-tac-toe on the fabric of my jeans.

We discovered that when he kissed me behind my left ear, I'd make a sound I hadn't known I was capable of. I discovered that my hands didn't tremble when I *wanted* to touch a man. I learned not to panic when his weight settled on me, that his hands would not bring pain.

I've always had difficulty remembering events of an intimate nature. I can never remember full sequences, only little snapshots. I don't remember everything that happened in Hamad's green jeep. Whenever I think of those nights, all that comes to mind is blue cigarette smoke, lights on the console, and his breath on my shoulder when he decided to write on me with a ballpoint pen. I hear the knocking of innocent limbs against dashboard, his hum against my pulse, and the interjections of the Turkish singer blaring from the stereo.

What we had (love?) was art, and we made each other art.

At one point I told him what had happened to me.

I see that conversation in snapshots too. Wretched silences. Bursts of rage, fists on a black steering wheel. 'It wasn't my fault.' A dead sky. 'I know, but . . .' Tears dripping onto the backs of my hands. 'It wasn't my fault.' A prominent nose in profile, sleepy eyes looking out of the sunroof. 'I know, but . . .' Hand moving, fingers inching across the center divide. 'It wasn't my fault.' Fists on thighs, clenched. 'I know, but . . .'

A couple of years later I was reading the newspaper, and my eyes drifted over the back page. His name was there, in bold black print, his much-too-young age in brackets next to addresses for the men's and women's funerals. Over the next few days I would see the small article about the accident, and the picture with the charred green jeep flipped on its back, and everything would feel terribly, terribly pointless.

I shook the recollections from my mind and returned my eyes to Mona. The anger flared in me again, like the catching of a candle's wick. 'It's not about love,' I said. 'It's about respect and affection and the fact that he doesn't deserve this. And even if I don't tell him or Zaina—'

'If?!'

'It won't change the fact that you did it. That for months, you lied to him, to all of us. I mean . . .' I shrugged my shoulders.

'What kind of person does that?' Her eyes were shiny again, but my sympathy was nonexistent, and I couldn't look at her anymore. I stood and grabbed my bags.

'Please don't tell anyone,' she said, but I was already moving.

The worst thing about knowing of Mona's infidelity was that nothing changed. For the whole of the following week, she continued to participate in our group chats with Zaina as though the betrayal meant nothing. She sent pictures of the record player Rashid had purchased (her husband squatting at its side and pointing at it with a big, goofy grin) because he'd suddenly decided to start collecting vinyl. She cracked jokes and suggested evenings for us to come to her place.

I'm lying. That wasn't the worst part. It was her nature to avoid an issue by pretending it didn't exist. We had that in common, I think. But this thing . . . the idea of adultery had always been very far away, an alien concept I never needed to concern myself with. But then it was there, a stranger sitting between us. I didn't know what to do with it. I kept quiet in our chats, but then I thought that seemed suspicious, so I overdid it. I spun plates on sticks while it seemed like Mona couldn't care less. I obsessed over the real-life implications of it.

I used to try and picture Mona and Rashid having sex. The first time was the night of the wedding, after they had walked out of the ballroom – him in his gold-lined black *bisht* and *ghutra*, her in a body-hugging lace number cut low in the back. Later, when I was home, in bed, with hairspray-stiffened hair and a full face of makeup I was too tired to wash off, I wondered how they would proceed. She'd told us, me and Zaina, that she and Rashid had done 'everything but' in the time they'd been together: she'd told us about the first time she blew him, in the front seat of his car, and how she'd cried after because it was the first time she'd done that and it wasn't supposed to happen like that and what would he think of her; Zaina and I could recount, with disturbing accuracy, every detail of their first kiss – right down to the song playing on the radio when it happened (Meatloaf's 'I'd Do Anything For Love', which we teased her about mercilessly); we knew when and where she'd let him touch her. We'd even been go-betweens when they fought, a two-headed Switzerland shuttling messages and apologies back and forth.

She'd said she was saving herself for him, or rather for whom-ever she'd end up marrying.

Would it be fast and frantic? Or slow and gentle, Rashid showing off his stamina? Would she cry that first time? Would he be patient when she tensed, or would the frustration show on his brow, in the line of his lips, the strain in his neck?

But now there was this nameless, faceless man to contend with. This nameless, faceless man pressing down on her, taking what she'd decided to give so freely. This usurper, this pickaxe scraping at their marriage. I hated him. I hated him for catching her eye, for worming his way in, for being whatever she thought Rashid wasn't.

I chewed over her insistence that she loved her husband, worrying at it like a chipped tooth. Intimacy and trust, I'd learned from a young age, were very different from sex or what passed for it in our society. It was easy enough to divorce one from the other, but for her to have that trust with Rashid, to say she loved him, all while giving her intimacy to someone else . . . I couldn't fathom it. My brain refused to process it. No, that's wrong. My brain had no trouble comprehending it. The part of me that struggled was something else. Something mobile. Something that slithered from my mind and sat heavy on my sternum.

Baba walked around his little kingdom, hands clasped behind his back like a general inspecting his troops, and admired the green shoots and little buds sprouting all over. His skin was darker than usual from hours spent in his garden while the weather was agreeable. He stomped up and down every so often, pushing to test the firmness of the dirt. If it was too soft, I heard him grumble about the houseboy over-watering – 'Leaves the hose on and goes to talk on the phone, that donkey.' Every so often he called to where I sat in my white plastic chair, soaking up the sun, and said something like, 'Look how tall the tomato plant has gotten,' and I would nod and smile like an indulgent parent. 'The radishes will start popping up soon,' he said, squatting low to the ground for a better look. When everything was deemed satisfactory, he pulled up a chair by me, sinking into it with a '*Ya'Allah*,' and a happy sigh.

We sat in comfortable silence for a while. Unlike Mama, my father never felt the need to fill pauses with mindless chatter. I inherited that, and some of my fondest memories of him contain no words – just blessed silences. That morning wasn't one of them, though.

'So nothing came of that boy then?'

I kept my eyes closed, feeling the sun through my lids. 'I guess not.'

'Your mother hasn't heard from them . . .' I couldn't tell if that was a statement or a question; either way I chose not to respond. 'It's fine.'

'I know it's fine.'

'I think she has another one lined up for later this week.'

My heart pounded, once, twice, all jangly, and I suddenly felt like crying. 'She hasn't said anything to me.'

'You know how she is. She likes to wait till the last possible minute to tell you. I think she thinks it makes you less likely to find a way to escape.'

'I don't know why she thinks the situation is so desperate.'

He chuckled, folding his arms over his gut. 'Your birthday is just around the corner.'

'Have you approved of the guy?' I asked, pushing my fingers through my tangle of curls.

'On paper, yes.'

I nodded; it was important for things to line up on paper. 'Do you know when they're coming?'

'Thursday, I think.' The houseboy passed us on his way to the gate, talking on his phone, and Baba took the opportunity to yell at him about over-watering and how he'd break that phone if he kept doing it. The houseboy pocketed it, nodding like a bobblehead, and scurried out the gate. Baba leaned back in his seat, attention once more on me, and said, '*Shidday hailich.*'

'What does that even mean?' I replied, sitting up and turning to him. 'Can you stop and think about that phrase for a minute? Really think about it. What exactly am I supposed to "try harder" at?'

'You know—'

'No, Baba, listen. You and my aunties and Mama, you spit out that phrase like it's no more than a punctuation point, like it doesn't cut me every time I hear it. How am I supposed to try harder at something I have zero control over?' I said, slicing the air with my hand. 'I sit here waiting for someone to choose me. Not only does the mother have to approve of me, but then I have to appeal to the guy. How can it work with odds like that?'

He accepted my mini-rant with a pensive nod, looking back out over his garden. My eyes followed. Was he thinking, like I was, how much simpler it would be if life followed such sure rules as seeding, watering, and reaping? Was he wishing he could control all our lives with such certainty?

It had worked with my sister. Nadia had played by the rules; she had never so much as had a personal conversation with a man until she'd met the one she would marry. Their marriage was arranged by Mama and her sisters when Nadia was twenty-three, and the first time she'd met Sa'ad had been at our house when he'd come to see her. Baba had given him an ultimatum; he could talk to Nadia on the phone for one week, by the end of which they would either make their engagement official or sever contact. Four months later they were married. That was fifteen years ago; Sa'ad had given her a beautiful house and an easy life, and Nadia had given him two sons and a daughter.

It had all worked out exactly as it was meant to. As sure as the cycles Baba went through with his garden. Almost too easy, some would say, which is probably why they got me.

4

A Marauding Heart

I am the tree that falls in the forest, needing proof of my own existence. When I look in the mirror, I don't always recognize the reflection. I don't mean in the way older people sometimes see their younger selves; I mean, I don't recognize *me*. The way my eyes, dark brown no matter the light, dip down at the inner corners like commas on their sides strikes me as new each time. I look at my hands and knuckles and think them strangers. The single tiny hair that sprouts from the top of my right foot is not mine.

I need reminders that I'm here, that I exist, that this isn't all just a dream within a dream.

Seeing myself bleed is real. Blood is a living thing you can't explain away. It pushes out, sticky and inconvenient. It demands attention. Simple and real. I only cut myself a few times, back in the days when I couldn't get the feeling of fingers creeping along my thigh out of my head, when I couldn't stop feeling the squeeze of a hand on the barely-there rounds of my newly adolescent butt, or the sensation of slimy rubber lips brushing my cheek. I swore I wouldn't make the cutting a habit because a) I liked the feeling; the pain (that was real), the blood, and the mark it left behind, and b) even then I knew it was something that would demand escalation, and I have a fear of scars.

I find a perverse delight in accidental bleeding, though. I cut my finger on a bit of broken glass once. It sliced through the knuckle, skinning me clean. I stood at the sink, finger under the tap, and let it bleed and bleed. The red streaming from my fingertip, swirling pink in the drain, felt more real than the wooziness in my head, more real somehow than the pain in my hand. I could see it. And I often believe what I see over what I feel.

My feelings are like my reflection, like the commas in my eyes and the hair on my foot. I struggle to verify them.

Thursday. Another dress on my bed. This one was cream with a floral pattern, big pink roses splashed across the bodice and down the full skirt. It was even frillier than the last, and I wondered whether Mama knew me at all, or whether she thought that was the mold I had to fit in order to land a husband, after which I could revert to being myself, the way some married women eventually stop shaving their legs.

I rubbed the fabric between thumb and forefinger. It was new, strong, and rich. Which shoes would I pair it with? In the closet was my black dress, fresh from the dry cleaners. I ran my hand over the comforting organza, fingering the small buttons down the front, and wondered if it was possible for a dress to be disappointed in me. Pulling it off the hanger, I spread it on the bed, pulling and draping until it covered the other one, until the flowers appeared more mauve than pink.

I would always hear them before I saw them. The suitors. Mama entertained them in the formal living room downstairs before I made my entrance. Even though no one could see me coming down the stairs, that was where the jitters hit hardest. My palm would get clammy on the banister, my heart would shiver in my throat, and the dress would suddenly feel too tight or too short or too low in the front. There was a moment, two or three steps from the bottom, where I was convinced I'd either fall or pass out, and I always hoped it was the latter because that, at least, could be blamed on something other than clumsiness.

I would make my decision based on their voices. Nothing more. Not looks or height or body, not beautiful hands or trimmed toenails peeking out from open-toed sandals. Pausing just around the corner, I would wait for the man to speak, and then I'd make my judgment. I didn't resort to any predetermined list; it wasn't about tone or pitch or how nasal the voice was. It was something unnamed. Call it a gut reaction. I stuck with it.

This one was an immediate and unqualified 'No'. I arrived in time to catch the end of some sentence about working at a bank, but it was enough. The voice was harsh and unforgiving, abrasive even. Like it was waiting to dole out some retribution. No.

The face that went with it was deceptively charming: straight, aristocratic nose, sun-burnished skin, wide smiling mouth. When he rose to greet me, I saw that he was tall with a broad frame that attested to some sort of regular athletic endeavor. Probably water sports, I thought, taking in his bronze face and hands.

Nadia was there to chase away the awkwardness with all manner of social niceties. She and the suitor got along perfectly. Mama and his mother got along perfectly. If only Nadia wasn't married, it might have been a perfect match. It turned out they had both gone through the same bank branch back in the days before Nadia became a housewife, and they reminisced about crazy managers, dunderheaded office boys, and insane clients. Finally, she turned to incorporate me into the conversation, asking leading questions to which I gave small, unremarkable responses. Mama's disappointment skipped across the sofa and into my lap, staring me in the face. But I was helpless to stop it. I couldn't be the engaging thing she wanted me to be. I'm not my sister. Maybe at one point I could have been, but the moment was gone, and we couldn't retrieve it.

My heart throbbed in my fingertips, and I pressed them into the fabric of the sofa. My scalp tingled like a million insects were crawling across it. This uncomfortable feeling, which I should have been used to by then, strangled me. I had an urge to bolt, to feign illness – and wasn't I sick? – and leave. But I stayed put and struggled not to fidget.

He tried, asking me what I liked to do in my free time, and I confessed my illustrations. He seemed genuinely impressed and asked what it was I drew.

'Monsters, mainly,' I said, gritting my teeth when Mama's fingers pinched the skin behind my knee. 'Big hairy ones with ugly teeth.'

Mama laughed it off, pinched me again, then quickly changed the subject. She hadn't seen my new Ariel obsession, only the Goyas that were multiplying on the walls in my room. She'd begged me to take them down, but I refused.

The Caprices. Eighty etchings in which Goya condemned the follies of eighteenth-century Spanish society. I often thought the Europe of that time was remarkably similar to twenty-first-century Arabia: the ignorance and shortcomings; vices and marital foolishness; the rationality infected by persistent super-stitions. It was all there, in those grotesque images, with the anthropomorphized asses and the scheming witches and the yawning maws of terrible men. I'd printed out a third of them already, taping them to the wall even though Mama had yelled at me that it would ruin the paint, and why would I do that for something so hideous.

They were hideous; I couldn't argue with that. At times, I confess, I struggled to see the 'art'. But there was something there that stayed in my mind long after I'd stopped looking at the prints, and perhaps that was essentially what art was. It was not light and shadow – those belong to Doré – nor was it the playground of Blake, full of prophecies and symbols. It was not the chilling details of Dürer or the Gothicism of Harry Clarke. I couldn't name it, but there was something there that required my continued attention.

*   *   *

When they were gone, Mama followed me upstairs to my room. I was already unzipping the dress, letting the petal skirt and cream bodice fall to the floor. I nearly tripped over it in my heels and did a little side shuffle in an attempt to stay upright. Mama watched from the door with a frown, but I managed to get the dress off the floor and into a heap on the bed without injury.

'Well,' she said, 'he's perfect, right?'

I chuckled, stepping out of my shoes and rubbing my toes. 'That's what you said about the last guy.'

'He was perfect too, and if you had put in a bit more effort maybe you'd be engaged to a doctor now.'

'So he was better than this guy?' I asked. She made a noise of frustration and threw her hands up. I shrugged on a robe and let down my hair, pulling out the strong, sharp bobby pins to free the heavy curls. 'Does it not matter at all who I marry?'

'No,' she replied. 'As long as it's a good match, I don't care who it is.' I turned to her, eyes wide, and she crossed her arms under her breasts. 'And if you don't like my choices, maybe we'll go to *khataba* and see who she can find.'

'A matchmaker?!' I gaped at her. 'Are you insane?'

She shrugged. 'Many people use them nowadays. What do you think, Dahlia, that there's one perfect man out there for you? Do you think you'll fall in love, and then he'll come seeking your hand?' It was on the tip of my tongue to mention Mona's love match, but I swallowed the words down and yanked out a tangled pin, pulling three long black strands with it.

'Children think that way,' she continued. 'You're much too old for such nonsense.'

'I've never said anything about a love match.'

'Your actions speak loud enough! Tell me; tell me what's wrong with this one? What do you object to?'

I shook my head down at the little mound of bobby pins before me, and I could only speak the truth. 'Nothing.'

I didn't have to look to know a smile had spread across her face. 'So, I can tell his mother "yes"?'

The moment felt monumental. The expectations, Mama's hopes and dreams, my fears and any courage buried in me seemed to dance in the air between us. It was not a dance; it was a battle, a frigid war I hadn't agreed to. I could have said yes, if only to avoid another fight, on the off chance that he'd say no. I saw his warm brown eyes, his white smile, his nods and jokes. He wouldn't object. And in any case, I couldn't risk it, not with a voice like that.

I shook my head, and it was all she needed. Crossing the threshold, she took hold of my arm and jerked me towards her, grabbing my other bicep and shaking me hard.

'Are you trying to kill me?' Her fingers dug into my skin; I was not at all protected by the flimsy robe. 'Why are you doing this to me, Dahlia? Why!'

'I'm not doing anything to you.' In my head it was a scream, but it came out as a whimper. 'This isn't about you.'

She was still shaking me, and she was so mad, when she spoke, I was hit with spittle. 'Is this your way of punishing me? Tell me! You're punishing me, aren't you?'

'No!'

'Then give me one reason, one good reason to say no to him.'

'I don't have to give you any reason!' I broke her hold, inadvertently shoving her away so she hit my dresser with her hip. The vanity swayed precariously, the big, heavy mirror threatening to tip over, until I rushed to steady it.

I was breathing hard. I didn't look at her, my eyes focused on where mirror and table met, trying to keep it upright. 'You can't force me to marry him, or anyone, no matter how much you wish you could.'

She was quiet for a long moment. Long enough for me to set the mirror right. Long enough for me to pick up the toppled-over perfume bottles and tubes of lotion. Long enough that I no longer had an excuse not to look her in the eye. So quiet, and I thought there could not be anymore to say and why wouldn't she leave and how much worse did she want me to feel?

'Do you never want to get married?'

There were tears now, but I wouldn't let her see them. 'I'm not even thirty yet. It's too soon to worry about that.'

'No, it isn't,' she replied, turning to leave. 'It isn't at all.'

In the shower I scrubbed myself raw, until my skin was an angry red – just like the showers when I was fifteen.

I realized a long time ago that, in a lot of ways, my body is not strictly mine. It's a shared entity, something to be criticized, guarded, commented on, and violated. I learned it at twelve when Nadia said I should start shaving my legs. She sat with me in the bathroom, showing me how to lather up with lots of soap, how to go against the grain – 'So it cuts at the root, idiot!' – and how to tear off tiny bits of tissue to plug up nicks. At thirteen Baba decided I wasn't dressing right. I had to wear skirts with hems below the knee and long shirts that fully covered my butt. Why I should have to hide my thirteen-year-old body from strange eyes I never asked, although I soon learned if you caught a man's attention, no amount of baggy clothing would deter him. Sleeveless tops were forbidden and V-necks couldn't dip too low (though at the time, there was nothing to conceal). At fifteen any sense of self I had, any sense of control, was ripped away from me, taken to a place where I feared I would never find it. At seventeen, when I was eating non-stop, Mama forced me to the *memsha*, a public walkway that stretches around our neighborhood, driving the car on the parallel road while I ran because nobody would marry a fat girl. At weddings, appraising eyes dissected me. In the street, men with greasy eyes let out catcalls.

That wasn't the point. I'm digressing. Besides, I relinquished control of my body a long time ago. I no longer have a connection to it. Perhaps I never truly did. My point is that my life was not my own either. It too was something to be controlled, commented upon, and directed to the will of others.

My mind drifted while I rinsed white, rose-scented suds from my hair. I tipped my head too far back and hot water pushed up my nostril and down my airway. It happened fast. One minute I was breathing, the next I was choking, like something had been shoved in my throat. In the steam and harsh jets of water, I was convinced I was dying. Scrabbling back against the cold fiberglass door I tried desperately to suck in air, but all I got was water and steam. It was blocking my nose and tightening my throat. I reached for the door, slipped and hit warm tiles.

The autumn of my thirteenth year was exceptionally warm, and we spent every weekend at the beach house taking advantage of the long days and pleasing tides. I was gazelle-brown by week two. Always the best swimmer, I had to be bribed into getting out of the water. They never worried about me, even though I swam out the furthest, dove the deepest, and opened my eyes underwater despite the sting.

There was one scorching day. My family stayed close to shore, splashing and lazing under umbrellas jammed into the mud. Maids came out with a succession of icy glasses of water, rainbow juices, and thick wedges of pink watermelon and orange melon. The youngest cousins, only toddlers then, decorated their sandcastles with blueberries and grapes, wailing when my aunties yelled and swatted at them.

I heard the wailing from where I was, treading water several meters out. Lifting my legs, I floated on my back and stared up at an empty sky. I leaned my head back until my ears were submerged. And then, it was silent. Blue above, blue below.

The boys in the neighboring chalet lowered their jet skis in, sending rolling waves that bumped me up and down, up and down. I righted myself to avoid water up my nose. With a roar of twin engines, they raced past me, the younger one skidding to the side so a sharp spray hit me full in the face.

I dived then, deep down in the blue where no one could find me. Open mouth for a big breath like I was about to swallow the sky. Then, like a dolphin, arching into a dive. Kick, kick, bigger kicks to propel me down, down. Open eyes, the sting will go away. Further down, until I hit it, the spot where the water is cold, where you're wrapped in this alien iciness, like a portal to another world. Look up, it's like a window in a thunderstorm, all wavy lines and squiggles. When the lungs are almost uncomfortable, start kicking back up; it's easier, you can relax because physics does the work, lifting you back to sun and safety.

I misjudged. I opened my mouth and nose and lungs too soon, sucking in warm, salty water. I flailed and splashed and couldn't breathe, couldn't scream. Flashes of light burst behind my eyes, and water sank into my ears. My *yathoom* wrapped his legs around my chest and squeezed. There were hands grabbing at me, strong arms lifting me and pressing me against broad shoulders, water draining off my body. Mama screamed at her cousin—a cousin who, orphaned as a child, had been raised in her house as a sibling, and who we called Uncle Omar—screams of panic and confusion and anger and still I couldn't breathe. His face swam before my eyes, blurry and indistinct, until they closed. My lungs gave up. Then there were fists on my chest, hitting much too hard, rattling my ribs. Then two lips, slimy and cold like fish, on mine, forcing my mouth open, forcing the air in, blowing me up like a balloon. Rough hands gripped my face when it wanted to turn away. Wet fingers, like sea cucumbers, made my mouth stay in place. Rubber lips, hot air, fists on chest, over and over and over. And still I couldn't scream.

5

The Architect

The next day my mother and I called a truce, unacknowledged and porous as it was. I'd woken with fingertip bruises and little crescent moons on my arms. There was a kink in my shoulder that I couldn't stretch out and a purple bruise, the size of a lemon, on my hip from the fall in the shower—a sour reminder of bruises long faded.

After my shower, after the panic, as I'd lain wrapped in a towel on my bed trying to connect with my lungs, I'd heard yelling from the living room. I got up and pressed my ear to the cool wood of my door to make out their words. In my head, there'd been the echo of a teacher from my childhood, telling me that the punishment for eavesdropping was flesh-eating worms blanketing you in the afterlife. It didn't stop me though, and I heard my father say, 'Leave her alone. Let her be for now.' 'She didn't even apologize,' Mama said. 'Pushed me into the dresser and your daughter didn't even apologize.'

I heard Baba's harsh breath and snort of frustration. 'I'm sure she will. It was an accident.' (It *was* an accident, but she got no apology from me.) There was quiet then, a quiet so long I thought perhaps my father had gone to their room, but then I heard her voice, low and resigned. 'I worry about her.' 'Of course, you do,' he said. 'Stop pushing her. Let her breathe a bit.' That was all I'd heard; any reply my mother might have made was too low, and I'd returned to my bed.

So, the day passed in silence, and as evening fell she asked me to sit in the living room with her while she watched an old Egyptian movie. I sat on the sofa opposite her with my sketch-book in my lap. I'd found a print by Fuseli the other day at work, depicting Ariel flying on a bat, and the lines and curves had me transfixed. I had the print stapled to a page in the sketchbook, and I'd started trying to replicate it on the opposite side. But as the actors in Mama's movie barked at each other in their rough dialect and my mind wandered, so did my pen, so that I was no longer moving it across the page, but across the bare skin of my thigh. I'd pulled the hem of my shorts up and was pressing the black ink into my flesh. I couldn't get much traction, but I kept at it until I had a basic outline – Ariel, balanced on the back of a bat in flight, one leg up behind him and one arm high overhead like a ballerina going into an arabesque, a cord of dripping stars whipping around his body.

The front door opened downstairs. 'Baba?' I said, thinking it was too early in the evening for him to be home.

'It's me.' Mona's voice came ringing up the stairs, followed by the clicking of her heels.

I sat up, putting my sketchbook aside. We hadn't spoken since that day at the mall. I'd avoided her calls and ignored her texts; the only time I replied was in our group chat with Zaina. She came into view, her pixie-cut hair standing almost straight up in what I called her punk look. Aside from thick black eyeliner wings, her face was bare. Her gray dress was loose, stopping at her knees and slipping off one shoulder. She headed to my mother, kissing her cheeks and asking after her health. Mama hadn't seen her for a while and made her sit for a chat. The next few minutes were filled with inquiries about the health of Mona's parents and invitations for them to come out to the beach house. She asked about her husband – Mona avoided my eye – and whether they were thinking of children yet. Her response was a bubbly 'no' and a fluid lie of how they were still enjoying their couple-dom. The answer strained Mama's belief, I could tell, their marriage being nearly five years old at that point. In Mama's mind they ought to have been on their second child. When the chit-chat was over and one last reminder of the invitation was issued, Mona and I headed to my room.

'So is this it?' she said as soon as I'd shut the door behind us. 'You're just never going to speak to me again?'

I turned to her and plopped down on my bed. 'I'm upset.'

'Yeah, I got that,' she replied, hands on hips, her face in a frown. Mona's first instinct was to go on the defensive, and I was not thrown by the aggression. 'But it's been like two weeks now. We should talk about it. You can't just shut me out.'

'I was processing,' I said, smoothing the cover of my duvet so I didn't have to look at her.

'Processing?' There was a lightness in her tone that hit me like the snapping of a rubber band.

'Yes, processing. It's not every day you have to deal with the knowledge that your best friend is cheating on her husband.' She had the decency to lower her eyes at that. 'And not just once, Mona! It's not like you did it once and realized what a shitty thing you'd done. No, you continued to do a shitty thing. You have this great life, this great husband who adores you, why would you do this?'

'It's been difficult, okay?' she finally said, shaking her head. 'Things with Rashid have been difficult.'

'Difficult how?' I replied. 'You never said anything.'

She shook her head again, blew out a breath and brushed a finger down the wood of the little human mannequin on my dresser that I used for drawing. 'Marriage is different, Dahlia. I don't come running to you guys with our problems the way I did with boyfriends. Zaina doesn't tell us about her marriage; do you just assume everything is perfect there?'

I did, I had, and Mona knew it. She looked at me like I was terribly naive, and I dropped my eyes back to the duvet cover. Ariel's upraised hand peeked out from the hem of my shorts; it was smudged now.

'Nothing is perfect,' she continued. 'My marriage isn't perfect and neither is hers.'

'She wouldn't cheat on Mish'al though.'

There was a beat of silence, but she had no choice but to

admit it. 'No . . . no, she wouldn't.' She came and sat across from me. 'Look, I know how awful it is, okay? I'm not denying I did an awful thing. But it's over.' She looked sincere and I wanted very much to believe her. Her hand with its myriad rings played with the hem of her dress. 'I hate that you know this about me. I was going to end it before anyone found out. And now you know and you hate me.'

'I don't hate you,' I replied. 'I'm just shocked and . . . hurt, I suppose. I always thought you were better than this.'

She winced and I wished I could snatch the words back, but they were out there and she accepted them with a nod. 'I'll be better. I'll *do* better. I don't want things to be over with Rashid, I do love him.'

I still found it hard to believe but I nodded all the same. There was another silence. I wanted to ask for details, for her to tell me what was wrong in her marriage, but she'd already deflected the question once, and I could not tolerate the idea that she might blow me off again. Finally she leaned in and wrapped her arms around me.

I returned the embrace, chin propped on her shoulder. I clung to her the way I used to with guys at parties when we were younger, the way I had with Hamad in his green jeep, with Bu Faisal in the back of a black town car in Berlin. I clung because I needed the contact, the verification that I was more than loosely bound mud. I needed to feel the heartbeat of another thumping against my skin, the rise and fall of their breathing, the illusion that I was not terribly, terribly alone.

Too soon she let go and stood. She wandered over to the

Goyas with a frown, taking them in one by one: the lunatics in the yard; the mad and frightened crowds; the beasts and flames and stakes.

'These are . . . dark,' she said, tilting her head and leaning closer to the prints.

'I know,' I replied, pulling at a thread in my shorts.

'Darker than the Dorés,' she added, glancing at the opposite wall with its black and white prints I'd picked up at museums in London and Paris and anywhere else I could find them.

'Yeah.'

She moved back down the line, pausing every so often. 'Your mother must love them.'

I chuckled. 'She hardly comes in here anymore.'

'Mission accomplished then.' She stood back, arms crossed, and surveyed the whole collection. I must have had twenty or thirty of them up on the wall. 'They're cool.'

I laughed again. 'I don't know if anyone's ever called Goya cool, but . . .' I shrugged. 'I like them. I don't know why.'

She turned to me, eyes dark and serious. 'You're okay.' It was not a question. Unlike everyone else, she never asked it as a question. It was always a statement, an opinion, a conclusion, as much then as it had been when we were younger. *You're fine, because I decree it to be so.* The world tended to bow down to Mona, so if she said it, it must have been true.

'Of course.'

She turned in a circle, taking in my illustrations that I'd squeezed into gaps between the masters' prints. She hadn't seen my sketches for ages. 'Did you do this one?' she asked, pointing at a replica of Doré's *Charity, Hope, and Faith*. The sisters were bedecked in black *djilabiyas* instead of Greco-Roman robes, their heads adorned with glinting jeweled headpieces rather than leafy wreaths, and they stood in an oasis racked by a raging sandstorm rather than the spheres of Dante's Paradise.

'Yeah.'

She turned to me. 'You're really good.'

I lowered my head, uncomfortable with praise. 'Thanks.'

'You should've become an artist.'

'Here?' I replied with a scoff.

She propped her hands on her hips and shrugged. 'Why not?'

'Art is a hobby, not a career,' I replied, mimicking Baba's voice.

She smiled at the impression. 'People are doing all sorts of things now that didn't used to be acceptable jobs – chefs, baristas, event planners. People never used to do stuff like that. Besides, it doesn't have to be art-art,' she added, pointing at the sketches. 'It could be something related, like graphic design or something.'

I huffed out a breath. 'With my relationship with computers?'

'You could go to school for that.'

Could I leave? Just quit my job and go to some art program somewhere? Would that stop my mother from pressuring me into marriage? The idea seemed ludicrous, so out of the blue for me, something I would never have the courage to do. I imagined how my parents would react to my wanting to leave, imagined the fight they would put up, the guilt they would instill in me.

'I don't know,' I said.

'Think about it.' She smiled, winked, and added, 'Come on, I owe you a fro-yo.'

When I was twenty-one Mama invited the first suitor over to see me. It was the Greater Eid, the Eid of the Slaughter.

That's not hyperbole. It was the festival of sacrifices, where sheep are slaughtered in the yard to commemorate Ibrahim's willingness to make a sacrifice of his son. It was a day that saw butchers in blood-soaked T-shirts walking the streets, stepping through gates as needed. It was a day for families to gather in the patriarch's home to watch the event: boys' sandaled feet slipping in the blood; the girls, past puberty, uninvited and left to hang out of windows or over balconies with their mothers to watch; the loud '*Allahu Akbar*' of the butcher; the helpless bleating of the sheep, or its terrible innocence if the butcher was good and kept the blade out of sight.

I recall being always on the brink of panic that week. Cheeks and lips numb. Heart in throat. A doom nimbus following me everywhere.

He wanted to be an architect, the first man she brought around. His name was Rashid. I've spoken of him.

He was the most beautiful man I'd ever seen in my life up to that point: thick hair the color of India ink; skin like tea splashed with milk; massive, dark brown eyes under thick brows. He had a nose like a falcon's, dominant and proud. He was broad with shoulders like rolling desert dunes.

We hardly spoke. His fleeting glances skipped over to me every few minutes and I kicked them away, letting them scatter like marbles – to the gold and brown tapestry on the wall above our heads, to the garden beyond the window, to the collection of ouds displayed in the corner, standing upright, strings gleaming against the dark wood of the pear-shaped instruments.

'No, I don't play.'

'Her father used to a long time ago.' Mama's hand squeezed then patted my thigh. A silent reminder to smile.

I had to serve the tea. A show of domestication. I cursed the delicate glass *istikans* and their delicate glass saucers. Gold spoon and sugar cube fighting the cup for space. It started to shake as soon as I lifted it. *Istikana* on saucer, spoon on saucer, sugar against spoon against *istikana*. This punishing jingle jangle. One or more of the items was going to fall, I was sure of it. It would all go crashing down, glass shattering on marble, the white of his *dishdasha* splattered in Lipton tea and saffron flakes.

The pass-off was almost complete, he nearly had control, I nearly relinquished my hold, when the sugar cube somersaulted off the lip of the saucer. It could have taken everything with it in some terrible domino effect. But he caught it, white cube in his beach-colored palm.

He smiled, I smiled, but still the terror flopped in my belly like a dying fish.

Later the four of us went outside; Mama showed his mother the garden while we stood on the front steps. Baba had the yard done up in lights: twinkling strings of white and icy blue hung from tree branches, so it looked like they were dripping lights; recessed spotlights were embedded in the floor of the pathway leading up to the house; and tall lamps cast a warm glow over the grass and flowers and vines climbing the boundary walls.

'That's Baba's radish plant,' I explained as our mothers bent at the waist to look at something.

'Do you garden?'

'No.'

'Neither do I.' He shook his head. 'It seems . . . unnatural in some crazy way, like we're trying to make this land something it's not.'

It was an articulation of my thoughts, that eloquent little statement. I looked at him with new eyes then, possibilities unfurling in my mind like hesitant flowers, but his dark eyes were scanning the yard. Our mothers made their way patiently around the greens. And so slowly, to give us some phony semblance of privacy.

'I hate this,' he said.

'Me too.'

The show went on. 'I'm just going to let Um Hamad see the other end of the yard,' Mama called out, leading the other woman around the bend of our house towards the back.

I took him on our own tour then, pointing out all the silly things my father was desperate to grow – the carrots and cherry tomatoes, even a baby olive tree (it would die within a month.) Rashid had a thing for cars so I drifted with him to the open garage, letting him tell me things about the Mercedes parked there. The hand that had caught the sugar cube ran over the metal, tracing the lines of the car, fingers dipping in and out of grooves, and I tried to imagine how those hands would feel on me. The *dishdasha* glowed in the glare of the neon lights, making him look darker than he was. His mouth was relaxed, smiles frequent and easy, and I wondered if there was anything in the world he feared.

Headlights swept the gate, and a car pulled up sideways to the garage door. Mona leaned over and stuck her face out of the passenger side window with a drawn-out 'Hi!' Zaina gave me a don't-blame-me shrug.

'These are my friends,' I said. He offered a small wave, but said nothing. 'What are you doing here?'

Mona rolled her eyes up into her thick black bangs. 'We're here to rescue you, obviously.' My face flamed in some combination of mortification and irritation, compounded when she scowled at him and added, 'She's not for sale.'

He took it with an easy smile and a laugh. 'Good to know.'

Mona slapped her hands on the steering wheel. 'Come on, let's go!'

I glanced sideways at him, but he was watching her with a smile, all white teeth and stretched full lips under the crisp folds of his *ghutra*.

'I told you not before nine,' I hissed at her, looking over my shoulder for signs of Mama.

She glanced at the console. 'It's fifteen till; what difference does it make?'

'Mona!' Zaina yelped, smacking her on the shoulder.

'What?' she asked. I gestured to Rashid, but she only shrugged and fiddled with the radio, clearly content to sit and wait.

'Go on.'

I turned to him with a frown, still listening for sounds of our mothers.

'Go on, it's fine.'

'Mama will kill me.'

'No, she won't,' he replied, waving away my comment. 'We're about to leave anyway, so it's fine.'

'It's rude is what it is,' I said, ignoring Mona's snort.

'Look,' he began, eyes drifting back to me, 'I'm leaving for graduate school in a few months and I'm not looking to get married now. I only came to shut my mother up. And she said my opinion was the only one that mattered tonight, and I'm not offended, so . . .' He petered out with another shrug.

I glanced over my shoulder one more time.

'Listen to the man,' Mona chimed.

'I'm going to kill you.'

'You've been saying that since we were five, now get in.'

Mama didn't speak to me for two weeks. Nadia was mortified. Baba thought it was hilarious.

Rashid told the story for years afterwards, saying he fell in love with Mona's scowl before anything else.

6

Snow Globes

'There's another theory that says Prospero is like a child who matures throughout the course of the play,' Yousef said as we settled into uncomfortable leather chairs. 'And that by being on the island, he's separated from society so he can mature.'

We had left work to drop in at one of the many coffee places sprouting up downtown. The place was an ode to steampunk-industrial, with concrete floors and walls and exposed piping. Brass and copper presses lined the counter, with glass beakers and high-tech milk frothers. Some nondescript World music dripped from the speakers. A newer place had just opened up next door, and their line stretched down the street.

'Hmm.' I leaned my head back against the fake leather and sighed. Yousef was going ahead with plans for his movie club. That *Tempest* film was the first one up, and it seemed he'd chosen me to hone his talking points for the discussion he had planned to follow the screening. Unfortunately, it meant I had to hear it all for the second time. I tried to contribute never-theless. 'What does that mean for Caliban and Ariel then? Are they still parts of his psyche?'

'I don't see why not,' he replied, sipping at his espresso.

'Caliban being his child-self,' I said, 'and Ariel the more responsible, adult side.'

'Ooh, that's good,' he said, pulling out his phone and making a note on it. He nodded and added, 'So, the whole play becomes a musing on individualism *and* becoming an adult?'

I slurped my iced coffee. 'It can be about more than one thing.'

'Of course,' he replied, still looking down at his phone. Finishing the note, he looked up at me and chuckled. 'Remember when you said all kids when they're born should be dumped to be raised in orphanages without parents? Or on islands even, like in *Lord of the Flies*? It's sort of like that with Prospero; he's dumped on this island to mature into a king.'

'When did I say that?'

'When we were in Germany a few months ago for that conference.'

I swirled my drink. 'I don't remember.'

'Of course you don't. You were high as a blazing sun at the time.'

'Shhh!' I hissed, glancing around us.

'There's no one here,' he said, gesturing around the cold, empty café.

'Regardless. It never happened.'

He made that sound again. 'Yeah, you tell yourself that,

sweetie.' He chuckled at my continued frowning and returned to his drink. 'Do you remember any of that night?'

I sighed. 'Parts of it.' I clawed through memories of cold November nights, of dancefloors cloudy with smoke and lights and sweat, bodies bumping bodies then pausing to test, to invite. 'I remember fluffy white angel wings. I was a bird, and we danced for a long time.'

There was a look of nostalgia on his face as he started shaking his head. 'I don't remember ever seeing you so happy.' I didn't say anything to that. 'God, do you remember that awkward breakfast meeting with Bu Faisal? I think I was still a little hammered.' He finished the rest of his espresso, and then his fingers wandered to the cookie sitting on a plate between us. I'd ordered it for us to share, but I could practically see him counting the calories and how many hours he'd have to put in to work it off. I reached over and broke off a piece of the oatmeal raisin goodness. He watched me chew and swallow, and yes, maybe I made a little hum, because he sneered at me then broke off a piece of his own.

We chewed in silence for a while, and I thought about Ariel. My replicas of him were multiplying; they were in sketchbooks, my monthly planner and notepads at work, and still on my skin. Beneath my work clothes – my nice trousers and blouse and blazer – that sprite was inked all over my body: I'd blackened the outline on my thigh; I'd drawn him trapped in a tree on my other thigh; he was crawling up my left forearm, looking up at me with eyes that yearned for freedom. I was sliding into obsession, I knew. Between *The Tempest* and the Goyas on my wall, all my sketches lately had been of monsters and sprites. There was something about Ariel that comforted me even while rendering me unbearably sad. The illustrations felt more real to me than my life, more real than my daily routine, more real than the circus and play-acting my mother put me through.

'I want to get a tattoo.'

No reaction. Yousef's eyes were on a group of guys that had walked in, all fancy suits and stiffly gelled hair. He studied them with an intensity he didn't seem aware of, and the last piece of cookie in his hand was returned to the plate.

'Did you hear me?'

'What?' He turned to me, seemed surprised and a blush crawled into his olive cheeks. He shook his head as though to clear it. 'Say again.'

'I want a tattoo.'

He cocked an eyebrow and wrinkled his nose. 'So not you.'

I fiddled with my straw. 'What is that supposed to mean?'

'A tattoo is permanent,' he said, like it was a sufficient explanation.

'So?'

'So . . .' He shrugged like he wished he hadn't said anything and glanced again at the guys getting their drinks. A blast of air hit us as the door was pulled open again. 'You don't really do permanent, do you?'

'Where'd you get that idea?'

He shrugged again. 'More a feeling than anything, I suppose.'

I looked out the door at the cars whipping up and down the

street and the stock exchange with its scroll of symbols and colors. Though it was a pleasant enough day, men in suits and *dishdashas* hurried across the road, trying to get to their destinations before they started to sweat. I wondered how many of them were happy, how many were resigned, how many were as bored as I was, how many wished for something more and if any were in the process of attaining it. I wondered how many of them had no idea how miserable they were.

'Besides, your parents would flip out,' he said.

'My parents would have an aneurysm,' I replied. I could just imagine it: my father too shocked to say anything, Mama going on about religion and hellfire and Allah's punishment for scarring your body. 'They'd lose their minds.'

He chuckled and started trying to fold a napkin into some sort of origami bird; he couldn't seem to manage much more than a set of wings before unfolding it and starting over.

I remembered more of that night in Berlin than I let on. A windy November evening, the air frigid and me sorely defenseless. Yousef and I had endured a long day at the conference and had decided to treat ourselves to a night out. He'd heard of a great club located in a former heating plant down by the river that played house and electronica and other kinds of music that had different names but sounded the same. He'd gone all out, in tight jeans and a button-down with most of its buttons undone. His hair was a dome sloping off his forehead, and he'd gone for a shave at some fancy barber he'd found online. He looked very much like he had at the party where I'd met him, when we'd both been on the brink of leaving our teens to begin our twenties. I opted for the only halfway-appropriate dress I'd brought – not having known that he'd want to go dancing – and I'd let my hair dry into its usual curls. Some makeup and my work pumps, and we were out the door.

He was right. It was a great club. Thumping bass, strobe lights, young half-naked bodies – all you could want on a Friday night. It was like an industrial warehouse inside, with high ceilings and cement floors and dark tunnels. We drank and danced and laughed and I put on some angel wings that someone was passing out.

It got late and I went outside for some air. The freezing wind slapped me in the face, jolting me from the haze of booze and whatever the pill I'd taken from Yousef was doing to me. He was nowhere to be found. I'd looked through two of the three floors, but then my head had started to pound, my stomach turning, and I'd needed to get out of there. I only just managed to grab my jacket, clutching it to my middle as I staggered out the door and vomited into a bush.

Yousef wasn't answering his phone, and I only had one other number to call. Having to call Bu Faisal was humiliating; he'd been my client for a couple of years at that point, but even in my haze I knew I could lose my job if he revealed anything to the bosses at work. I couldn't even contemplate what might happen if word of the night got to my mother. But I was outside on a quiet street, littered with construction cones, and it was cold – the kind of cold that makes you forget you've ever been warm. I didn't know where I was, and the little pill was telling me I'd die if I got in a cab alone, or if I tried to walk to the hotel alone, or if I did anything alone.

What seemed like minutes later, Bu Faisal showed up in a car from the hotel, leaping out and throwing a coat over me. He hustled me into the back seat, murmuring reprimands about catching my death out there and not wearing clothes appropriate for German winters, and what protection was that flimsy jacket against the elements?

The seats were black and shiny and the heat was on full blast. I sighed happily and mumbled something about my wings and I needed them to fly. He shined a light in my eyes, and then gave two little tsks of his tongue. He removed his coat, pulled off my angel wings and put them in my lap, then made me put the thick, wool overcoat back on properly. My shoulders and arms and all of me was dwarfed by it. It smelled of him, of cigar smoke and woodsy whiskey, and I suddenly felt very calm and safe.

He spoke softly, as though he knew how badly my head was pounding. 'There are bad people in the world, Dahlia,' he said, like this was something I didn't already know. 'You're young and beautiful.' My belly dropped at that, but in my haze, I attributed it to the speed bump we'd just gone over. 'People will take advantage of it.'

'I'm almost thirty,' I murmured.

'Life begins at forty,' he said, shushing me. He said I was special and had to take better care of myself, but by then my head was on his bicep, my eyes were closed, and I was no longer listening.

*   *   *

77

The summer of my thirteenth year we took a big trip, and by big I mean that as well as my family there was Zaina's and Mona's. Our parents rented three villas in a gated compound in California – the other end of the world. It was populated by health nuts in short shorts and sports bras and Persian families who drove fancy cars and wore white doctors' coats and knife-pressed suits.

They were used to Arabs and accepting of us descending on their compound. The mothers pushing prams smiled at our mothers and gave us sticky cakes and date cookies. The fathers invited ours over for cigars and poker nights. We had communal barbecues by the compound pools, the men arguing about how best to cook the kebab while us kids whined about wanting hot dogs.

I remember walking around the property at dusk, when the night sounds were just kicking up – the crickets and buzzing things whose names I did not know. So different from the dead nights of Kuwait, where you heard nothing but cars on the road. The nights were alive in California, in this green and golden oasis with its flashing billboards and theme parks you could see into from the highway. I never heard cars though from where I stood amid the dark, thick trees at the end of the property, just an orchestra of night sounds.

Reza would often find me there. He was two years older than me and lived with his parents in one of the nicer villas, one on higher ground, with a view of the whole compound spread out beneath them – all spider-web alleys, turquoise pools, and multipurpose courts – like a modern-day Cordoba. His mother, a beautiful woman with dark eyes and long silk for hair, who I knew only as Aunt Sheri, was the social director of the place. She organized charity dinners, picnics and pool parties, Scrabble tournaments and Pictionary nights. She knew the best caterers and where to find the freshest seafood. She wore cashmere and dainty heels and jeans that looked too nice to barbecue in. Her jewelry was big and loud, huge stones hanging from her ears and throat, massive bangles jingling on her wrists. So different from my mother, who wore her house *dara'a* to the park and jammed a baseball cap over her *hijab* when we went to Disneyland, and whose everyday jewelry consisted of a gold wedding band and tiny diamond studs that no one saw.

Reza favored his mother, with big, dark eyes and the softest, blackest hair I'd ever seen. He had her build, tall but with delicate bones, his features fine and smooth as marble. He was nothing like his father who, squat and fleshy, looked like a lump of dough someone had given up on.

Reza kept to himself a lot, rarely showing up at his mother's events, and when he did, he was removed. He'd be on a lounge chair, brown chest thin and shining in the sun, while we splashed in the pool; he'd only get in the water when we'd migrated to the food. At picnics, while we kicked footballs and threw frisbees, he'd be under a tree, his nose in a book with a terrifically adult cover – something monochrome with an austere, gray-haired man gazing into the distance.

I was the only one he talked to, always at night when I roamed the compound. Sometimes I'd have to wait until everyone had gone to bed, then I'd sneak out of the villa and make my way through the maze of pink and blue hydrangeas and water fountains to the edge of the property where the trees were tall shadows and the air was alive with sounds. Reza would find me there. We'd walk through the sharp grass and he'd name trees in the dark, plucking up fallen leaves to show me the differences and I'd nod along even though I couldn't see the veins or edges he was talking about. He explained how to calculate the temperature by counting cricket chirps and when it worked I thought he was a sorcerer. From him I learned that my name was a flower that grew in Mexico, and it was beautiful and wild as a goddess. He said it in the same breath in which he gave me my first and only nickname – '*Kol Kokab*' – which he said was Dahlia in Farsi. I found this dubious since in Arabic it meant 'every planet', but he just laughed when I said that. He talked about phases of the moon and knew the Latin names of constellations and the love I felt for him that summer might be the loveliest emotion I've ever had, which is terribly sad, but which, in my more charitable moments, I regard with a kind of sentimental awe.

Those emerald grounds were our paradise. We kicked through tall grass, searching out little treasures: shiny coins, camouflaged GI Joe figures, and a rainbow of hair clips. We split our finds; he'd march toy soldiers across my shoulders and I'd slip pennies into his pockets.

He unearthed a *nazar* on the night he gave me my first kiss. It gleamed blue and white against the dark earth, like early-morning dew. He picked up the hard stone. It was a pendant, the silver chain dangling loose in the breeze. We bent our heads over it and he wiped it clean with his thumb. It shone like a beacon, reflecting the streetlights and the moon like a blinking eye. The 'pupil' was black and rough to the touch as though the dirt were permanently embedded in it.

Reza reached out to put it on me, but I backed away.

'It belongs to someone,' I said with a shake of my head.

He tried again, smiling as he replied, 'Finders keepers.'

He clasped the pendant around my neck and then he kissed me. He kissed me there, beneath an orange tree, with that night concert going on around us – the chirping and hooting, the rustling leaves, and the wet sound of our mouths pulling apart and coming together.

I hold those moments in snow globes in my mind, perfectly preserved miniatures of our trees and grass and night orchestra and endless sky. And every so often I'll come across that *nazar* in an old jewelry box, or a constellation will flash across the screen in some movie, and those snow globes in my mind will shake until our leaves rustle and our stars tumble and fall.

7

They Spin Finely

It was like some bizarre *voir dire*, I thought as Um Khaled walked us through the questionnaire. Mama and I hadn't been there long, only enough time to be shown to two winged armchairs and receive two glasses of tepid water. Enough time for Um Khaled to apologize profusely for the state of her 'office'.

As far as my admittedly meager knowledge went, these things were normally conducted in the home, but we'd been directed to an apartment building in a questionable part of town. Rundown and derelict, built in the 80s by the look of it. Barefooted children ran through the street, clothes and rags hung from windows, and the elevator was a ramshackle Otis with a scratched-off maintenance card. Um Khaled's office was a spartan apartment: white *kashi* tiles, the kind they don't use anymore; white walls; wide aluminum-paned windows looking out over nothing. There was a tapestry of the opening verse of the Quran on one wall and a blue evil eye talisman hanging by the door.

There was a rolled-up prayer rug in the corner. Our seats were opposite a metal desk littered with papers and files, and she sat in a rickety, swiveling desk chair behind it.

Um Khaled was what I expected a matchmaker to look like: wide, expressive black eyes, laugh lines and crow's feet, large mouth. She looked like someone who'd brought peace of mind to a lot of people. She had a broad nose that she kept passing a hand over, as though afraid it might have wandered off. On her head was the standard black *hijab*, but her *abbaya* was lightweight and loose. It said, *Don't be nervous. I'm just like your mother beside you.*

Mama was indeed dressed just like her. They spoke the same language and got along perfectly. They had a shared history of experience, a shared frame of reference. It was not completely alien to me, this talk of how much easier it had been in their day, how much more seriously people had taken the business of marriage, but it was foreign enough for me to be unnerved by it.

'Fill this out, *Habeebti*,' she said, turning to me with a toothy smile and sliding the pages across the desk. 'You can have your mother help, or you can do it on your own, as you like.'

I wondered if just letting Mama fill it out for me was an option, but Um Khaled got up and disappeared into another room, leaving us alone with this exam and a pen.

'*Yella*, let's see,' Mama said, positioning the top page between us. 'Obviously he must be a college graduate . . . Sunni . . .' She started ticking her way down the line. 'He must make more than you, what a stupid question! Older or younger, it doesn't matter.'

I leaned back in my seat and left her to it. I couldn't believe she'd actually dragged me here. I couldn't believe Baba had allowed it. It was humiliating for everyone involved; couldn't she see that? What would people think, if they knew she'd had to resort to a *khataba* to sort out her problem child? Did she honestly think this Um Khaled was going to find someone remotely compatible with me?

'You've never been married,' Mama murmured with a tick on the page.

That wasn't the real question, though. It was just a subtle way of asking whether I was a virgin or not.

I wondered what else she planned on lying about.

Several moments later, she turned to me. 'Dark, medium, or fair skin?'

'Does it really say that?' I leaned over to look.

'Hmm, we'll put medium, it's better.' She ticked that one. 'Widowed or divorced is okay. Children are fine, right?'

'I don't know, are they?'

She pursed her lips and frowned like all this was my fault, which I suppose in a way it was. 'I want to say no, but we have to be realistic, Dahlia.' She ticked yes, but said no to sons. I asked what the difference was. 'Daughters will stay with the mother.' She'd thought of everything. She let loose a laugh. '*La baba*, we don't need your beach house. We have our own, *hamdilla*.'

'Ha?' Um Khaled said, leaning around the door frame. 'Is everything okay in here?' She waved a Filipino maid in.

'*Hamdilla*,' Mama answered.

The maid replaced our empty glasses with fresh ones and set down two *istikans* of strong, brown tea and a small plate of butter cookies in their transparent wrappers. 'Thank you,' I said. She scurried out without a word; Um Khaled followed her back into the other room.

Mama was still ticking away, thankfully without consulting me, and I plopped sugar cubes into our drinks, stirring them with the same tiny gold spoon until the white sugar melted into a swirl at the bottom of the glass and then disappeared completely. I took a sip of mine. Too hot.

'How much did you pay for this?' I asked, blowing the steam off my tea.

'A nominal fee. It was nothing, don't worry.'

'I'm not worried,' I replied with a scoff. I was sure we'd spent more for less. 'I'm only asking.' She ignored me, tick, tick, ticking away. She must have been on the second or third page by then.

'Yes, please God, a quick engagement,' she said with another tick.

I sat up and stopped her hand. 'What?'

She looked at me, her thin black brows dropping into a frown. 'It's asking if you'd prefer a long or short engagement.'

'Define long or short.'

She glanced down at the page. 'Less or more than six months.'

'Are you insane?' I grabbed the pen from her hand and put a dark tick on the 'more than' space.

'Dahlia—'

'No, Mama. It's enough I let you drag me here; you're crazy

if you think I'm going to let you ship me off to the first man Um Khaled brings by. It should be a year – six months is nothing!'

'Your father and I were engaged for less than three months. It was the same with your aunts and uncles. Your Aunt Norah was only engaged for three weeks if I remember correctly.'

Three weeks. It seemed impossible. You might as well just marry someone off the street. I shook my head and said, 'Well, that was a different time, as you insist on reminding me.'

The last trip our families took together was perhaps our most eventful. It was not uncommon for entire families to undergo a mass exodus to Europe to escape the brutal heat of summer in the Gulf, and it seemed like everyone joined our vacation that year. We had rented apartments within blocks of each other and did everything together. Bu Faisal and his wife and kids had taken an apartment down the block as well, and as always, we'd folded them into our family outings.

I was unhappy with the vacation. I had begged to return to California, to that state, that country, that Mama's family finds too far to manage, but nobody listens to kids. I'd spent that spring avoiding the family beach house. Feigning a fear of my usual summer brown and a sudden hatred of sea water, I'd stayed behind with a maid each weekend. Not Mama, Baba, Zaina or even Mona could induce me to go. I stayed home with my colored pencils, my paints and easel, and my coffee-table art books that Baba ordered for me. I got very pale that year. Not dark to begin with, I paled to Wednesday Addams-level white.

I was nothing but papyrus skin, blue veins and angry scratches. So translucent, it was like you could see right through me. I should have liked to disappear.

The family chalet meant Uncle Omar – Mama's cousin – and I already had a hard time avoiding him at the weekly family lunch. What had started as 'accidental' touches had become the pressing of his body against mine as he moved behind me to take his place at the dining-room table; his eyes crawled all over my body when I stood to go anywhere; and his hand often found its way under my hair to squeeze my nape like I belonged to him.

If it was hard to avoid him at home, it was damn near impossible to do in London. The family went everywhere together – on walks in Hyde Park, to theme parks outside the city, on trains to visit historical sites out in the country. The only time we separated from the men was when we went shopping, and so I became a shopper. Every day I would beg and beg to go to Selfridges or Harrods or just up and down Oxford Street for hours on end. It was easy since Nadia was getting married that fall, so there was always that justification for a shopping day. But my sister has never been much of a shopper, and she found her dress the first week we were in London. By the end of that first month, she had shoes and a veil and honeymoon clothes, and it became harder to convince her to go to the stores. When I would suggest it in the morning over breakfast, she'd shake her head and frown and Uncle Omar would glance over at me with narrow eyes and an unkind smirk on his lips.

I could not tell anyone. I did not tell anyone. The shame of it would have dissolved me from the inside. The longer I stayed silent, the harder it was to say anything. Was I complicit? Was it, on some level, my own fault? Was I inviting the attention? I couldn't open myself up to that possibility, could not make it real by speaking of it.

That summer might have been the final time Mama held Bu Faisal up as the ideal husband, but it was also the first time I saw something heroic in him – something more ideal than his generosity towards his wife or his unusual tea etiquette.

I never knew what exactly the fight had been about. It was a sunny day, and the families were all in the park – the younger kids running around like manic chickens, crying over kites that wouldn't fly and skinning their knees and falling off bikes. Us older ones sunned ourselves on the sloping grounds and watched the people go by. The mothers were huddled up on blankets beneath the trees, gossiping and laying out food and tea and coffee for a picnic while the men wandered around and around the lake.

The commotion started far away from us, down at the bend in the lake with the restaurant and the horses lined up for rides. We heard shouting; the harsh, Arab sounds that Westerners find so threatening. Hyde Park in the summer is full of Arabs, and so, at first, we paid it little attention. Nadia and I turned our faces back to the sun, but then one of our cousins said, 'Isn't that Uncle Omar?' We turned to see him being whipped around and pushed to the ground, identifiable only by the tight jeans he wore and the black leather jacket with the Tommy Hilfiger stripe, like he was eighteen and not pushing forty.

It was Bu Faisal who had him on the ground. I could tell it was him by the salmon pink shirt he wore, which all us girls had giggled about that morning. He was straddling Omar, punching him repeatedly in the face while my father and others tried to pry him off. It took all four of them to do it, only managing to get him off by the time we'd all rushed over to join the crowd growing around them.

Omar's face was red and wet with blood. Mama kneeled beside him, wailing and dabbing at his face with the fabric of her long tunic. He was groaning in pain, clutching his bleeding nose then his side then his arm as though the pain were slithering around beneath his skin. It reminded me of the nervous energy I was suffering under more and more – the days where it felt like my heart was wandering around my body looking for something to do, like it was a little jumping bean that flicked at my throat or jangled in its cavity or tap-danced across my ribs then down to tickle my fingers.

The men were still physically restraining Bu Faisal. I looked up at him; he was like some furious Bedouin warrior, glorious in his wrath. Lips pulled back in a sneer, eyes like twin burning bits of coal, he spat curse after curse at Omar. He broke loose once, lunging forward to kick him in the ribs. Uncle Omar wailed and gripped his side, and Mama screamed at Baba to stop him. My father went to pull Bu Faisal back, but it was unnecessary. He was backing away, calling his wife and kids to join him. He sneered down once more. I looked down as well, at the tears leaking from his slimy eyes to meet the blood coming from his nose and mouth, and I smiled. When I lifted my eyes, they met Bu Faisal's. His eyes narrowed, face falling into a frown, but his wife pulled on his arm and he allowed himself to be turned around towards the park gate.

I didn't see them for the rest of the holiday, and I spent less time with my family. I would cajole my older cousins into taking us away from the adults, to the Trocadero or Madame Tussauds or London Zoo, though I felt too old for all of them. More and more, Nadia and I would abandon the family to go to art galleries and museums.

I discovered Fuseli, with his contortions and exaggerations and perfect colors, on a gloomy day trip to the Tate. I pored over his work – the biblical, the literary, the mythological. And when I found *The Nightmare*, I felt, for the first time, the unbroken thread of history. For the first time, I felt like I was more than a collection of matter floating in empty space. I felt part of something larger, my experiences no longer my own, but shared with others. I remember staring at it for hours: the woman stretched out on her back, in that position which the *yathoom* finds so inviting; the wide-eyed incubus, that demon, mounted on her ribs; her hand droops, lifeless, to the floor. He's killing her. Every night, he kills her.

8

The Sleep of Reason . . .

The party was nearly over when Yousef and I arrived. You could tell because the soul-eradicating noise that was popular at those things had been replaced with something slower and moodier. Atmospheric, new wave strumming in lieu of bombastic 808s. There was a guy in a white vest and low-slung jeans talking about a show he'd seen in London – all I heard was 'show' and 'London' and then he stomped onto the wooden trunk-cum-coffee table, gripped the brass chandelier over his head and swung. Back and forth he went, kicking his Docs out with every go-around as girls screamed with laughter.

The coffee table was wet with glass rings; bits of dry leaves and thin paper said that most of the fun had already been had. The lights were dim, blue and white, and the word 'Hallelujah' blinked in pink neon from the corner. Through the sliding glass door there were people who'd decided that swimming in March was a good idea. The bottles and glasses around the pool should keep them warm, and if not, well, the human body was a pretty good conductor of heat.

'I thought he was doing *Phantom*,' Yousef said as the guy was pulled back to the ground. 'You know, the bit in *Phantom of the Opera* when the chandelier swings over the audience.'

'Never saw it.'

'Uncultured swine.' He sniffed at me. He wrapped an arm around my neck and led me further into the room. There were eight or nine of us in there, and Yousef and I ended up squashed into a large, black armchair.

He dragged me to one of those parties every few months. I was the reason we were so late. Showing up when it was in full swing or, God forbid, at the start was unthinkable. It was difficult for me to be in crowds. I ended up clinging to Yousef like he was a pacifier. I didn't know what to say to people, how to connect with them, and our conversations were stilted and disappointing for all involved. The start of a party was the worst, before a rhythm was established, when couples and groups were unbalanced and still coming together. It was the easiest time to spot those that didn't belong, and even Yousef couldn't shield me then. So, we arrived later, when you could almost pretend you'd been there the whole time.

Chandelier Boy came to sit on the couch. I now recognized him as Zacharia-Don't-call-me-Zach, the curator at an art gallery by the airport. I saw him every once in a while – at parties, farmers' markets and exhibits – and we rarely spoke, which I suppose meant we were friendly enough. I was always surprised by how thin he was, like rakishly, unhealthily thin.

Whenever I saw him I got the sense it might be for the last time.

He bummed a cigarette from Yousef, who passed me one in the same round, and they started chatting, elbows to knees, heads together like co-conspirators. There was a blonde at the far end of the couch, leaning back, eyes to the ceiling, having a very poor trip by the looks of it. Her eyes, lashes like moths, blinked rapidly; her chest, in low-cut, tight velvet, just heaved and heaved; and her hands pressed against her belly like she was holding something in. I hoped she wasn't about to be sick. She flinched when Yousef flicked on his lighter, looking around with big, horse eyes like she didn't understand how we had come to be there. Her knees were bare and pale, ghost knees, and they jiggled incessantly as she returned to blinking at the ceiling.

'Is she okay?' I asked, breaking into the guys' conversation.

Zacharia turned to her for a moment, his dark eyes flicking up and down like she was a canvas he was appraising and said, 'She's fine. Go to sleep, Kim.' She obeyed, shutting her eyes as Zacharia turned his attention back to Yousef.

I recognized her now. Kim. She was an American who taught English at one of the private colleges. She'd become a regular at these parties. We'd spoken a few times, but had never found much in common. I hadn't seen her in months, and it surprised me to find that she was still in the country. I would have expected the strangeness of life here to have scared her off by now. Americans and Brits came over to teach, usually only for a couple of years, just long enough to make a buttload of money before heading off to their next posting.

Further down the sofa were TT and whichever boys were fawning over her that month. Everyone called her TT; I didn't know her real name, though we'd hung out a dozen times or so. She was just back from some course in Paris – diamond grading or something – and she was all in black. A tight black top. Black leather pants clung to her long legs, ending in gold-tipped stilettos. A teardrop pendant hung above her cleavage; a big, shiny yellow diamond, probably real, but you never ask such questions. She sucked on a long, slim cigarette, white with green trim, blowing smoke right in the guys' faces, but they didn't seem to mind. I'd never met them, but they looked like brothers, both with bland features and mouths that talked and talked. The words 'photo shoot' and 'model' were bandied about, and TT threw her head back at the absurdity of modeling her own designs. 'Who better to represent your brand?' Thing 1 asked. 'A professional,' she replied, the smoke crawling up her feline features as she released it. She could be a model; she had a face that made one think of a Turkish harem – all angles, high cheekbones, and sculpted jawline. Her eyes were big and dark and heavily lined, eyebrows thick and perfectly arched. Her lips were Parisian red that night, ruby and wide and looking for trouble.

'You have the look,' Thing 2 protested. 'You should use it.' TT tossed her head and tapped her cigarette in the direction of the full ashtray on the table. 'I'm a serious designer with a serious business. I'm not going to model my own stuff like some singer hawking perfume.'

Someone stopped the music. A guy, dripping wet from the

pool and clad in gray boxer briefs, crouched by the sound system. Was this his house? Was he the DJ, or just some random guy deciding to take control? After some shuffling, opening and closing of cabinets, the warm pop and crackle of a record about to start filled the air. 'I Heard It Through the Grapevine' spun out and now there was dancing. Our DJ moved in on a girl in a purple tank top, matching underwear showing through the soaked white fabric of her skirt.

TT was still shaking her head, tossing her long black hair from one shoulder to the other like an agitated cat flicking its tail. I noticed she'd shaved the right side of her head so that there was a buzz-cut strip under the hair there. The sight left me in slightly nauseated confusion. It made me feel very old all of a sudden, like I should turn down the music and ask everyone whether they wouldn't like to go on home to bed.

I was too sober to dance, so I finished off another cigarette while everyone but me, TT, her boys, and Kim got up. Yousef had left his man-bag with me, a little black leather bag like the kind you use to hold toiletries when you're traveling. I rummaged inside and found a little bottle of pills. They were prescription, but Yousef had said you could get a pretty good buzz off them. They were only little and white, and though I knew better than most the dangers of little white pills, I popped one in my mouth anyway, washing it down with the remnants of the glass Yousef had left on the table before me. The swimmers had all come in and as they danced they flicked drops of chlorinated water our way. There was one girl with long, soaking wet hair who was a particular nuisance, and it wasn't long before someone threw a towel on her head. Zacharia and Yousef were dancing very close together, the kind of closeness that would be fine for two girls, but was not for them.

After the Motown medley came one side of a jazz record that hurt my head, then it was back to screaming guitars, bass that hit you low, and lyrics that a five-year-old could have written. The party was getting a second wind. They danced and danced; even TT got up to join, trailing Things 1 and 2 behind her. I stayed where I was and went through the rest of Yousef's pack, one cigarette after the other, until I reeked of smoke and tar and whatever else was moving through the dark air.

If our behavior is nurture rather than nature led, then how come I couldn't envision a 'me' that was up there dancing? Maybe hopping onto the table and taking a swing from the chandelier. It seemed impossible in a way that it shouldn't have. Perhaps I should have had another drink or two, or rustled up something else to inhale, maybe then I'd have learned how to navigate those things.

Sometime later I ended up by the pool. It was late and nearly empty inside, and I wondered when Yousef would want to leave. I couldn't see him in the living room anymore. The air was dead, empty and cold, raising goosebumps on my bare arms. One or two bright stars blinked down, or maybe those were airplanes flying very far away. The moon was a silver coin on black velvet, hazy and weak. I sat at the edge of the pool, dangling my legs in the cold water until they went a little numb, and then it was like they were someone else's feet kicking in the shimmering blue. I tipped the drippy remains of glasses and bottles into the water, dark browns and caramels and crystal clear swallowed up by the chlorine scent.

'How long was I out?'

Kim, our sleeping blonde, was squeezing through the crack in the sliding door. She rubbed her brow, her hair long and messy around her shoulders. When she looked at me, I saw raccoon eyes, the mascara and eyeliner bruising her lids. Her skirt looked made of taffeta and was very wrinkled, the creases and folds glimmering in the pool lights as she walked out to me.

'I don't know,' I replied, 'a couple of hours.'

'Fucking Mohi,' she growled. Another nickname for another person I didn't know. She pulled her hair back, twisting it around and around into a smooth bun, then released it, so that she really hadn't done anything at all. Her face and chest and legs were shiny, and I couldn't tell if it was lotion or sweat or something else. Her bare feet took her to the edge of the pool and she talked the whole time. She told me about how she didn't usually behave like this and that yeah, she may be blonde and she may have gone to college in Miami, but that didn't mean she was some hard-partying whore and why didn't Mohi understand that. In the middle of this rant, the top was peeled up and off, the taffeta skirt was dragged down curves and hips, and she slipped into the water like some mermaid. And then the long hair was soaked and moved like a yellow silk cape, and I thought she must have been a siren. Her voice dropped lower, like she was talking to herself, like I wasn't even here;

she said that this was the last time she'd go to a party with him, how he always bailed at some point and went God-knows-where to do God-knows-what.

I decided that maybe she would rather be alone and stood to go.

'Why don't you get in?'

I shuffled my feet.

'It's nice,' she said, moving her pale arms through the water, her aqua eyes fixed and lucid. 'Cold, but nice.' I looked through the glass door. It was still empty inside; the music had played itself out. 'Most of the guys have gone,' she reassured me. 'Just TT and her fags in the kitchen.'

Before I could talk myself out of it, I removed the black dress in quick, efficient movements. No zipper, no buttons, just slid it up over my head and let it fall to the ground in a puddle of cotton. I was no mermaid, and there would be no dainty sliding into the water for me. I took three steps back, then lurched forward into a run and cannonballed into the deep end.

When I broke the surface, Kim was laughing hard, water dripping down her face and off the tip of her ski-jump nose. I apologized, but she just waved it away and dove down. From where I was treading I watched her white torso and yellow hair, with those bands of blue across her bottom and back, wiggle and shimmy as she swam underwater to the shallow end. She splashed about over there, doing handstands and forward rolls, while I stayed by the edge floating on my back. At some point she settled for just standing there, twirling around and around.

'It's so strange,' she said, her voice high across the water. 'I was talking to this girl in there earlier.' She nodded towards the glass doors. 'And she was telling me how she lied to her parents about where she was going tonight, telling them she was "hanging with the girls".' Her fingers, trailing water, came up for the air quotes. 'Can you imagine? The girl has to be thirty-five or so, and she's lying to her parents like that, like she's a high school kid or something.'

I tapped my palms on the surface of the water, making wet slapping sounds. 'Maybe they wouldn't approve.'

She furrowed her brows. 'It's a party. Parents never approve of that, but I mean, she's an adult.'

I had no response, and she turned away to spin more circles and send little waves across the pool. How could I explain to her that in our culture a daughter is not thought an adult until she's married and no longer in her father's care? That until then we just played at being adults – going to work, hitting the gym, watching our money – but remained impotent when it came to making any real decisions about our lives. I bet Kim had difficulty fathoming that a thirty-year-old had to ask permission to leave the country, or that she had to hide her male friends from her parents because 'good girls' didn't socialize with men. My parents had no idea who Yousef was; in the ten years I'd known him, as a friend, then as a colleague, they'd never met him nor heard me so much as mention his name. How could I make her see the myriad paradoxes in our culture? That while a few families were like Mona's, who'd actually encouraged her to get a degree abroad and had been disappointed that she'd chosen to stay with us, most of them were like mine and Zaina's, who thought we shouldn't do anything without considering what society might think of it first.

Our lives were these elaborate plays, and we all wore masks. There was a life that people saw, where you were respectable and did all the right things, a life where people thought highly of you and you were firmly set on a predictable trajectory. But there was another life as well, one inside you, a life where you thought things you were too ashamed to say out loud, where you lied to people and you lied to yourself. It sometimes felt like I had put my past in a hole and spent my time shoveling dirt into it, but like some cheap horror movie, it kept trying to claw its way out.

9

. . . Produces Monsters

When I was seventeen I was enveloped, finally, in silence. I functioned, but barely. I went to school; I came home. My grades weren't slipping anymore, and senior year passed in a blur of ditched classes, bare minimum assignment hand-ins, and avoided eye contact.

It had been two years. Two years since I'd had to sit in front of Mama and Baba, bleeding where I shouldn't have been, and tell them what had happened. Two years since Baba had driven like a madman to Uncle Omar, nearly killing him but settling for breaking his nose, collarbone, and three ribs. Two years since Mama had pleaded and wailed and pleaded some more for Baba not to tell anyone, not to bring shame down on us all.

Finally I had silence. The noise that had raged in my head was quieting. I no longer flinched when any male so much as brushed against my clothes, although that might have been because the worst had already happened and there was nothing left to fear. I had a candle ritual, involving flames and melted wax, that was down to once a month, and I'd only cut myself twice in two years; both times when the noise had gotten so great that the veins in my wrists pumped and trembled in invitation. Slicing into my inner thigh had been an unworthy but sufficient substitute.

The three of us were on the *memsha* – Mona to my right, Zaina to my left – when I told them what had happened on that suffocating August night. The egocentricity of adolescence had prevented them from asking too many questions about how I'd changed during that time. We'd all become moodier; we'd all severed contact with one another every so often, only to come together again without questioning the root causes of our separations. They'd hung out at the chalet, and I didn't return to those beach properties for years; and so, for a time, our threesome had become a twosome. I was left at home with my bleeding ink flowers and itchy skin while they tanned and talked about boys. Our fathers took the families to islands – to Kubbar and Um AlMaradim – to swim and snorkel and tan some more. And not once did they push, really push, for the reason why I didn't join those weekend trips.

I finally told them, on that balmy evening, when the sun was a pink grapefruit low on the horizon and kids whipped past on bikes without helmets or padding of any kind. I had to say it twice before it registered; we were still walking when it finally got through. There was sputtering and gasps and a scream from Zaina that made people walking ahead of us turn and tsk (there are always reprimands from society elders – strangers who you nevertheless must address as Aunt and Uncle.)

They both stopped then, like a frame locking into place, but I walked through it. They called after me, 'Dahlia's that were questions, exclamations, even whimpers. But I kept walking, letting them volley the Whys and Hows between them. I kept walking because I could not answer those questions; I didn't know Why and I couldn't think on the How, otherwise I was liable to stray from the path and bury myself under a tree.

They eventually caught up with me, across the road on the second half of the *memsha*. Quiet, short, and seething breaths on my right, sniffles and fingers rising to swipe under eyes on my left. Other than that, silence. Not outer silence, of course. Around us were revving car engines and boys doing wheelies on their motorbikes; there were children screaming in the play-ground and chattering groups passing us. The fourth *Azzan* of the day rang out, a staggered call echoing from mosque to mosque.

There was an inner silence, though. A calm in my soul now that they knew, now that the secret was no longer there – a leech on our friendship. There was the silence of relief, of knowing I would no longer have to pretend to be whole. I was free to be the stunted, half-formed thing he'd left behind. There were no recriminations from them, only a solitary 'Why didn't you tell us?' from Zaina which went unanswered. She slipped her hand in mine, squeezing tight, her left hand passing over her face every now and then when she couldn't sniff back a tear.

The muezzins' calls were winding down, men and boys in *dishdashas* hurrying across the roads to the mosques to join the prayers. A kid on a red bike pedaled past, nearly tripping us over, and hopped down and up the two sets of curbs before racing across the empty lot, kicking up clouds of dust in his wake. He skidded to a stop, letting the bike crash to the ground and skipped up the mosque steps, yanking off his sandals as he went.

'I don't understand how this happened,' Zaina whispered. 'He was always so nice.'

'He wasn't nice.' My voice was a flat monotone. I didn't want to talk about it. I wanted them to accept it in silence.

'And your parents . . .' Mona shook her head. 'Your parents know and haven't done a thing.'

'Baba put him in the hospital. Beat the shit out of him.'

'He should have killed him,' she growled, kicking at a loose stone on the path.

I let them toss their rage back and forth, keeping my head low, eyes on the ground. I had passed rage a long time ago; that space in my chest was hollow. Fury, sharp and acidic, radiated from Mona. This ire that sliced us every time she spat out a word. She threatened to tell her father, saying that unlike my spineless parents, hers wouldn't hesitate to involve the police. It was only when I'd stopped walking, sobbing and red face in hands, that she'd backed off, promising – along with Zaina – to tell no one. Zaina's reaction reminded me of Nadia's: that horrified sadness I'd seen wash over her, the look that said she'd never imagined the world could hold such things.

We kept walking, both their hands gripping mine, and rounded another playground, with mothers and nannies shouting up at children to be careful on the jungle gym. Girls pushed each other on swings and boys pushed one another off seesaws. The sun was nearly gone, in that in-between period that could herald a new day as easily as it could the night. The streetlights flickered on, one by one, orange and white lights bathing the *memsha*.

'He rubbed up against me once,' Mona said, 'a few years ago, at the chalet.'

Zaina and I pulled her to a stop, my eyes wide and searching her face for any sign that this was one of her stories, like telling us a guy had said he loved her when really all he'd done was smile at her or something. But there was no sign of that. Her eyes were dark, her brow troubled, her lips a dash across her face.

'Why didn't you say anything?' Zaina yelled, looking very much like the world was falling apart around her.

Mona's eyes were on mine. She hadn't said anything for the same reason I hadn't – because it was humiliating, because we weren't sure whether or not we'd invited it somehow, because telling someone made it real. That hollow in my chest was filling up with something new, something sulfurous that I didn't yet have a name for. My heart broke, right there and then. Shame and guilt washed over me. I couldn't look at them, couldn't think too deeply about what it meant. I just turned around and ran all the way home.

10

Who More Is Surrendered?

I was a dormant volcano, stretching, yawning, and rumbling awake.

The Caprices of Goya, that gallery of social condemnation, were calling to me. Did he mean what I thought he meant? The man slumped over the table, over his art, legs crossed, surrounded by beasts: bats flapping at his back; owls looming overhead; that panicked lynx at his feet. Did it mean what I thought, that abandoning reason brings about calamity? Or was I infusing it with my own preoccupations and prejudices? Is art about seeing what's there, or discerning how it relates to your existence? My reason had abandoned me. I was shattering from the inside, cracks widening, visible where they'd been so well covered.

I'd tried to stay with Shakespeare's benign isles and forests. Yousef kept wanting to discuss *The Tempest*, unsatisfied with the discussion yielded by his film club showing, which I'd been conspicuously absent from. He was preoccupied with the psychology of the play – what it said about the human soul and Freud's facets of the ego and how he now thought it was ultimately about freedom and service – but all I could contribute was a liking of the aesthetics that surrounded it. Miranda's wild and flaming hair, soft curves, and milky white skin as she watched the shipwreck and the angry waves of the eponymous tempest in John William Waterhouse's imagining of it. Showing him Walter Crane's illustrations of the play I told him how I'd spent far too long staring at the one of Caliban kneeling before Stephano and Trinculo. Caliban beseeches the would-be rebels, reminding them that he is 'subject to a tyrant', but those weren't my feelings, not really. I didn't identify with him any more than I did with the tree Ariel was trapped in. I didn't feel as if it was saying something to me – unlike the Goyas, which never stopped talking. The Crane illustration calmed me; I found a muted joy in the stones at Caliban's feet, the leaves all around, the fold of Stephano's tunic.

The Goyas, by contrast, were dark, maybe even dangerous. They gnawed at me when I was asleep, flashed across my mind at morning meetings, superimposed themselves on family gatherings. His entire gallery was open in a hundred tabs on my browser, and I had a habit of clicking from one to the next, searching out a print I might be able to try. And this one, number 43. The sketch is monotone, like all the others. Color gone, seeped into the abyss. It is dark, dense, and consuming. Hues are swallowed, shapes disintegrate. Everything implodes. No, implodes is the wrong word. It's entropy, decay, and a stain that can't be cleaned. Loneliness, too, is a constant. It had been with me so long I'd forgotten how to connect . . . like those Romanian babies that never learn to love.

The bats were acquiring faces. The big round owl eyes looked familiar. And the lynx curled on the floor was looking like a 'me' that was dangerously close to being real.

Friday evening, Yousef and I met for sushi. We were scandalous and unapologetic, showing up at the crowded Japanese place in our workout gear and wet hairlines. Yousef at least had showered at the gym, but I had come straight from the *memsha*, just pulling my hair into a matted bun and dousing myself in perfume on the way.

'Jesus,' he said when we greeted each other, waving a hand in front of his nose.

'You'd prefer my natural musk?' I asked, dropping into the seat across from him.

He winked. 'I think I would actually.'

The waitress brought over green tea and an amuse-bouche of avocado and salmon. There were more people there than I'd anticipated: groups of girls in spiked heels and caked foundation and guys in *dishdashas* or jeans and polo shirts, all eyeing each other up like chattel at an auction, wondering who would be the next to go.

'Oh, I meant to tell you,' Yousef said, dipping an edamame pod into some spicy mayonnaise. 'I showed Zacharia some of your art, and he loves it. He wants you to put on a show at the gallery.'

'What?' My eyes went wide, my bite of salmon pausing in the air before my mouth. 'When was this?'

'I told him about it ages ago,' he said with a wave of his hand. 'But at the party the other night, I showed him some pictures of it on my phone. I mean, the pictures weren't super clear obviously, but he loved the work and wants to see the sketches for real.'

'Why would you do something like that?'

He frowned at me. 'Because if I don't, you never will. You've been drawing for ages, Dahlia, but you don't do anything about it.'

'I'm not trained. It's just doodling.'

He looked at me like I was an idiot. 'It's more than that and you know it. And anyway, who cares? You think all those people who sell their "paintings" for thousands of dinars are professionals? Or those photographers with shit pictures of Buddhist temples and Asian street markets? Nobody here is a pro. They just act like it. And you have actual talent.'

'I don't want to sell them,' I said, horrified by the prospect of parting with my sketches.

He waved that away too. 'You don't have to sell them if you don't want to. He has some open dates towards the end of the month, and he just wants to display them for a few days, have an opening and everything.'

An opening, like those pompous events staged by the glitterati all over the city, like it was Manhattan or London's East End. The hipsters with their thick-framed glasses and perfect hair, with the designer clothes and fancy cars, they showed up to be seen. They did it for the Snaps and the posed Insta-shots, for the appearance of it all. Yousef dipped his toe into that scene, but the girls and I never got into it. We preferred to spend our free nights parked in front of a TV show instead of standing in line at a pop-up coffee shop.

'I don't know,' I said, making way for the salads the waiter was arranging on our table.

'I know you hate shit like that, but it would just be for a few days.'

'What would be the point, though?'

'To do something with your art, to feel a sense of accomplishment about it, to show people your talent; who knows where it might lead?'

'They're just flowers,' I said, thinking of the dahlias and orchids that most people saw.

He looked down at his plate and mumbled, 'I'm not talking about the flowers.'

I stared at him, quiet until he met my eye again. 'The replicas? How did you even get pictures of those?'

'Don't get mad, okay?' he said, holding up his hands. 'I take pictures of the sketchbook when you're at my place. When you're done with one, you take them out of the book, so the sketches I've shown him probably aren't the final versions, but they're enough for him to want to show them.'

I shook my head. 'Those are replicas of classic work by world-class artists; there is no way I can show those. I'd be laughed out of the gallery.'

'By the kind of people that show up to those things?' he

asked mockingly. 'Sweetie, most won't even know the pieces aren't originals.'

'But some will, and if it is as you say then why bother at all?'

He huffed and said, 'Because they're beautiful, Dahlia! And they're more than just replicas. You put a spin on them, you don't just try to copy them.'

'Some might say that's worse,' I replied, thinking it's one thing to copy a famous work, it's another thing to make changes to it, as though I don't have the talent to replicate it, or – worse – think I can do it better.

'Come on,' he said. 'It's just a little show. It won't be that bad. You might even enjoy it.'

'Hmm.' I left it at that, but I could tell he would take it as acquiescence.

Maybe it wouldn't be so bad. And if the reception was good, it might give me the confidence to go further, to apply to an art program, to bring up the idea to my parents. I could point to the success of it – provided it was a success – and leverage that into an argument.

Our main dishes came and I changed the subject, telling him about my experience with Um Khaled; at first he was cackling, then he was horrified. 'Do people actually use a *khataba* anymore?' he asked. I told him that, judging by the state of her 'office', not as many as Mama thought.

He pushed the food around on his plate. 'We could get married.'

'What?'

'We' – he indicated the pair of us, like he could possibly mean anyone else – 'could get married.'

'Why . . . would we do that?'

'Well, it would certainly shut people up.'

I shook my head at his suggestion. 'What people?'

He looked at me like it was obvious, linking his fingers into some sort of prayer fist beneath his chin. 'Your family . . . mine.' This last he said in a mumble.

'Yousef.'

'It makes sense though,' he said, leaning forward, his features alive and determined. 'We're really close, we adore each other, what's the problem?'

'What's the prob— What about love?'

He looked genuinely confused, his eyes flicking down to the table for only a moment before they were back on me. 'What about it?'

I shook my head again. 'Don't you want a marriage of love?'

'I love you,' he said with a schoolboy shrug.

'You know what I mean.'

He sighed, dark eyes wandering this way and that, avoiding mine. 'It would be for convenience, so if one of us, later on, fell in love with someone, we could divorce.'

'So you think I would fall in love with someone who thinks I have a morally lax attitude towards cheating?' I asked with a frown, Mona and Rashid's faces flashing against the wall of my mind.

He shook his head and ran a hand over his neatly combed wet hair. 'It wouldn't be cheating.'

112

'I agree, but he wouldn't know that, not at first. This is Kuwait; one of the first things he would learn is that I was married. Or should I get "Married for Convenience" tattooed on my arm?'

He chuckled, nodding to the waitress when she came by with the pot of green tea. 'Well, you were thinking of getting one.' I laughed as well but turned my face away, shaking my head at the proffered tea. 'It doesn't have to be so complicated.'

'But it is,' I replied with a shrug. 'Say I do fall in love. You can get on fine as a divorcé, but what happens if you want out? People won't be so kind to me.'

He frowned, but his response was quick and on point. 'No offence, but divorced at, what, thirty-two or whatever might play better than having never been married at all.'

'Ah.' I nodded, poking my chopstick at the wasabi. 'It would take care of the what's-wrong-with-her question.'

'Exactly,' he replied with a wink.

I shook my head again. 'Crazy man.'

His laugh was quiet and sincere, but his voice when he spoke again was painfully earnest. 'It's not that crazy.'

'Maybe not, but you are.'

I was being dismissive and he wasn't pleased. He took up his baby chopsticks, with the rubber band holding the tops together, and inhaled three pieces of sushi in rapid succession. With a mouthful of avocado and shrimp and crab there was no more talking to be done, and his eyes remained locked on his plate. I rescued a saturated bit of tuna, set it aside and reached for a fresh one.

The idea that Yousef might have been facing the same pressures was a new one, and I found myself looking at him differently. That his parents hounded him about marriage struck me as impossible. He was young; he had plenty of time for all that. More than that, he was a man. Unlike me, his eligibility didn't plummet further each year. If anything, he would become more desirable as more and more women remained single for longer. Why were they, our parents, so eager to push our lives forward? Why were they so keen to see the next phases of our lives start? What if there was no next phase? Certainly there were people – even here, where being alone struck such fear into the chest – who never found anyone to share their lives. Surrounded as we were by the divorced and cheated on and jilted, all slinking back to the family home, often with multiple children in tow, was it even worth it?

Did it not make more sense to just give up on the whole enterprise?

11

Tantalus

My mother went to the market every Saturday to load up on provisions for the week ahead. She loved it – scrutinizing the fruits and vegetables, haggling over the price of fish and meat, seeing what spices and oils were on offer. On Saturdays she could pretend all was in order with the world, she could pretend there was nothing for her to worry about. She headed out early to ensure she was home by the time the noon prayer was called.

Finally dragging myself from the warm covers, my coffee and I joined Baba in the yard. I settled in my wicker chair while he surveyed his kingdom. The tomcat had been in the herbs again, but my father didn't seem as annoyed by it; he just shook his head and repositioned the nets. It was overcast, not as nice as it had been. The sky was a suede blue, tentative and blobby with clouds, sun barely peeking through. It felt like spring was coming to an early end; it had been a mild one.

Like clockwork, we heard her pull up around the other side

of the yard, rolling to a stop and popping the trunk. The maids climbed out of the back seat and went to get the groceries. Minutes later she came over to the front garden. She was pleasant with Baba, smiling and telling him about the massive shrimp she'd found at the market. She hadn't seen me yet, and I remained quiet, watching her unguarded behavior with him, wondering if this was what they were like when we weren't around. There was a young quality to their interaction, a washing away of years when all they needed to discuss were pesky cats and the best way to cook fish.

She saw me and the moment was over. The smile was replaced with a frown and she marched towards me as visions of calls with Um Khaled flashed through my mind.

'*Ta'alay*,' she said, wagging her finger as she approached the porch. 'Come here, you – we need to talk.' Baba returned to his plants, though he was still within earshot, and I tried to suppress a sigh. 'Where were you last night?'

I frowned. 'What do you mean?'

'Last night,' she repeated, standing in front of me with her hands on her wide hips, her *abbaya* bunched up between her fingers. 'Where did you go?'

I glanced at my father, but he still didn't seem to be paying attention. 'I went to the *memsha*.'

She shook her head, scowling down at me. 'Was that before or after you had dinner with some man?'

My head whipped up. Baba's eyes flicked over to us at the mention of 'dinner' and 'man'.

'Your cousin Ahmed saw you there, having dinner with some

man. Who is he?' And then my father was wandering over to join her, propping one foot up on the porch, hands at his waist.

I shook my head. 'He's no one, just a guy from work.'

'Just a guy from work,' she mimicked, trading a look with Baba. 'Who is he?'

'Just a friend. Yousef. We've worked together for years. He's the one that goes with me on business trips.'

'Men and women can't be friends,' she shot back, shaking her head. 'Tell the truth, Dahlia. What are you doing with him?'

I snorted and shook my head in turn, wondering how she would react if I told her that Yousef had proposed. 'I'm not doing anything. He's a friend from work and we had dinner, big deal.'

'Do you embrace all your male friends from work?'

'Oh my God!'

'Embrace?' Baba repeated, looking from me to Mama, a definite frown on his face.

'He said she was embracing him.' She gestured at me with an open palm of accusation, like I was a whore she'd found loitering outside her house. Baba looked to me for an explanation.

'It wasn't an *embrace*,' I said, dragging out the word in a mock sing-song. 'We said hello and goodbye, that's all.'

'*La, ya mama*,' my father said, shaking his head, eyes dark and disappointed. 'You can't do things like that. You know better.'

'Of course she knows better,' Mama chimed in. 'But does she care? No! She wants to ruin her chances any way she can.'

It was like she refused to acknowledge how 'ruined' my chances already were. It was like she denied all that had happened, denied that it might have had any sort of permanent effect on me, denied that a man might not want someone who'd been through that. It was like she rejected reality, living in her little world of tradition where if you were good and followed the rules, you were rewarded.

She still believed in a life that made sense.

'You can't do things like that,' Baba was saying. 'I don't care if he's your friend or work colleague, you mustn't embrace men in public. Ever.' He shook his head and scratched at the patchy hair there. 'And perhaps lunch after work we'd be able to explain, a lunch meeting or something, but dinner . . . No, dinners are too suspicious.'

'Suspicious?' I barked back. 'I was sweaty from the *memsha* and he'd just come from the gym! Obviously, it wasn't a romantic thing.'

'People don't know that,' he retorted.

Mama looked horrified. 'You went to a nice restaurant straight from the *memsha*?' She shook her head, unable, yet again, to fathom her daughter. She looked at Baba and splayed her hands out in a gesture of astonishment. Then, she turned to go inside, shaking her head the entire way.

'That cousin doesn't take long,' I remarked once the door had shut behind her. I crossed my arms and legs, trying to take up as little space as possible in the chair, hoping my father would smirk like he always did and return to the garden.

But he didn't. He stood there, hands still on his waist,

inscrutable look on his face. I couldn't tell what he was thinking and it troubled me.

'I'm not doing anything, Baba.'

He scratched his head again and sighed. 'You know that, I know that, even your mama knows that,' he said, gesturing to the door. 'But people don't. People will see you, and they'll talk.'

'So what if they do?' I replied, leaning forward, arms crossed like I was doubled up in pain. 'Who cares if they talk? Do you honestly think a harmless "hello" in public is the worst thing anyone is doing? At least when I "embrace" men,' I added sarcastically, 'it happens in public where people can see the nature of it rather than in private where who knows what's happening.'

'You shouldn't be doing it in either case,' he said, in that tone that said he was uncomfortable and didn't want to continue talking. He moved off the porch as though if he tried hard enough, he could shuffle out of his problems. He wore an imploring look that asked why matters with his daughter couldn't be as straightforward as the garden, with its segmented plots and predictable fluctuations.

When we were nineteen we took small, escalating steps to rebellion. They were not pre-planned, these things we did, but they might as well have been. We had our driver's licenses and were heady with freedom. We stayed out too late, talked to boys, and tried anything that was handed to us. Our evenings that year followed a predictable pattern. At around six one of us would pick up the others and we'd stop for a caffeine fix. By eight we were on the road again, doing circuits on the Gulf Road while Mona figured out where we were headed. The night usually culminated somewhere we weren't meant to be – at a party too loud to talk in or a chalet of dubious repute.

Mona had befriended a new group at university – guys who'd gone to different, wilder high schools, girls who didn't give a damn about societal rules, and Kuwaitis who'd transferred home in a post-9/11 world. We moved en masse across campus like some primordial sludge, attending the same classes, getting lockers in the same corridor, descending on the cafeteria as one. We congregated under gazebos and laughed at the girls who came to class in coiffed hair and a full face of makeup. We tried to ignore how our guy friends ended up dating a lot of them even though they'd laughed right along with us.

We developed a reputation; the 'good girls' talked about us behind our backs, and the boys called us sluts for running around with so many guys. It didn't matter that none of us – not me nor Mona nor Zaina – had any interest in the males of the group, it was decided that we were fooling around with some, if not all, of them.

Our parents found out about all this at various points through the year, with predictable if dissimilar results: Mona's parents shrugged it off – they were progressives who rejected the conservatism of society anyway; Zaina was repeatedly reprimanded; and my parents just sighed a lot. They were still walking on eggshells around me at the time, and I got away with a lot. We all did.

It was anarchy, and we moved like a *pas de trois* of dissidence.

There was one night. The party was at a house out by the water; it was a big house, big and white with a wide concrete veranda. An infinity pool spilled off it, down towards the beach below. The house was all lit up with spotlights shining down on white marble and multi-colored strobes darting in and out of sliding glass doors. Music blared from all corners, a loud, thumping bass that took up residence in your head and would stay there for days after. The house had no neighbors, standing alone along a stretch of desert road halfway between town and the beach house district. It was a popular place for this sort of thing, and we'd all been there before.

We separated quickly, like always. We wouldn't be at a party five minutes without drifting away from each other. It just happened, almost as though we were ashamed to let each other hear the words we said or see the things we did. Mona's new guy found her and dragged her out towards the beach, Zaina plopped onto one of the sofas with some girls, and I migrated towards a loaded table in the corner.

The party swelled to mammoth proportions, too quick for the eye to catch, more and more people streaming in through the wide doors. The air grew thick and heavy with smoke and scents and the sweat of bodies in motion. The walls and floor and windows throbbed to the bass; it hammered my ribs and settled at the base of my skull. I fell into a happy haze, moving from sofa to chair to the floor in the corner where a small group played some game involving matchsticks and dice. I lost track of Zaina; she'd left the room and Mona hadn't come in yet.

I leaned against the entertainment center and let the beat fill my head until my brain shook. Eventually the party splintered, half heading outside while the others stayed and opted for a game of poker. I was never one for card games, so I went for a refill.

That was when I met Yousef. I was pouring some questionable-looking orange juice into my glass when over my shoulder I heard someone say, 'The music sucks.' This was a common opener, a complaint I was used to and sick of hearing. Rather than turn, I just replied, 'So change it.' In the pause that followed, I glanced at him out of the corner of my eye. His black hair was cropped short at the sides and stood straight up on top. He wore a too-tight shirt and too-tight jeans gripped by a belt with a shiny brand logo for a buckle. He also wore an expression of thorough befuddlement, as though taking matters into his own hands had never occurred to him.

Turning on his heel, he marched over to the sound system. He was small, half a head shorter than me in my heels, and narrow with a tiny waist. The hard rap stopped, to the protests of many, and was followed by some rapid-fire dance number sung by an out-of-breath female. He danced back over to the table, out of time with the beat and clearly uncaring that people were bemoaning his choice. Nobody changed it though, and he returned to my side with a sigh of, 'That's better.'

I disagreed but kept it to myself.

'Having fun?' he asked.

'Oodles,' I replied, taking a swig of my drink and gagging at the sourness of the juice.

He carried on bobbing his head to the music, still on the downbeat. 'You don't look like it. Your face is all . . .' He froze, his features still and bland, like a half-finished statue.

'Yeah, well, it's a party on the inside,' I replied, tapping my temple. I emptied my cup into the punch bowl and surveyed the bottles on the table.

'I got this,' he said. He picked up bottles and sniffed at their contents before setting them aside or putting them back. When he was satisfied, he poured and mixed and found some lime to squeeze into the glass before mixing it all some more. Finally, he dropped a maraschino cherry into the pale green liquid and handed it over.

'Not bad,' I said after a sip.

'*De rien*,' he replied with a theatrical little bow.

Before the song ended I was privy to many of the more salient details of Yousef's life: I found out he was the lone boy among five siblings; he had a thing for clothes and wanted to open his own boutique one day; he was studying psychology at one of the universities because FIDM in LA had rejected him; he was still upset about this but had to hide it because no one knew he'd even applied. He talked and talked, and I found out more than I probably needed to know. We stood against the wall and he tried to get me to gossip about what people were wearing or how they'd done their hair, but I couldn't tell what worked from what didn't, so I just nodded and laughed at what seemed to be the appropriate moments. Rap music came back on and he gave a groan of annoyance, knocking his head against the wall behind him and complaining about the lack of originality.

'This song is pretty popular,' I said. It was the closest I would get to admitting I liked it.

'This song is shit.'

A couple were going too far on the couch – she looked Indian, with skin like caramel, while he was a luminous white with fire-engine hair – and people started snapping photos. Freeze-frames and flashes: fingers danced down torsos – flash; tongues flicked out and in – snap. She bit his earlobe and the crowd roared their approval. She threw her head back and laughed, a loud, piercing sound, and he took it as an invitation to suckle at the skin of her neck like a babe seeking a teat.

'What a whore,' Yousef said, tilting his head so that it rested lightly on my shoulder.

'She's free,' I replied.

'Hey.'

It was Sultan. Too-cool-for-school Sultan who flitted in and out of our group like he couldn't decide if he liked us or not. He liked me though; since we met he'd been trying to make something happen. He flirted with us all in a natural, unthreatening way – a hand on the arm, a touch of lips to temple, innocuous little actions that bothered no one – but the attention he paid me was more intense and less divided than that which he gave to the other girls.

I was both flattered and repulsed by his attention. Flattered because he was good-looking in the most obvious way possible – tall, athletic, sharp features perfectly balanced in a tan face. Repulsed because he touched too freely, too easily, without any thought as to whether his touch was wanted. As though it baffled him, the idea that his touch was unwelcome . . . perhaps it never was with anyone but me. The other girls, even Mona and Zaina, giggled and beamed when he favored them with a tickle to the ribs or a rub of his big hands across their shoulders. I was the only one who gave him any trouble.

'Hey,' I replied, leaning forward to accept his kiss on my cheek. His lips felt like rubber, waxy and soft.

I introduced Yousef, and Sultan's dark eyes swept over him once before apparently deciding he wasn't a threat. He leaned against the wall on my other side, cradling his drink to his chest, and we watched the show.

Things with the couple were progressing. Her shirt was pushed up her torso, revealing flat white skin and the edge of a hot pink bikini top. Their audience had grown bored though, talking over one another, tossing nuts and chips at the couple and yelling at them to get a room.

'Looks like she's having fun,' Sultan murmured near my ear.

'Hmm.' I had hoped this would sound apathetic, but it came out breathier than I intended.

'We could have some fun,' he said, louder this time as someone had turned up the sound system.

I glanced at Yousef, but he just lifted his brows and drifted away. I turned back to Sultan, gripped by a sudden urge to scratch the smirk off his face.

'Who's the lady boy?' he asked, nodding towards Yousef's retreating form.

'I just introduced you.'

'I meant, who is he? I haven't seen him around.'

'Me neither,' I replied. 'We just met.'

'He wasn't trying something with you, was he?'

'The lady boy?' I asked in a mocking tone. I shook my head, eyes on the couch. 'Not everyone moves as fast as you.'

His laugh was a dark rumble that made me lean closer to him. I didn't understand myself. I let him drape his free arm around my shoulder and when those rubber lips ghosted over the shell of my ear, I didn't pull away.

'Why do you torment me like this?' he whispered. The movement, the breath against the delicate skin of my ear made me shiver. He delighted in my reaction, pulling me closer, letting his arm fall and tighten around my waist. He pressed lazy kisses to my neck, his nose burrowing in the mass of my hair.

'Aisha's getting upset,' I said, my eyes falling on the girl glaring at me from the doorway.

'Hmm?' he mumbled, opening his mouth against the point where my neck met my shoulder.

I flinched. 'There's something going on between you two, and she doesn't look pleased.'

'We're just fooling around.'

I didn't know if he meant us at that moment or him and Aisha, but I replied, 'Does she know that?'

She sent daggers at me, then turned away with a flick of her long chestnut hair and flounced back out onto the veranda. She nearly knocked over Mona, who scowled at her as she dragged her boyfriend into the house. She looked around then met my eye with a slight shake of her head and a quizzical look. I replied with a mirrored shake of my head that no, I didn't know where Zaina was. She frowned, shrugged, and let herself be pushed to the drinks table. Sultan tried to pull me to a vacant armchair, but I refused to budge. He brushed the hair off my face, his fingers stopping to feel the scar in my brow and I backed out of his grip, turning my face away when he tried to kiss my lips. He gave a frustrated sigh, but returned to my neck. Mona and her boyfriend were pouring drinks for each other, laughing and joking with an ease I couldn't emulate, much less feel. And in that moment I was Tantalus, just like in illustrations I'd seen, standing in a barren well, craning my neck to the fruit, but never touching its sweetness. I saw Yousef out of the corner of my eye; he was hovering by the sound system, looking through the stacks of CDs there. Sultan opened his mouth against my shoulder, biting down on the skin there. I yelped in shock and pain and shoved him roughly to the side so that he bumped against a table.

And then, many things happened at once.

Sultan was righting the glasses and bottles on the table when a flurry of activity erupted by the front door. We watched, all of us frozen like a paused film, as a troop of men – uniformed and non – burst in and began shouting orders.

Yousef yelled something I didn't catch, and then he was a bolt of lightning, streaking past me and out the sliding door into the night. Shouts of 'Police!' rang out as people tried to get out of the house. Yousef's escape over the veranda scattered everyone on the beach, and all I saw were blurry streaks of color as they ran for cars or somewhere to hide.

I was frozen where I stood, and Mona came to me rather

than flee with her boyfriend. Some in the living room managed to slip away, but the rest of us stood under the watchful eyes of three officers. The others were systematically moving through the house, yanking sobbing girls and arrogant, big-talking boys out of rooms.

'Where is she?' Mona hissed.

I just shook my head as one of the officers came into the room, followed by Zaina and the guy she'd been found with. Her face was folded in on itself, blotchy with tears and snot and saliva as she sobbed uncontrollably. The guy behind her was nursing his jaw and cursing under his breath. The officer glared at her like she was filth.

We were allowed to go to her, and Mona and I formed a cocoon around her, which only made her wail harder. The music cut off with a suddenness that left a vacuum of silence in its wake, but it was quickly filled with more barked orders, Zaina's sobs, and Mona's soft, comforting murmurs.

In the lieutenant's office there was the lingering smell of sweat and saffron and fried food. The walls were yellow with water stains, the furniture bulky and an ugly taupe color, like a cracked desert plain. The desk and coffee table and filing cabinets were arranged like blockades, as though the dough-faced man before us expected a battle.

We sat in a row in front of his desk, Mona and I with crossed arms and legs – little signs of continued defiance – Zaina quietly crying between us. The lieutenant's lips were massive, made more so by the smallness of his other features – beady eyes and flat nose. The lips protruded far off his face, turned down like those of a grouper fish, and I could focus on little else but how they flapped and flopped with his words. In my mind I was already sketching them, trying to figure out the mechanics of how he could function every day with such an encumbrance. Vaguely I heard him speak about shame and tradition and fathers who had been called and were on their way. Sarcastically, he asked if we knew that alcohol was not only illegal but forbidden by God himself, and had we not been paying attention during our religious studies classes at school? He said that as young women we were the bearers of family honor, and what damage such actions would do to our reputations and that of our family name, and did we not care about such considerations?

'Obviously not,' he grumbled in answer to his own question. 'Otherwise you wouldn't have been found in such a place.' He leveled a dark gaze on Zaina. 'Or in such a situation.'

We did not know what situation he was talking about; she'd been far too upset to say anything during the drive, but Mona and I could certainly guess. Then she started talking and she said all the wrong things. Lies about how it was the first party we'd ever gone to. Lies about Aziz giving her a drink that tasted funny, and more lies about what he did to her in the back room, how he'd groped and touched and she'd fought him off and how grateful she was that someone had shown up before something terrible had happened.

Lies. Mona and I stared at her, gobsmacked and silent. She and Aziz had been sniffing around each other for months; there was no way she'd needed to be forced into anything.

Lies. Her fabrications sickened me – they trivialized what I'd gone through, what she *knew* I'd gone through – but the lieutenant ate it all up. Those grouper lips nearly wrapped around his chin as he switched to a tone of compassion and understanding, pouting and clucking his tongue. He told her young men were evil and that was why our society was built on firm segregation of the sexes, that it was to prevent these sorts of situations. Mona scoffed and shook her head, bringing his anger back to us. He decided that we were a bad influence, that Mona and I had led Zaina astray (and who knows, maybe we had). He reprimanded us in language we only ever heard from our mothers. We'd shown poor judgment in going to such a place and poorer judgment still while we were there. He asked what sort of person allowed their friend to just wander off, who didn't then check on her to see that she was all right. He told Zaina she ought to rethink her friendships, that she had to choose very wisely the people she decided to spend her time with.

'May Allah conceal your sins,' he grumbled as we were led out of his office – a figurative veil for three girls who refused to wear one.

The arrival of our fathers brought more yelling and cursing and demands that Aziz be presented to Zaina's father, who felt he deserved to exact his own revenge. The fact that there was no rape to avenge didn't sway him; he still wanted a shot at that 'son of a whore'. He was still fuming when we were led away fifteen minutes later to sign our pledges – the pieces of paper wherein we confessed our sins and promised not to repeat them. I didn't know what such papers were meant to accomplish, but it appeased everyone to see us sign them.

And weeks later her father continued to rage when Zaina had to recant her story because he'd contacted a lawyer and was searching for a legal charge to level at the 'swine'. He was glorious in the defense of his own. He swore up and down that he would not let such ignominy stand, that he would see Aziz and all the other men at that party in jail. She was forced then to say what Mona and I already knew – that none of it was true, that she'd participated in it all, that the mistake had been hers.

We learned all this from overheard conversations and the single sides of phone calls that happened between our parents. We were forbidden from calling, much less seeing, each other. Mona and I avoided Zaina at university even, so furious were we at the havoc she'd wreaked.

It was a long time before we invited her to another party, and they were invitations she never accepted. Some people don't repeat their mistakes.

12

He Cannot Make Her Out

Zaina's little girl took afternoon tea very seriously. My niece Sarah and I realized this as soon as we were shown into the living room. A pink and cream floral tablecloth was draped over the low, square coffee table, and squat pink and blue stools were arranged at the four sides. A short, round vase with pink and red roses sat in the center of the table. The splash of color stood in stark contrast to the minimalist, monochrome look of the room, with its gunmetal grays, chromes, and dark chocolate tones.

Mariam acted like she was receiving the queen, taking my niece by the hand and pointing out the four little bone china plates, cream with blue embellishment, with their matching teacups and saucers. She exhorted her not to pick up the buttercup yellow sugar bowl – 'It's real and delicate. From China.' Zaina and I exchanged smiles as Sarah oohed appreciatively. We'd all dressed the part: Mariam and Sarah both had on pink, puffy dresses, almost matching but for the Peter Pan collar on Mariam's (they both had on Mary Janes as well, and I began to wonder if Zaina had called Nadia to coordinate); I'd broken out the floral cocktail dress Mama had bought me for when suitors came by, and Zaina was wearing a navy blue dress with mint green polka dots.

Tea was served promptly at four. Sarah and I were made to sit on the stools while Mariam carefully loaded the mini-sandwiches, slices of cake, and jam cookies onto the three-tiered serving tray. Zaina poured out the tea, and in no time we were sipping Earl Grey and nibbling on cucumber sandwiches.

I hadn't really spoken to Zaina in a couple of weeks. I'd been avoiding her, fearful of letting Mona's cat out of the bag. I eased into it, letting her rant about a new employee she was supervising and filling her in on my boss's missive about wanting to put together a company-wide recycling initiative – never mind that our tiny department wasn't in a position to enact anything company-wide. She told me about her summer plans, and I talked about a gym I might join and Yousef's film club that nobody was actually into. Our talk happened in dribs and drabs, bending to the rhythm and whims of the children.

I gave her a summarized version of the trip to the match-maker, and she was appropriately horrified. She refused to believe my mother would have dragged me somewhere like that, and remained in that state of disbelief until I started listing the questions we'd had to answer.

'That's insane,' she said, when I recited the question about skin tone.

'That's my mother.'

She shook her head, scraping jam off a cookie and onto her plate before she took a bite. 'What's gotten into her?'

'She's panicking,' I replied. I shouldn't have had to explain this to Zaina.

'So, you're turning thirty? Big deal,' she said. 'She's overreacting.'

'You think?' I asked sarcastically, though a part of me knew Zaina would be singing a different tune if she'd still been single on the cusp of thirty.

She shook her head again and finished off the cookie. 'But a *khataba*? That's like a last resort.'

'Many people use them these days,' I said, mimicking Mama's voice.

'Not that many,' Zaina replied disapprovingly. 'She better not go around telling people you went to a matchmaker. That really won't look good.'

I shrugged again. 'Whatever. I don't even care.'

'How can you say that?' she exclaimed, replacing a cookie on her daughter's plate with a cucumber sandwich. Mariam, deep in conversation with Sarah, didn't notice. I took a long drink of tea, hoping I didn't have to reply, but Zaina wouldn't let it go. She glanced at the girls and said in low voice, 'This isn't about . . .'

I looked up when her sentence trailed off. 'God, no!' I replied. 'No, not at all. I'm just sick of it. The whole thing's such a sham. I hate feeling like my whole life hinges upon this one event, like if it doesn't happen, then I'm just taking up air.'

She shook her head in sharp, tight jerks. 'No one thinks that.'

'Mama does, or she seems to at least.' I played with the sandwich on my plate, pulling out the cucumber slices and eating them first.

She looked at Mariam. They were talking about a clown day Sarah's school was having the following week and how she hates clowns and didn't want to go. Zaina and I smiled as Mariam reached over to give a consoling hug, explaining to Sarah that there was nothing to be scared of.

'Maybe I'll just go away to school,' I said when the girls had quieted down again.

'For a master's?' Zaina asked, distracted by the mess her daughter was making. She tsked and leaned over to reposition the napkin on Mariam's lap.

'Or something,' I replied, thinking there was no way I'd get into a postgraduate graphic design program and that I'd probably have to start all over. Panic flared in my chest at the thought.

'That's a lot of money and time to spend just to get away from your mother.'

'It's not just about her,' I murmured, pushing the remnants of sandwich around on my plate.

'What then?'

I shook my head, unable to articulate my thoughts. How could I explain to her that nothing in my life felt real? That in a country like Kuwait, where everyone knew everything about each other, the most monumental thing to ever happen to me was buried and covered over? For the sake of my reputation, my future, my sister's and cousins'; the family honor sat on my little shoulders, so no one could ever know what he'd done to me. Society would never have shut up about it.

The result was that my life was not real *because* society had no idea what had happened to me. And I was left to play the part of a normal, late-twenties woman. I was supposed to care about clothes and makeup and getting lip fillers and fake lashes in the hope of catching the attention of men everywhere I went. I was supposed to put my best face forward at receptions and weddings, get up and dance and show off in the hope of snagging the attention of some woman with a marriageable son in mind. I was supposed to care that I wasn't married and should be actively pursuing the goal by doing the rounds at popular spots and events around town and splashing my face all over social media.

If society had known what I'd been through, no one would have expected me to play along. They would have given up on me from the very start.

'You know what we should do?' Zaina broke into my thoughts, turning back to me with an excited look on her face. 'This girl at work was telling me about this woman who reads *fenjals*.'

'What?'

'She's a coffee reader. You drink Turkish coffee and then she reads the grounds and stuff left behind.'

'Reads them?'

'Yeah, like reads your future or helps sort out things in the present, I don't know . . . alerts you to things you might not be aware of.'

'Like the fact that my friend believes in such rubbish?'

She grinned. 'Come on! If nothing else, it'll be fun.'

'Fun?' I replied, raising an eyebrow.

'Sure. It's been ages since we did something silly. I'll get in touch or make an appointment or whatever.'

'Mommy!' Mariam whined, grabbing her mother's sleeve. 'Tell her that the prince in the movie is the one who cut Rapunzel's hair, not the witch!' Sarah was glaring at her, arms crossed, with the kind of conviction only four-year-olds are capable of.

'I think it's time to talk about something else,' Zaina said, smoothing her daughter's hair.

'No! Tell her, tell her.'

'*Khalas, mama,*' she said in a sterner tone. 'No arguing.'

Mariam subsided with a huff and Sarah smiled triumphantly, but soon they were diverted into a discussion about spring shows at their respective schools. Sarah started singing the song from her school's show. And then they were up, bunching dresses in their tiny fists, showing off and comparing the dances they'd been practicing.

'I can't believe we were ever that small,' Zaina said, smiling as we watched them bounce across the floor.

'Yeah, crazy.'

On our way back we stopped off at the grocery store where, in my distracted state, I allowed Sarah to wander through the aisles at my side munching on mini-chocolate cookies from a little tub. Her mother would be furious at my giving her that much chocolate, but I was too distracted to stop her. I found myself considering Yousef and his suggestion.

A part of me was tempted by it. We were very good friends – best friends, you could say – and it would have been a fairly easy arrangement. He came from a family comparable to mine: same tribal origins, same religious sect, same class, etc. On paper, it all lined up perfectly – and didn't I say it was important for things to line up on paper? He'd come to the house with his mother and sisters; they'd chat with my mother, who would already be aware, of course, of how Yousef and I know one another. 'I knew it was a date!' she'd probably hiss at me triumphantly at some point, to which I would have to blush and smile and pretend to be coy.

And that would have been it. If we'd put our minds to it, we could have been married inside of two or three months.

As Sarah and I left the store I heard someone calling my name and turned to see Bu Faisal coming towards us, his mouth twitching into a grin. He greeted me with an easy smile then directed his flowery praise to Sarah, asking her name and age and all those other things you ask children while she shuffled and hid behind me in embarrassment. That done, he and I traded pleasantries; he inquired about work, I asked if he had any trips coming up and he said he was staying put for a couple of months. Sarah quickly grew bored of our conversation and started pulling at my skirt, pointing at the playground between the store and parking lot.

'Oh, no, baby,' I said, shaking my head down at her. 'We need to get you home.'

'Please, please, please,' she whined. 'Just five minutes.'

'*Haram*, let her play,' Bu Faisal said, winning a beaming smile from Sarah.

'Fine, but only for a little bit.' She took off before I finished speaking, and I had to holler after her. 'Be careful with your dress!'

We followed at a slower pace, Bu Faisal offering to take the bags from me, but his hands were full as well so I didn't let him. We ended up at the boundary of the playground, right where hard pavement turns to soft, green mats. There were kids crawling all over the place, climbing the jungle gym, swinging from monkey bars, screaming down slides. Some parents stood on the sidelines watching, but most of the adults were Indian and Filipino nannies who talked to one another or texted on their phones.

'You look very nice today,' Bu Faisal suddenly said. I turned to him, but he was looking at the children.

I turned my face back to the playground. 'Thank you. Sarah and I were at a tea party.'

'That's sweet.'

'It was.'

'Work is good?'

'Yeah, fine,' I replied, though he'd already asked that, and I glanced at him from the corner of my eye.

His brows were low and drawn together, mouth pursed into some odd facsimile of a frown, and I wondered if he suddenly wished he hadn't called out to me. An awkwardness descended between us, one which was unfamiliar. I wondered if it was because we hardly ever saw each other outside of the office; the times when our families had traveled together felt very far away, like they'd happened to other people in other worlds. They didn't seem connected to the person I had become, or to the relationship he and I had. Occasionally I'd run into him at the mall or grocery store or riding his bicycle on the seafront, and we would stop and say hello, but most of our interactions happened at the office or during business trips, which usually involved Yousef. Plus, there was a safety in being abroad, in being able to converse without having the sense that someone was always there to watch, to listen, to judge.

I couldn't imagine Bu Faisal worrying about such a thing as the opinion of others, but the silence was stretching between us, and I felt an impulse to fill it with something.

'Yousef asked me to marry him.'

It was the worst possible thing to say. It firmly pulled him into some murky, more intimate territory that I couldn't name. He knew Yousef; why not tell Mona or Zaina, who only knew him as someone who occasionally joined us for coffee? I don't have an answer for that. Perhaps a part of me wanted to push him into another category, wanted to reclaim that moment of intimacy from Germany, that sense of comfort and safety, which neither of us had tried to extend or explore.

I tried to laugh it off, but it came out as some pitiful half-sniffle.

'Well,' he said in a slow, measured tone, 'that's nice. I hadn't realized . . . I mean, I didn't know.' He glanced at me. 'You kept it well hidden.'

'There was nothing to hide.'

His brows dipped further, and he tilted his head, dark eyes searching my face. For what, I didn't know. I couldn't stop now.

'We've been under a lot of pressure . . . from our families . . . to marry. Separately, not each other,' I rushed to add. 'And getting married would put an end to all that. We would be able to relax and not be hounded about it all the time. It would be . . . like a back-up but in reverse.'

'A back-up?' he repeated, tripping on the unfamiliar term.

'Yeah, you know, you make a deal with a good friend that if neither of you is married by a certain age, you marry each other?'

The look on his face told me he'd never considered nor perhaps even heard of such a thing. 'That's ridiculous.' I shrugged, unable to argue. 'What would such a marriage accomplish? You say your families are hounding you about marriage. Let them hound you! What are they going to do, drag you to a *milach* by force?'

'Of course not, but—'

'Everyone goes through this at some point, if they haven't married early. It's normal. The answer isn't to have some joke of a marriage. That's not something to take lightly.' He shook his head, eyes on the children running in manic circles.

His disapproval, though its essence aligned with my instincts, wounded me. I felt his disappointment, like he'd expected more from me, and I rushed to restore my standing.

'I said no, of course.' He turned, scanning my face again, and I continued, 'I told him it would be a lie, that I couldn't live like that, that it would be . . . dishonest.' I petered out with a limp shrug, unsure what I was fighting for or against.

'That's good,' he said. I didn't know if he was talking about my saying no, the reasoning behind it, or some combination of the two. In any case, I was unwilling to ask.

Sarah, who'd been chasing after some other girls, went tumbling into the dirt. I took a step forward to help her, but she just leapt to her feet and resumed running. I could see smudges and dust on her beautiful dress, what looked like a rip in her white tights, her hair was a mess, and I knew I was in for a lecture.

'I need to get her home.'

13

What One Does to the Other

It took two weeks to shore up my courage. Two weeks of hand-wringing, web-searching, and abhorrent navel-gazing before I dared approach my parents with the idea of leaving.

I would leave on the pretext of going to school; I'd found several graphic design programs – some undergraduate, some of the continuing education sort – both in America and Europe. Going to school was a smokescreen, though. I'd get a degree, but I would also find a way to stay there – a job, asylum, anything. Anything so I wouldn't have to come back to this. Perhaps thirty was a sell-by date of sorts; take control of your life by then or forfeit any right to happiness. No, that couldn't be it. There were plenty of people floating along on the whims of others who seemed perfectly happy. Were they happy or did they just seem it? Was there such a thing as 'happy'? Were they in fact following the whims of others or had they made their own choices? Nadia married the first man

Mama presented her with; did that mean it wasn't ultimately her choice?

I wasn't sure. There was a lot that I wasn't sure of. I probably should have gotten those things straight in my head before approaching my parents, but I hadn't. I jumped in with little to commend me aside from some printed-out pages from university websites.

And then they sat there, at opposite ends of our L-shaped sofa, staring at me like I was a puzzle they had no hope of ever deciphering, like I was an alien they wished they could strap to a table and dissect, like they couldn't fathom how a few minutes of copulation had resulted in this thing who thought and spoke in all those ways that they didn't condone. I empathized; often I couldn't understand myself. My thoughts, my actions, seemed strange to me, to spontaneously *be* rather than emanating from some clear source. I struggled to understand my past and the series of events that had made me what I was. Likewise, my present could feel just as foreign, just as tenuous, just as delicate.

'What do you need more schooling for?' Mama asked, breaking the silence.

'You can never have too much education,' I mumbled in reply.

She puffed out a breath, not bothering to turn from the television. They both ignored the papers on the coffee table.

'What's wrong with your job?' Baba asked.

'It's not . . .' I began, my voice too timid for my liking. I took a deep breath and tried again. 'It's boring. It's not challenging enough or interesting enough. It's just not . . . enough.'

What I meant to say, but could not say, was that life here, in this country, wasn't enough.

He scrutinized me for a long moment. 'That's no reason to give it up,' he finally said. 'You're doing well there. They keep promoting you, and the job pays well.'

'Not everything is about money,' I replied, shaking my head. 'I never chose that job, Baba. I took it because everyone expected me to work in finance.'

'Because I wanted you to have a good job, and those are the best. There's no other option.'

'Maybe not then, maybe not ten years ago, but there are now.'

'It's too late to change your career now. Why go through all the trouble? You have to learn something new and start at the bottom all over again. If you're bored, find something to do outside of work.'

A perfectly reasonable response. 'I want to go back to school,' I said, nudging the papers their way, 'to learn.'

He picked up the stack, going through the pages one by one, though I couldn't tell whether it was just a token gesture or not. In the long silence of his contemplation, Mama switched channels, refusing to involve herself in the discussion. When Baba was done, he looked at me again, eyes dark and unreadable, a deep wrinkle marring his brow.

'Abroad?'

'Of course, abroad,' I replied. Mama shook her head, but she let my father do the talking. I had no idea where this sudden shrinking violet persona of hers had come from, but it unnerved me.

He shook his head as well, held up the papers, and said, 'This isn't anywhere near your field. This is art.'

'Art?' Mama repeated, turning to him and glancing at the papers.

'Graphic design,' I said.

'What is that?' she asked, wrinkling her nose.

'It's art,' Baba replied with a frown. 'We agreed that art was a hobby.'

'No,' I said, 'you decided art was a hobby and I didn't disagree with you then, but I am now. It can be a job now, Baba. Look at the career prospects.' I gestured to the papers again.

'What prospects?' he huffed, dropping the stack back on the table. 'You leave a good respectable job in a respectable field to work in what, an advertising agency or a magazine or something?'

'We don't want you mixing with those sort of people,' Mama added.

'What sort of people?'

'Good people from good Kuwaiti families don't work in those kinds of places; why should you work there?'

'Because . . . it's what I like to do.'

'And we're not saying don't do it,' my father said, his frustration beginning to show. 'Keep drawing, do exhibitions, sell your pictures even. You don't need to go to school for that.'

I hadn't told them about the exhibit Yousef had pushed ahead for me. He'd confirmed the date and I'd already taken my sketches down so Zacharia could see them. He'd shown me the space and we'd talked about how best to show them. Telling my parents about that wouldn't help my case; they'd see it as confirmation of their argument and a subsequent weakening of mine. 'There are techniques,' I said instead. 'Technical things I want to learn.'

'And you need four years abroad to learn it?' Baba retorted.

'Four years?' Mama exclaimed, turning her full attention on me.

'It's another bachelor's degree,' he said, tossing the papers back on the table. 'You'd be starting over, like the last seven or eight years were just a waste of time.'

It felt like they had been. Like with Mama's suitors, my job was just another play I was acting in. It felt like my life had been just a series of situations that I'd fallen into, like I had no agency or control over anything. I was through living like that.

'Four years abroad? Are you crazy?' Mama said. I leaned back against the cushions and crossed my arms. 'No, Dahlia.'

'What do you mean, "No, Dahlia"?' I said. 'We can't even talk about it?'

'There's nothing to talk about,' she said. 'You can't live somewhere, alone, for four years. I'm having a hard enough time getting you married with you here all the time.'

And there it was. What we always came back to. The damnable event upon which my entire life hinged. The big disappointment. The one concession I'd been unwilling to give my parents. I traveled to the future, envisioned a future me who married, a marriage of convenience – with Yousef or one of Mama's choices. It would be an unhappy marriage, one that would naturally end. A part of me was beginning to believe I wasn't made for another person. Was that kind of marriage the only way to secure a life of my own choosing?

'You've never said anything about this before,' Baba said. 'Why now?'

'Because I've worked for a while now, and I think it's time for a change.'

'You want a change?' my mother replied. 'Get married, that's an enormous change.'

'Mama . . .'

'Be serious,' Baba added.

'I am serious,' she said, turning my way. 'You would be thirty-four or thirty-five when you got back – who'd marry you then?'

I shook my head. 'There are more important things in life than marriage.'

'Like what, art school?' she said. 'That's a stupid answer, Dahlia. Do you want to live in this house your whole life?'

'I definitely don't want that.'

'Don't be disrespectful,' my father said, and there was genuine sadness in his eyes. I turned my face from it and stared blankly at the television.

'Four years is too long,' Mama said. 'It's impossible. People will forget you exist.'

I should be so lucky, I thought. 'What about one of the shorter programs,' I asked, gesturing to the papers, 'would that be better?'

'No, it wouldn't be better,' said Baba. 'Who will take care of you, living abroad? Who will protect you?'

'Protect me from what?'

He had no response. He stared at me for a moment then turned his dark eyes back to the television.

'You can't take care of yourself,' my mother added. 'Here, everything is done for you. Who will cook for you, who will clean your room and wash your clothes?'

'I'll learn.'

She made another scoffing sound. 'You have this dream of going away. You think it will be like the movies. You have no idea how difficult it will be.'

'Neither do you,' I snapped. 'You went straight from your family's house to Baba's family house, so don't pretend you know any more about it than I do.' When she opened her mouth to retort, I cut her off: 'You might think I'm useless, but I can learn how to do all those things for myself.'

'And what will I tell the family?' my father asked. 'Your aunts and uncles? How will I tell them that I let my daughter go off to America by herself, like I don't care about her well-being?'

'It's a little late to be caring about my well-being.' The words launched themselves from my mouth before I had even thought them.

It was below the belt, I knew that. The words hit their mark and sliced deep, right into a very old, very infected wound. My parents stared at me, speechless for once. And when the shock receded, the expression that settled on my mother's face transcended anger. If expressions could speak, I imagined hers would have said something like, 'I wish you weren't here.' On my father's face was something I couldn't articulate, but it cut me as deep as my words had cut them.

I took back my papers and retreated to my room.

We are, all of us, accumulations of memories, reservoirs of revised history. Like magicians, we pull stories from our pasts – some we remember, some are pieced from the memories of others, some are partially or entirely appropriated.

There was a time when I saw evil eye talismans everywhere – *nazars* and *Hamsas*, blue and white and shiny, everywhere. I found them tucked into pillowcases, dropped into sock drawers, affixed to silver and gold chains. My memories are distorted; at times I don't quite recall my own life. Perhaps the talismans were Zaina's. She has a belief in the occult that some *sheikhs* might find uncomfortably close to blasphemy. Are the *Hamsas* hers? She used to wear one, with a diamond for an eye, around her wrist. The memories might be hers; I sometimes feel like the three of us have a shared pool of history, a common pond that we dip our toes into when recalling stories of our child-hood. Mona tells the story of Nadia pushing her off the top of a slide, but the scar cuts through my eyebrow, not hers. I have a strong memory of emptying a jar of strawberry jam when I was six, digging my fingers into the gooey sweetness and licking and licking till it was all gone. I feel the sticky pips and pulp on my face, around my lips, I see the redness under my finger-nails and in the grooves of my palms. But I'm allergic to strawberries and always have been.

We like to think of ourselves as a well-traveled, cultured, and thoroughly modern people. Xenophiles who welcomed expats long before Dubai. We are the ones gamboling from Knightsbridge to Mayfair; we're the ones who love, who've adopted, Beirut with an unbridled passion; and we're the ones who brought cellphones and commercial airlines to the Gulf. We're the ones on a constant search for the new, the wondrous, the techtastic.

It's a kind of masked secularism though. Lurking in the breast of every Kuwaiti are the superstitions of our pearl-diving days. We have a hundred different phrases to ward off evil. '*Istaqhfir Allah*', and '*Mashalla*', and '*Hamdilla*' – rapid responses for any comment that crosses our path. '*Bismillah*' to bless our food or protect our footing on unsteady terrain. The ritual of a sneeze entails the exchange of three phrases. There's the miming of spitting at the thing you wish to protect from evil eyes. All these rituals are second nature now, but beneath them are very real fears, very concrete beliefs. Who knows if they work; I suppose the comfort alone must be worth something.

I was possessed by a demon as a toddler. Most two-year-olds are, but mine necessitated the intervention of a holy man. He prescribed a ritual that entailed the reading of Quranic verses and the sacrifice of a sheep whose blood would then be smeared on my deviant form.

Knowing my parents as I do, their deference to a holy *sheikh* seems unlikely. Baba never had time for such things; he's a rational man for whom the only unprovable thing to believe in is God. Mama had some superstitions, but they were mild and mostly asserted themselves when something vital was at stake. A blood ritual seems over the line for her. Nevertheless the story is there, lodged in my consciousness. I see the white *kashi* tiles of our old yard, the grayish wall with its crayon graffiti, and the black iron gate. I can see the sheep, also grayish, by the driveway, where the blood can be easily hosed out into the street gutter. I hear its bleating, that distressed sound that doesn't say 'let me go' so much as it says 'I've seen the knife'. If I put my mind to it, I can feel the blood, warm and slick and metallic, painted across my forehead and dotting the apples of my cheeks.

My parents swear it never happened, but the memory has been with me for ages. Is it a repression? An appropriation of other stories? Or an utter fabrication?

14

Hunting for Teeth

The reader's palms were orange. Not ochre, or sienna, or some other quasi-romantic sounding tint. Orange. Like a particularly ginger orangutan. They were black where the henna had seeped into the cracks in her skin, like sticky tar or a fresh tattoo. And the smell of it. My God, the henna smell burst from her skin with each movement of her long, bony hands. Wafts of that cloying scent climbed up and into my nostrils to gather like a cloud at the front of my mind.

An orange cloud, with black veins. Like the sky after the war when the oil fields were still burning.

Zaina was speaking to the old woman, Um Dawood, in low, nearly reverent tones, but I wasn't listening. Quranic verses lined the wall opposite me. Short verses, longer ones, all swirling lines and sharp accents. I recognized the more familiar ones, traced their letters in my mind, let them dance silently on my tongue. They were embroidered on tapestries, etched in mirrors, and burned into wood. It seemed nothing else was allowed on the walls. In the corner was an old TV set on a teetering glass and metal table that matched the coffee table before me.

Um Dawood ignored Zaina, only giving the occasional *insha' Allah* or nod in response to whatever was said. She spread a green cloth over the table; gold tassels dangled over the edge and tickled my knees. I should have worn a longer dress. I wondered if she found it offensive. Her smoky black eyes had passed over me benignly when we'd arrived, but they soon began darting little glances that pinched my bare legs.

She smoothed the cloth, her fingers like withered carrots stretching my way, sending another wave of that oily scent. I turned my face, meeting Zaina's eyes. She smiled, but it was tight and pinched, like she was the one about to get her future read. She had nothing to be nervous about. Her future was secure, a book whose last page she'd read several times over.

'*Ya Allah.*' Um Dawood sighed, reaching up to adjust the black *hijab* draped loosely over her head. The hair that peeked through was burgundy, with tell-tale henna stains in the part. The stench was overwhelming, poking at my gag reflex.

As if on cue, a maid entered with a stainless steel tray that she set before us. On it were two handle-less coffee cups, small enough for a cupped palm. They and the saucers they sat on were a stained and dulled white with no embellishment or decor. They'd been used many times. I welcomed the strong scent of the Turkish brew as it overrode the henna, leaning in and taking a deep breath.

She was not a woman of many words. Um Dawood only

extended a hand to indicate I should begin drinking. I was surprised to find my hand shook; the *fenjal* rattled against the saucer, coffee threatening to spill over. I looked to Zaina again, but she was blowing on the surface of her own coffee. I pursed my lips to do the same, but Um Dawood stopped me with three rapid tsks of her tongue. When I looked up, she shook her head and motioned again that I should drink. I winced as the first sip seared me, the bitter coffee latching onto my tongue.

'*Shway shway*,' she said, shifting in her straight-backed chair. 'Take your time.'

I'm not a fan of Turkish coffee, but I could be obedient, so I sat quietly, letting my gaze wander around the room while I sipped the tarry liquid. The grounds were already coating my tongue, gritty and dry. Zaina tried again to engage Um Dawood in conversation, and the old woman was more receptive, lamenting the dry winter, recounting the number of girls in my 'situation' who'd come to her the past few months, boasting about her well-trained third eye.

'I was eight when I read my first *fenjal* for Mama, *Allah yer'hemha*,' she said, tapping an orange and black finger against the wooden arm of her chair and looking up at the ceiling. I followed her gaze, only half listening. 'I saw a dust storm, huge clouds of dirt blowing towards the center.' There was a mount in the ceiling for a chandelier, a white, circular eye with a pocket. Wires dangled from the hole, looking for something to illuminate. 'Anything near the center means it will happen presently, *insha' Allah*. "Shoofee, shoofee," I said to her. "A storm is coming." The next morning, bah!' She swiped her palms across one another with a thwacking sound. 'You could see nothing. Blinded by dust.'

'My God,' Zaina said, turning to me with an awed expression, though I didn't think predicting a dust storm in Kuwait required much in the way of prescience.

'Your predictions are very specific,' I said, wanting to take a sip of water to wash down the grinds, but wary of getting another set of tsks.

I got them anyway. Um Dawood sat forward and shot me a rapid half-dozen of them. 'I make no predictions,' she said, wagging a pruney finger. 'I'm not a witch.' She turned to Zaina, thin lips drooping into a frown, eyelids buckling over kohl-rimmed eyes. 'Did Um Humoud say I deal in magic? There's no magic here!' She made that swiping motion again with her palms.

'No, no, of course not,' Zaina said, sending me an accusatory glance. I looked down into my coffee. 'She said nothing of the kind. Of course not. Allah protect us from such devilry.'

Um Dawood scrutinized us for a long moment, her glare darting between us like a ping-pong ball. Finally, she seemed satisfied and relaxed her face. I tipped my cup towards her, showing her that it was empty but for the soupy sediment at the bottom. She nodded and plucked the saucer from my lap, laying it on the rim of the *fenjal*. 'Now, three times, at the chest,' she said, demonstrating for me. I followed suit, holding the cup and saucer at my chest and moving it in three horizontal circles. I felt silly, but it would have been bad to laugh. When I was done, she took the items and flipped them over, setting them back down on the cloth to let the coffee grounds slide down the sides of the cup and into the saucer. She placed a large silver coin on the upturned bottom. I wasn't sure why. Then, she leaned back in her seat with another sigh. Talking time was over.

Tasseography. That's what it's called. And despite Um Dawood's vehement denial, it is a form of divination. I'd looked it up the day before. I liked to be prepared. And so, I knew about dividing the cup into positive and negative halves; I knew certain practitioners didn't believe the cups could divine things more than forty days into the future (perhaps Um Dawood was one of them); and I knew about the present and future sections she'd mentioned.

She removed the coin, touching the sides of the *fenjal* to test its temperature. Satisfied, she turned the cup over, tipping it my way as she gazed into it. The coffee grounds had coated the sides in wavy lines – thick and thin, weaving up and down around the inside, like a Joy Division poster. Arches like domed crescents leapfrogged around the rim. Sediment remained at the bottom, murky and chocolate brown.

Um Dawood shook her head with a clicking of her tongue. 'So dark.' Surely I couldn't be blamed if the brand of coffee was too strong. I glanced at Zaina, but her attention was on the old woman. 'If you keep looking, the lines will take shapes. They will tell you who you are, what your life is. Events can begin to make sense, perspective can be found.'

I remained skeptical, but Zaina was enjoying the show, leaning forward, hands on knees as though the reading was for her.

'Ah, see here now,' Um Dawood said, pointing to the bottom of the cup. 'Shapes are coming, triangles, maybe angels. Very good.' She nodded, holding the *fenjal* steady. 'Animals. Many animals. And ants!' She pointed at an indistinct cluster of grounds. 'Ants are hard workers, very determined.' I glanced at Zaina again. No reaction. I should have brought Yousef; I'd have at least gotten an eye-roll off him. 'Hmm,' she continued, peering this way and that, examining the cup from all sides. 'There are quarrels, I think. See these?' She pointed at a section of lines that had oozed together into some globular shape. 'Cats. Definitely the backs and tails of cats. Whiskers, too. There are quarrels in your life. Wavy lines indicate instability, uncertainty.' Zaina glanced over at me, eyes popping. Um Dawood tsked again, shaking her head at the cup.

'That looks like a horse,' Zaina offered, pointing at the goopy bottom.

'Many animals,' the old woman replied with a nod. She cackled, startling us. 'Horses, cats, ants. You've given me a zoo!' Zaina laughed a little nervously, but I only smiled, smothering an urge to apologize. 'Horse; yes, there's a horse. It means you are strong and independent, but it can get you in trouble. Look at these cats.'

'There's a bear,' she added after a moment, eyes snapping up to meet mine. 'Think carefully about what you're planning to do.'

'What are you planning to do?' Zaina asked me with a confused look.

I shook my head at the pair of them. 'Nothing.' Um Dawood was unconvinced, I saw that immediately.

Her beady eyes narrowed into little black-rimmed marbles of scrutiny. 'There will be trouble ahead. You must think carefully on your course of action.' I wondered if she could see into me. If her third eye had popped clear open. I wondered if she could read my mind.

'I thought you didn't make predictions,' I whispered, forcing my eyes to stay on hers. She said nothing, but a storm kicked up on her face, a cloud passing over her thin brows. She studied me for a long moment, the cup and its globs and lines forgotten in her hand.

A door opened down the hall, and the melodic tone and elongated syllables of Quranic recitation spilled into the hall. Zaina and I jumped at the sudden sound. It was a man's voice, a recording rather than someone reading live, I thought; but it was loud and shrill and Um Dawood withered a bit in its presence – almost like it reminded her of the nature of her work.

She refocused on the *fenjal*. 'There is a beetle, yes, indicative of a difficult task. Ants and the horse show you to be strong and determined; this may be of help to you. But I would beware the bear.' She glanced up at me again, eyes hard and unforgiving. 'These triangles may be the spokes of a wheel, indicating change or progress. Perhaps you will be successful in your plans.' There was a note of finality there, and she returned the cup to the saucer, ignoring the mucky grounds that had pooled there.

'All right,' I said, unwilling to argue.

'Is that all?' Zaina asked.

She spread her hands. 'The cup says no more.'

'All right,' I repeated, turning to Zaina with a shrug. I made a move to stand. 'Well . . . thank you. This was very . . . interesting.'

The smile didn't sit comfortably on Um Dawood's face. It twitched like it was trying to run away. 'Would you like to open your heart before you leave?'

I slumped back in my seat. 'Sorry?'

She leaned forward and placed her right thumb in the goop left on the saucer and gave it a small clockwise turn. There was an impression left behind; a thumbprint, surely, but with spikes like fire sparks going off the end. 'Do the same for the bottom of the *fenjal*,' she said, 'and I can tell you the feelings you have deep in your belly, the things you hide behind your heart, the things no one can see.' Her voice was low, steady, and sure. It pierced me. I couldn't breathe in that air.

I shook my head. 'I don't think—'

'*Yella*,' Zaina interrupted, nudging my arm. 'It's the last thing, and we're here so you might as well.'

The twitchy smile returned to Um Dawood's face. The reciter ended a verse and started a new one; I heard the turning of the page on the recording. Extending my arm, I dipped my right thumb into the mouth of the cup until I hit sediment, then quickly gave it a 90-degree turn. She stared at the resulting shape for a long time, all unwavering eyes and firm lines. To me the shape was as unremarkable and indistinct as the others. I saw nothing in it. I told myself I saw nothing in her. She was a fraud, as phony as everyone else.

Finally, she looked up at me, eyes dark and confident. 'Horses are strong and ants may be determined, but neither is known for its bravery.'

'I mean, she basically called me a coward,' I complained as we climbed into my car.

It was dinnertime, the acidic rumbling in my stomach said so, and I resented Zaina for dragging me there. I hadn't eaten much of anything that day – an orange, a couple of crackers, a spoon of rice and yoghurt – and the Turkish coffee wasn't sitting well, churning in my gut. There was a bitter taste in my mouth and my tongue was dry.

'I don't think that's what she was saying,' Zaina murmured as she buckled her seatbelt.

'Why are you defending her?'

'I'm not.'

I repeated what Um Dawood had said, that ridiculous thing about horses and ants, doing my best to mimic her gravelly whine. 'What does that even mean? It's a load of crap. I can't believe you brought me to such a quack.'

'She's supposed to be really good,' she mumbled, fiddling with the radio as I pulled into traffic.

The highway was bumper to bumper. It was always bumper to bumper, giving plenty of time for in-car arguments and road rage-fueled venting. Zaina hit SEEK over and over, running through all the stations, and I gritted my teeth and fought the urge to slap her hand away.

'So, you agree with her, then? I'm a coward.' It didn't matter that I may have thought it; I didn't want to hear it confirmed.

'She wasn't saying that.'

'My ears are connected to my brain, same as everyone else, and that's exactly what she said, Zaina. And stop that, please!'

She returned her hands to her lap, folding them primly over the smooth fabric of her skirt, and looked out the window. The cars were backed up all the way to our exit, at least half a kilometer away. Too long for us to remain silent. I felt an urge to argue, to assert something, to wrestle some sort of acquiescence from her. I tried to ignore it, to redirect my anger to Um Dawood where it rightly belonged. That old hag, with her henna palms and greasy hair and her fingers like rotting vegetables, sitting there talking about me like she knew me, like she knew anything about my life.

'What are you planning to do?' Zaina asked, her voice low under the heavy bass coming out of the radio.

'Huh?'

'She said you were planning to do something – what is it?'

I snorted and pressed SEEK until I got to a station with talking. 'Was that the cats or a koala, maybe?'

'It was the bear. She said it meant you were planning something.' She turned to me, and I could feel her gaze.

I darted my eyes to her then back to the road. 'You don't really believe her, do you? She's a quack! Who knows what she was talking about?'

'But she said you were planning something; that's very specific.'

'Is it?' I scoffed. 'Who isn't planning *something*, Zaina? I'm thinking of going away to school, you're planning to have another baby, Nadia's planning a vacation. Everyone's thinking about doing something.'

'You were serious about that – about school, I mean?'

'Maybe,' I replied with a shrug. We'd barely moved and I tapped my fist on the horn impatiently. It wouldn't make the cars go, but it would make me feel better. I told her about the talk with my parents and their reaction and how things had ended.

'Wow,' she said when I was done. Understatement of the century, I thought. 'Well, they always say no at first; you can try again later.'

I shrugged again, trying to move one lane over. I never drove in the Emergency lane; I hated it when people did that, but I was starving and mad and didn't want to talk. The radio was on Voice of America, and there was a man talking about ISIS, the US response, video beheadings, and a world gone madder than usual. It was a crossfire-type show, the opposing side talking about how an Arab problem required an Arab solution. 'Thousands are dying,' the man said, 'and you want to wait for the Arabs to agree on something?' The other one, a conservative by the sound of it, was indignant, like they were talking about something terribly personal – 'Why should our men and women continue to die while they sit around twiddling their thumbs?'

It's hard to argue with that.

If Zaina and I started talking about it, she'd use it as a teaching moment. 'Remember that picture I sent you of the dead kids?' she'd say, a deep frown etched into her face, made deeper by the night and console lights and shadows. 'Or the one with the children in school with the hole in their chalkboard from a bomb?' I would nod even if I wasn't sure exactly what picture she was talking about. 'I mean, we're so lucky. Imagine if I had to worry about that every time I sent my baby to school.' She'd shake her head, twirl her wedding band around her finger, and murmur a quick *Hamdilla* or prayer to Allah to keep such catastrophes far, far away from us. I would nod through it all and agree with her, because how could you not? We were lucky. Our lives were stable.

I was too young to remember the war as our family, like many others, had been on summer vacation at the time. But for years after the liberation, alarm sirens would blare out across the city. There would be a warning of an impending system test, but I didn't always know about it. Still, even on those days when I hadn't been told, I never took it seriously. For some reason I always assumed it was a test. I mean, Iraq was no longer a threat, and Saddam had been returned to the role of the crazy cousin at the barbecue that no one talks to. What was there to be afraid of? I remember once though, maybe ten years after the war had ended, I had been in bed sketching when the alarm wailed. It startled me and I lost control of my line, the pen zig-zagging to the edge of the page like an erratic, inky lightning bolt. I was still far too jumpy then, always sensing danger at the slightest sound or a shadow of movement. I felt the anxiety snowball as the siren screamed on, and I covered my head with my hands, like that brace position they show you on airplanes. On and on it went, louder then softer, closer then further. And I remember thinking, God help people who live like this every day.

Yes, we were lucky, but if you weren't supposed to feel sad because other people had it worse, then you couldn't really be happy either, could you?

My stomach let out a mighty roar, a plaintive cry that vibrated my insides.

'Your stomach is playing me the song of its people,' Zaina said with a small smile.

I let out a little laugh, shook my head and pressed down on my belly with one hand.

Her voice was low and tentative. 'I don't think you're a coward.'

15

A Cowslip's Bell

Fen Gallery was out by the airport, in an old warehouse surrounded by rundown factories and empty complexes in need of demolishing. If you stood in the courtyard long enough, you would see the gleaming belly of planes overhead and your ears would fill with their deafening roars. The building was white-washed in its entirety, so that it stood like a beacon among the forgotten structures around it. Zacharia must have it repainted every couple of months. It wasn't the best neighborhood, but he somehow made it seem desirable – a destination that people would gladly go out of their way to get to.

It was only six in the evening when I parked my car down the street and made my way to the gallery. The sun had just descended and the twilight was hazy. The season of the *sarayat* had begun; the wind blew from the south, bringing with it dust and clouds the color of wet tarmac which exploded into sudden, angry storms. We'd had one the night before, the shutters on the windows of my room shaking from the violence of it, the thunder cracking like bombs. The rain had fallen, kamikaze rain that hit the windows and roof hot and fast. It was gone by morning, the earth left wet and strained at its parting, the hard sand struggling to absorb the water.

Zacharia had had some trouble at the gallery. The wind had ripped some branches off an old palm tree in the courtyard, and these had been left to litter the ground like he had intended it, like it was some art installation. The white walls bore rain tracks, long and ragged streaks that looked like the concrete was split in parts. I hoped they'd not had any flooding inside, and if they had, that my sketches were well protected.

As I moved through the courtyard I saw food vendors in various states of setting up: there was a burger and hot dog truck parked at one end, the workers busy with grills and aligning condiments on the serving shelf; there was a little stand preparing a crepe station to go with the spiced milky chai the restaurant was famous for; there was a vintage pink caravan parked in the opposite corner, setting up American pies and brownies, with little wrought-iron chairs and tables to sit at. It wasn't my idea, but Zacharia had said that you couldn't get people to go anywhere without serving them food.

I found him in the gallery, barking at one of his assistants to sweep up outside and that he didn't care if it was still windy. The walls were white, the same white as the outside, and the floor was a lighter concrete that I didn't think was the original flooring for the building. There were warm glowing lights spaced out along the walls, and beneath them were my sketches.

It was strange to see them like that. I had a sudden urge to run around the space pulling them down and stuff them in the trunk of my car. They were lined up in the exact order we'd agreed on. On the near wall, as soon as you walked in, were the Doré reproductions – of his *Paradise Lost* work and *The Inferno* – but looking at them up there, right by the door, seemed like a colossal mistake. Who would not look at them and laugh? I kept my head down and moved to the back wall. Here they'd hung the John William Waterhouses, but where his were vibrant, mine were all in black and white, and I'd chosen his least charming girls to replicate – the angry one standing over a cauldron with its tower of smoke, another standing with a stern expression on her face, her head tightly wrapped in what I had turned into an elaborate *hijab*, and still another with her veil whipping loose around her so that you did not know where veil ended and hair began. They all had Arab faces as well – strong brows and noses and full lips – and as they stood staring down at me, I had no idea how they would be received. The Shakespearean reproductions were on the last wall. I had tried to space them widely, but they still looked like an ode to Ariel: there was the sprite as Rackham saw him, trapped and anguished in a broken pine; there he was as the childlike fairy of Edmund Dulac's imaginings, a bright spot in a sea of darkness; there he was as William Hamilton's robust, Georgian blond. I had no idea I'd drawn so many of him over the last couple of months. I hadn't brought the Goyas; they were too raw, and I'd not done more than basic outlines of them.

Turning in a circle, I felt exposed, as though they were nudes of me up there hung for everyone to see.

'There she is!' I heard sometime later as two thin arms wrapped around me from behind. I turned to embrace Mona.

She'd gone all out for my big night and was more glammed up than I was. Her hair was teased into a mohawk and her ears glittered with diamonds and jewels slotted into multiple piercings. Her arms sported high-end diamond and gold bracelets and thick cuffs and tinkling bangles, her fingers stacked with rings. She wore a body-hugging, aqua blue dress by a designer I was sure I'd never heard of and nude pumps that made her legs look like they went on forever. Her brows were dark and perfect, eyes shadowed in golds and browns and hints of blue eyeliner.

I scanned the room, catching sight of Rashid over by the Doré replicas. He was more laidback in jeans and a black button-down, though the shirt seemed to glint as though it were threaded with a metallic version of the same aqua as his wife's garment.

'It looks amazing!' Mona gushed, gripping my upper arms. Her face glowed, all bronze and pink cheeks. 'I'm so proud of you, Dahlia.'

'Thanks,' I replied, squeezing her arms in return.

She looked around the space. 'I had no idea there'd be so many of them.'

'Neither did I,' I said with a small laugh. 'I was surprised when I went digging in my cabinet. Some of those,' I added, pointing to the Waterhouses, 'I barely remember doing.'

'Well, it looks great,' she said with a nod. 'And I see the bloggers are all out and taking pictures.' She nudged me and winked. 'You might go viral tonight.'

I chuckled. 'Another tick for my bucket list.'

Rashid was still at the first Doré. It was a replica of the Fall from Milton's *Paradise Lost* that I'd done a few years before. The angel was larger, his wings spread wider than the original and the earth below looked dark and uninviting. It barely looked like Doré's, was far below Doré's. I never should have included them. Rashid was an architect; he knew all about proportion and lines. I was struck with a stomach-plummeting shame at my shortcomings.

Zaina came through the door, understated in black trousers and a floral silk blouse, and made a beeline towards us. She pulled me and Mona into a three-way hug, her squeal of excitement landing right in my ear canal.

'I can't believe how great this is!' she exclaimed, doing a little hop of excitement in her heels, so that her long hair swished around her shoulders. 'My best friend is going to be a famous artist.'

I laughed and shook my head. 'It's just a little show at a little gallery.'

She gestured around the room. 'This isn't little, Dahlia. It's seriously impressive.'

'Thanks,' I said, watching the door as more people streamed in. I heard some grumblings about not being allowed to bring their tea and coffee and food in from outside. I was pleased that Zacharia was so strict about it. 'Are you alone tonight?'

'Yeah,' Zaina replied, running a hand through her hair so that her studs caught the light. 'Baby Girl's asleep and Mish'al is watching her since the nanny's traveling.'

I nodded and furrowed my brow as I caught sight of Yousef coming my way with a frown. It had flipped into a smile though by the time he got to us.

'Hello, ladies!' he said as I shuffled aside to make room for him. 'You all look beautiful tonight.'

The girls thanked him, Mona adding, 'You did an amazing job. Dahlia said it's more your exhibit than hers.'

'Lies,' he replied, giving me a quick squeeze on the shoulder. 'I'm just the manager.'

'Seriously though,' said Zaina, 'she never would have done it if it weren't for you.'

He looked at me and smiled. 'See? Told you I was good for you.'

I gave him a tight smile and pretended not to see the confused look that passed between the girls. 'There's a ton of food, you guys,' I said, shooing them away. 'Eat, drink, and be merry.'

'If only,' Mona mumbled, linking arms with Zaina and pulling her towards the door.

I turned to Yousef, but he was backing away, claiming he needed to check with Zacharia about something.

People came and people went. The volume rose around me, so that laughter and chatter bounced off the high ceiling, and then it dropped until the clacking of my pacing heels sounded crude and slightly menacing. There was an acoustic guitar playing out in the courtyard, a solemn voice rising and falling in song, a smattering of applause following each tune. What Zacharia called social influencers stopped me for chats, filming little Q&As and taking pictures to filter and caption and post. It was uncomfortable, but I smiled and laughed and pretended it was just a normal evening. A young group, high schoolers by the look of it, tried to come in with their loaded hot dogs before Yousef shooed them out, looking so much like my father trying to scare stray cats from the garden that I laughed long and loud. People came and went, and through it all I remained, pacing back and forth between the two walls.

'I'm shocked.' I turned to see Rashid at my side. I hadn't heard his approach. He was looking at one of the Arabized Waterhouses. 'I had no idea you were so talented.' My face heated under the praise and I mumbled my thanks. 'It's stunning, Dahlia,' he continued, shaking his head. 'It's really stunning.'

'Well, it's no skyscraper,' I quipped and his mouth twitched into a smile.

'How do you come up with that?' he asked, gesturing towards the girl in the picture, with her kohl-rimmed eyes and shaded veil whipping around her head.

I shrugged. 'How do you decide what to put on a building?'

He chuckled. 'A building's design is mostly dictated by needs.'

'So's a sketch,' I said, inclining my head.

He looked at me like I'd said something profound when I was pretty sure it meant nothing at all. 'I'd buy it if I could,' he said, turning back to the wall, stepping closer to study it.

'I'd never sell it to you.' His eyes narrowed in confusion. 'I mean, I wouldn't take money for it.'

He smiled and turned back to the wall. 'I love it.'

'I'm glad.'

We stood in silence for a while, staring at the wall of illustrations. I expected him to say he needed to go find Mona – perhaps I should've asked about her or suggested we go together to find her and Zaina – but there was an elysian closeness in the air between us, and I was loath to see it end. It seemed like the gallery had faded away, like the clocks had turned back and we were in my yard and I was pointing out the herbs Baba was planting. We were young and there were possibilities everywhere. It was a moment, a decision had been made there, a choosing of paths, and I couldn't help but imagine where all those other choices and paths might have led us. A world in which he'd chosen me, in which there was nothing to prevent me from pursuing him, in which he was at my side as a husband supporting his wife and there was no wonder on his face because he'd been there to watch me draw the illustrations. There was a world spinning out there where Dahlia had a normal life and nothing bad had ever happened to her.

'She cheated on me,' he said, his voice low and soft.

I wanted to pretend I hadn't heard him, that I had chosen to walk away in search of the girls, or that he had. But that wasn't the path we were on now. We were on this one, where I had to decide whether to lie or be honest. More choices, more paths. I sighed instead.

'I know you know,' he said.

A choice made for me.

'I couldn't say anything.'

'Your loyalty is to her, I know that.'

I sighed again, because what was it if not loyalty that had made me hold my tongue? 'I'm sorry.'

He shook his head, still facing forward. 'Not your fault.'

'She loves you.'

He smiled, but there didn't seem to be any joy in it. 'I know.'

'And you love her.'

His eyes were unfocused; he wasn't looking at the illustration at all. He was looking at memories of the two of them in his mind: trips to Koh Samui and the Maldives to snorkel in crystal waters and rappel down waterfalls; driving her crazy while decorating their apartment, their opinions so at odds, and the makeup sex that followed; watching her fluttering lashes as she napped or the way she danced whenever she cooked.

I heard him agree with me, but his voice was so low I could pretend I hadn't heard it.

It was near the end of the night. Zaina had left first; she needed to go home and check on her babies, she said with a wink. Mona and Rashid had left not long after, her clinging to his arm and him pulling her close with another of his quiet smiles. Yousef was outside with some friends he'd found, and I'd not seen Zacharia for hours. I glanced at my watch, a quarter to eleven – fifteen minutes and I could head for my car and pull off my heels and go home. I had been longing for my bed for an hour already. All I wanted was home, a shower, and sleep.

Hearing shoes on the threshold, I turned to the door. Bu Faisal was walking in; my stomach fluttered, and I told myself it was nerves from our last conversation. He grinned and I returned it, shuffling my aching feet until he drew closer.

'*Mabrook*,' he said, reaching for my hand. His was warm as it shook mine, and he pulled me in slightly for air-kisses on the cheek.

I felt my face flush again and I drew back, folding my hands behind my back. 'Thank you. How did you hear about this?'

He looked around the gallery, eyes twinkling as he took in the work. 'Yousef sent me an invitation. This is wonderful,' he added, turning in a circle to take in the whole series of illustrations. His mouth dropped open, his features slack with awe. 'And here I thought it was only flowers.'

I laughed and followed him as he moved towards one wall. 'The flowers are for work doodles, I guess.'

He gestured to one of the larger pieces, a replica of *The Destruction of Leviathan*. In deference to local customs, I'd excised God and his avenging sword, so that all you saw were the dragon's scales and forked tongue and the froth of the angry waves. Everything else was darkness. 'That wouldn't fit on your little monthly planner.'

'No,' I replied with a chuckle.

'How are you?' he asked.

'I'm good,' I said with a nod.

'You look good.'

175

I turned to him in surprise then glanced down at my simple gray and pale pink dress. I faced the wall, but my stomach continued to flutter annoyingly.

'I mean, you look happier than the last time I saw you, which is not to say you don't look nice tonight.'

I smiled. 'Thank you.' Shaking my head, I added, 'I wasn't upset when I saw you that day.'

'Seemed like there was a lot on your mind. I assume it was the issue with Yousef,' he replied, looking around as though expecting him to pop out at any moment.

'Oh, no,' I said with a wave of my hand. 'I mean, yes, it was strange and out of the blue and . . .' I petered out. 'I've known Yousef a long time.'

He nodded and moved down the line of sketches to the other wall. He was nonchalant as he asked, 'Are you reconsidering?'

His interest was a question mark I wasn't sure I wanted the answer to. Twice now he'd complimented me, and it wasn't in the manner I was used to hearing from him. It felt different in a way I'd never considered. Different like how he'd been in Germany, protective and caring. His words enveloped me like that big overcoat, leaving me feeling warm and safe. I looked at him again, my mind conjuring his wife and kids, and I berated myself for the turns my thoughts were taking.

'No.'

He nodded, but his eyes had landed and were fixed on Fuseli's Ariel. I had stayed up many nights perfecting it. The only liberty I'd taken was to erase Miranda and Ferdinand. I had no need for them. I wanted Ariel to be the focus, and he was. He was *en pointe* on the back of a black bat, its wings stretched in flight. The sprite was leaning into an arabesque. His features were leaner, more delicate, than those in the original, and he was aglow in the light of the cord of stars whipping around his body.

'Beautiful,' Bu Faisal said.

'None of them are originals,' I replied. 'They're copies of famous work.'

He looked over at me, eyes gentle, a smile lifting his mouth. 'Still beautiful.' I turned back to the wall. 'Tell me about it.'

I bit my lip and pointed at a little card affixed to the wall by the illustration. 'The words that inspired it,' I said, though they were in fact the words that had inspired Fuseli.

'I don't have my glasses,' he said.

I breathed out a little laugh, but stepped closer and read,

> 'Where the bee sucks, there suck I;
> In a cowslip's bell I lie;
> There I couch when owls do cry.
> On the bat's back I do fly
> After summer merrily.
> Merrily, merrily shall I live now
> Under the blossom that hangs on the bough.'

He was quiet for a long moment, perhaps struggling, as I had, with the meaning behind the lines. Though, unlike me, he didn't at that moment have the benefit of the internet to help. 'What does it mean?' he finally asked, and I felt his eyes on me.

'He's a spirit,' I said, 'a sprite, but he's held captive. He serves a master, Prospero, and does his bidding. Prospero is not a terrible master, just reluctant to release him. There's always one more thing to do, one more thing expected of him. That,' I pointed to the card, 'is the song he sings when he's about to finally be set free.' I took a step back and looked at the whole illustration, feeling something in me lift. 'It's a flight of freedom.'

'On a bat?' he asked with a smile.

I turned to him. 'Why not?'

He nodded. 'Why not.'

The next day at work, Yousef passed by my desk and we headed for the balcony of an empty office space upstairs.

The day was nothing but endless sky of blue and cotton-candy white, the breeze carrying only sweetness. It was the kind of day that should not be spent behind a desk, hence our escape five floors up. The abandoned office had been used by an old accounting firm. There were still some generic posters of land-scapes and inoffensive abstracts in their cheap plastic frames stacked against a wall. The gray carpet was pulled up here and there, electrical outlets gaping up through the holes. The windows were tall and wide but so grimy with dust and muddy streaks that the office was dim despite the high sun.

Once Yousef got the joint going he passed it over and I took a tentative, mousy puff. I tried the stuff once every few months to see if my reaction differed, but, with only slight variations, it hardly ever did. The first time I'd tried it was in the beach house of a friend of Yousef. Some Cape Cod hipster whose name I couldn't recall. He was not actually from Cape Cod, of course. He was from Haifa by way of Amman, but dressed prep with a dash of hashtag hipster, which may or may not have been ironic. I didn't know him well enough to tell. Anyway, I hadn't been prepared for the effect it'd had on me, namely that on my way to his living room my legs would forget how to negotiate stairs. I have a vague recollection of tumbling down the final three steps onto my hands and knees to the sound of people giggling like I was a child who'd done something terribly cute. I spent the rest of the party on Cape Cod's couch, eyes closed, fully convinced my body was a record spinning round and round, my head at the center, the needle hopping over my feet when they went by.

We talked about the exhibit, and Yousef told me how happy Zacharia had been with it and that the reception had been good.

'You were happy with it, right?' he asked, grimacing as he released a long breath of smoke.

'Yeah,' I said, turning my face towards the sun like a flower. 'It was good. I'm glad I did it.'

'You're welcome.'

'Thank you, Yousef,' I said in a sing-song voice, making him bark-slash-cough out a laugh. When he quieted down, taking a swig from the bottle of water he'd brought, I asked, 'You think I could turn it into a job?'

'I don't see why not,' he said. 'People do all sorts of weird shit now.'

We sat quietly, watching the birds dipping and lifting, the

cars honking, and the people moving about like toy soldiers, marching here and there. I hadn't told him about art school. I didn't want to hear him say that it was unnecessary, that I could turn it into a job without going to school, that he could help me bullshit my way into making money off it. Instead, I told him again that I wanted a tattoo, and he was more receptive, asking where and of what.

'No, don't tell me!' he said, holding one hand out while the other handled the cigarette. 'A dahlia.'

I laughed, my eyes tracking a little bulbul soaring down to a garden in front of the building next door. 'Maybe. I was thinking of here.' I pointed to the inside of my left wrist.

'No, no,' he croaked. 'Somewhere less visible, like around your boob or something.'

'My boob?'

'Yeah, like here.' He stuck his chest out and pointed to his side, near the right pec. I wrinkled my nose and he shrugged.

'It has to be less conspicuous, though.'

'Maybe,' I agreed, even as something in me insisted I make it public.

He took one last drag before stamping the cigarette out underfoot, grinding it beneath his patent leather brogues until there was nothing left but scrapes and dregs of black and white. 'Why do you want one?'

Why indeed? I wished I had a sketchpad – maybe then I could make him see, in lines and curves, in the absence of light and deepening of shadows, how futile I felt, how utterly inconsequential it all seemed, how oppressive, intolerable, it was becoming.

Maybe Ariel and his bat would get the point across, or Goya's condemned women and upright jackasses, or Fuseli's nightmare. Maybe those prints would say what I couldn't find the words for. Although there they'd been, lined up on a wall in that gallery, and no one had seen beyond the lines and precision of them.

'Have you thought any more about what we talked about?'

It took me a minute to get what he was referencing. 'Should I have?'

He scowled and pulled a pack of cigarettes from his shirt pocket. 'You can be a bitch sometimes, you know that?'

'You can't be serious.'

'What if I am?' he said, looking away from me as he twirled the pack in his hands. 'What if I'm being totally serious and this is me laying my cards on the table? What then?'

'Then I'd say you should probably quit smoking those things,' I replied, nodding down to the remains between his feet.

He made a noise between a hiss and a growl, and I laughed, which only made it worse.

'Come on,' I said, nudging his arm. 'I've known you a long time. And I know you well enough to know when you're serious, and this isn't one of those times.'

'Yes, it is!' I recoiled from the sudden anger in his voice, but he carried on. 'Maybe not about the love thing, although I do think I love you enough to do it, maybe not in the way I should, but well enough—'

'Yousef . . .'

'Well enough to marry you, for sure. We know each other better than any couple getting married this year.'

'I know, but—'

'I'm solving your fucking problem, Dahlia! Your parents are pressuring you to marry, well, guess what? You're not the only one going through it. It's not like my parents aren't hounding me. I'm their first-fucking-born.'

'So, why don't you get married then?'

'Why don't you?'

I looked away to buy time, though I hardly needed to think over his question. The drug was doing me in; I must have only had three or four turns, but there it was, the spinning was taking over. I rubbed my palms across my knees in an effort to feel them.

'It's different for you,' I finally said. 'You're the instigator. You can choose. You can make it happen.'

'So can you,' he argued. 'You could say yes to any of the guys your mother brings around or to someone from the matchmaker.' I snorted, and it seemed to anger him. 'You act like such a martyr sometimes, like you're the only one being pressured to do what you don't want to do. You sit here talking to me about shit like tattoos and how all of these great guys your mom brings around are shit and then say I'm the one not being serious.'

'That's not fair,' I said, but my voice was weak and my mind was rotating.

He stood up with a sigh. 'Whether it's fair or not, it's the truth.'

He waited, a sky-blue and navy shadow at my side. I didn't know how many minutes passed, but when it became clear that

I had no more to say, he turned, picking his way over boxes and around dusty furniture and out of the office.

And then it was just me, staring at a spinning city, hoping it would stop.

16

Fifteen Candles

A quiet Friday. The morning sky was overcast, just godly rays breaking through every now and then. The air was muggy with rain, but I was outside anyway. My attempt at Goya's number 23 sat in my lap: the condemned woman on the platform, head down and trussed up in a dunce's cap; the official reading the charge, or perhaps the sentence – it doesn't seem to matter. A crowd is gathered, surrounding the platform, packed so tight they can't breathe. And they're bored, barely a face turned to the condemned. They could be asleep for all the attention they pay her, all indistinct faces and lowered eyelids. Why are they there? Why attend a hearing they have no interest in? What is this morbid curiosity we are so afflicted with, this rabid *schadenfreude*? It's disgusting. The etching is grotesque; there is no beauty there, nor in any of his other Caprices. But it is sublime; sublime like Dürer's *Melencolia* or Doré's *Inferno* series.

Nadia came through the gate. The children weren't with her,

and there was a serious expression on her face. She said nothing as she approached, nothing as she climbed the steps, and nothing as she took the wicker chair by mine. When she was seated and settled, handbag on the ground by her feet, hands in her lap, she turned to me.

'Uncle Omar died.'

I looked straight back down at my sketchpad, pencil poised over the dunce cap. It was a reflex. Whenever I heard his name, I looked down.

'You didn't hear? It was a car accident.'

I shook my head. I hadn't seen my parents yet that day, and if Mama had been told she would have rushed to the family house to see her siblings.

'How do you feel?'

I brought pencil to pad, darkening a shadow, but careful not to press too hard. Light shading. Hold the pencil so the point is sideways on the paper. The garments were tricky. They had lines, vertical and horizontal, that did most of the work, but there were also folds and draping. It was almost impossible for me to recreate.

'Dahlia?'

'What do you want me to say? I feel nothing.'

She looked out over the garden with a sigh. 'I should probably go to the funeral.'

'Sure.'

'I don't want to.'

I smiled down at my sketch. 'I know.'

There were clouds rolling in, big and dark and too convenient.

The sun was trying, peeking in and out between the smoky grays. It was no use, though; we'd definitely see rain.

'He's not why you don't want to get married, is he?'

'Who said I don't want to get married?'

'Mama was saying—'

I cut her off with a scoff. 'Mama was saying!'

'She just doesn't know why it's taking this long for you, and I was wondering if it was because—'

'It's been fifteen years, Nadia.'

'That doesn't mean you're over it.'

'I didn't say I was,' I snapped.

'I know. I just mean it would be awful if what happened, if what he did to you . . . if that was making you not want to be with a man and stuff.'

A sound escaped me. It might have been a laugh, or another scoff, or something that didn't yet have a name. 'That's got nothing to do with it.' She seemed unconvinced, so I was forced to meet her eye, to say it again with emphasis. 'It's not about that.'

She studied me for a moment, and my eyes returned to the pad and the curves I was trying to create there. I abandoned the fabric to focus on hair. The condemned's hair was curly, I remembered. Three little tangled balls at the nape of her neck, with wiry bits poking out here and there. But I was distracted. I was distracted by the expression on her face. It was not right. The brow was more troubled, not as resigned as the original. The eyelid was too dark; my light was wrong. And the mouth, the bottom lip should be fuller. It was wrong. All wrong. I had a violent urge to tear the page into ribbons.

'Do you maybe want to talk to someone about it? Like a professional?'

I looked up at her. 'I didn't see a shrink when it happened. You want me to talk to one now?' She was contrite, ducked her head, picked at a loose thread on her sweater. I felt bad; she only wanted to help, but it was too late for any of that. 'When was the last time you saw him?'

'Oh God,' she said, folding her arms over her chest and looking up into the heavy sky. The sun had gone away again. 'It must have been when everything went down with him and Baba. What about you?'

She saw her mistake immediately; I didn't have to react. Her hands went to her eyes then her mouth then my arm. She gripped me, pleaded with me to forgive her, said it was a stupid thing to ask and she knew it. She was more agitated than I was. Not just about that, but about the news in its entirety. I had no feeling where he was concerned. I couldn't even muster up a proper rage anymore. He might as well have been dead for the last decade for all I cared. I had no contact with Mama's family, not her phony siblings and cousins or her evil parents. I would not mourn him, not even for appearances' sake.

'I saw him at the bank once,' I heard myself say, 'when I got my first job.' Far away there was thunder, a low steady rumble. And then the rain came, in small unobtrusive smatterings, darkening the red tile of our yard with spots. 'I turned around at the take-a-number machine and walked back out. I made it to the car door before I threw up.' I wondered what the sketch would look like wet, and I was already moving. Out of the chair and off the porch into the drizzle. Nadia said nothing. What more was there to say about any of it? I held the sketch up to the sky like an offering, watching the splattering dots and fading graphite.

'I've never gone back to that branch.'

The bathroom tiles were cold. Cold beneath my butt, so I didn't know if the numbness was from them or the fact that I'd been sitting there so long. Around me were fifteen candles; shall I enumerate them? There were two black ones with round bottoms, emblazoned with crystal skulls; there were two flat ones, either suns or starfish – one was red and the other tangerine; there were two tall ones (why did they all come in pairs?) that were white like fresh cream; there was a generic purple one, unremarkable with a label of lavender sprigs; I had two beeswax yellow votives and five pasty tealights; and there was one more, a soup bowl of a candle, pink as flayed flesh that burned heavy with the scent of rose bushes.

I was not suffocating yet. I'd only just started. All the candles were assembled in a semicircle before me. Tile was good, spilled wax would dry and flake right off – same as when it hit me. I was not aiming to hurt myself, but I hadn't done it in a while and pain could be nothing but a bonus.

I'd been staring at the pink candle too long. That was why my butt had gone numb. The candle had burned low through the years, but there was a sinkhole on one side, scooped out over and over like the favored side of a tub of ice-cream. I tried to do the math: how many years had it taken? How many times had my two fingers dug and scooped into the soft gooey wax? Why hadn't I spread it out, like I had with the others? If anyone saw the candle, there'd have been questions. Mama would probably have thought I had some bizarre fetish.

I lit them all, one by one, indiscriminately. Only the pink one was deliberately left till last. I leaned back against the wall and let them work up a burn. The flames flickered and jerked in the late-afternoon light. There were dust motes in the air, thrown up by the hanging robes I was leaning against and the bathmats on the floor. They sunk into the candles, vanished without a sound. I shut my eyes against it all – crawling hands and alcohol breath, Baba's face when I'd told them, the shouts, Mama's screams, and the bloody noses. It was an effort to not bang my head against the tile and robes. I rocked instead.

I used to do this all the time. Back when he'd still been welcome in our house, when he'd stopped at lingering hugs, or his hand pressed low on my body. I used to do this, run upstairs to the bathroom and wax myself in until he was gone, until the bathroom stank of lavender and cinnamon and roses and whatever else I could find in the house. It was the only way to block out the noises, the only thing I could focus on.

I couldn't wait any longer, already the panic was in my throat and my head swam. My *yathoom* played me like an accordion, blowing his tar onto the back of my tongue; my lungs were surrendering bellows in his claws. I tapped at all the candles, looking for the most malleable. Always the tealights. I scooped out thick fingerfuls of wax, warm and safe, and pasted them to the crack where door met wall. Scoop, work into a long strip, and plug into place. From the bottom and roll up, it was easier that way. Thick strips of wax, reds and pinks and creams and yellows and lavenders, climbed the door-jamb like a vine of melted crayons. Sitting down, I could only reach as far as the handle, so I started on the opposite side. Three fingers down the crater of the pink candle; it had a fierce flame that burned my knuckles, but I didn't care. Three fingers down, and I pasted the door hinges, covering the brass till it was nothing but pink. I wished I had clay, or cement, then I could have stayed in there forever, but there was only that weak wax. And still I filled the gap between door and floor with beeswax yellow until it looked like a line of spilled curcumin.

Baba was the one who found me, just like when I was fifteen, and sixteen, and seventeen. He pushed against the door. The bottom of it pinched me awake and flakes of wax cascaded down like falling snow. The candles were dead; only the pink one persisted, and he squatted down to blow it out. His coal eyes looked me up and down for signs of injury, and I felt more than heard the little relief that puffed from his lungs. He smelled like dirt and grass and air.

'*Ya Allah*,' he said, dropping into a cross-legged position with a sigh and groan and popping of weak knees. 'Your baba's getting old.' He started picking up the dried wax, pinching the flecks and flakes between thumb and forefinger and releasing them into the trashcan. He cupped his palms, scooping the line of yellow until it was a manageable mound and depositing it in the bin as well. 'Mama's not coming home tonight. She'll stay with her sisters. She and Nadia can give our regards.' He tried to smirk, but there must have been something in my face that stopped him because he turned his attention back to the wax. He pinched and scooped and scraped until I was lying on clean tile again, until the door was clean and white with only tiny flecks of pink in the hinges. He lined up the candles like toy soldiers underneath the sink, stood and washed his hands, then looked down at me. 'I can't carry you anymore, *mama*.'

He pulled me up by the biceps and splashed water on my face, flicking his fingers like when I was a child. Only I didn't laugh now, I just tried to spit the residue of panic into the sink before he led me to my room.

It was a field of dahlias: single dahlias, blooming pale pink and cream; dwarfs clustered in threes and fours; and fat, bushy spheres of orange and red. All of them alive and perfect, clamoring for the ceiling and spilling over edges. They were in glass pots and wooden pots and plastic pots, covering every surface of the room, every shelf and dresser and table.

'Baba . . .'

'That's why it took me so long getting home.'

He was behind me, in the doorway, and didn't see the tears that dropped to my cheeks. But he felt it, he must have, because he wrapped his arms around me, squeezed and gave me a kiss on the back of the head before leaving me alone with my flowers.

I got into bed, under the covers, wrapped up tight and coiled, to wait out the day.

*   *   *

Dahlias everywhere, but all I smelled was incense. I could see the funeral, the patriarch's basement dense with *bukhoor*, the spicy woody scent that clung to the hair. I could see the rows of black *abbayas*, the prayer booklets, and I could hear the Quran ringing out from a CD player tucked in the corner.

Legions of women would trudge up and down those stairs, morning and evening, for the next three days while the men would hold court in the family *diwan*. Mama and her sisters and aunts would sit nearest the door, so people would know who to offer their condolences to first. There would be weeping, the sobbing and wailing that accompanied untimely death. There would be whispering behind cupped palms and questions about my absence that Mama would deflect with claims of some debilitating illness that had incapacitated both father and daughter. There would be shaking of heads and appeals to Allah for mercy. There would be little improprieties: those not close to the family who might end up not greeting my mother at all; water spilled or a nervous chair toppled over; young women with perfectly sculpted curls and precise brows, aware even then of possible prospects.

How many of them knew he was a monster? How many of them had glimpsed his proclivities? Did any of my cousins know what his weight felt like?

How many of us were keeping his secret?

They came for me. I'd known they would. As I dozed among the flowers, Mona and Zaina pushed into my room and climbed into bed with me, wrapping me up until we were one being, like Aristophanes' origin of love, only with three sets of arms and legs. They let me cry and shudder and shake – I didn't even know what I was mourning. Zaina's tears met mine and Mona took over the comforting of us both, rubbing our backs like we were children and this was a nightmare.

Eventually, they led me away, bundled me up in the car as the sun was dropping into sand and drove me to Mona's place.

And then we lay like a trefoil on the floor, immovable and heavy with things we couldn't say. Zaina's hand would not release mine, hadn't since we'd left my house. Only Mona defected from time to time, getting water or tissues or changing records. She was struggling to find one that fit the mood. I stared at the ceiling with its recessed lighting as she went from U2 to The Doors to Tom Waits, muttering all the while under her breath, 'Too sad', 'Too angry', '*Laish?*' Finally, she plopped back down with a huff, a record sleeve hitting the floor and disturbing the air between us. I saw the cover out of the corner of my eye: Neil Diamond. I'd never heard of him, but he looked confident.

It was dark, a light on in the adjacent kitchen, another in the hallway; car lights from the street below flashed across the ceiling like fireflies. Neil Diamond's voice was pure, clear, and accepting, a voice that gave without taking, and I sank deeper into the floor. He sang of walking on water and night-time shoes; I floated on the words, clinging to syllables like life-rafts, and ignored the chaos in my chest. He sang of music in the head, but I wouldn't examine what was in mine. I shut myself off from my body, from the skin that was starting to itch, from the brain that couldn't find anything to latch on to, from the veins and the poison they carried.

It was over. I should have been happy that it was finally, truly over. Even if I hadn't seen him for ages, even though we hadn't spoken in fifteen years, there was the knowledge that he was there. He was out there, living and breathing and free. Free to marry, to have children of his own, to walk into bank branches and through malls. Free and innocent to everyone but us, like those fingers punching in ATM codes hadn't crawled over my skin, like those knees he used to walk and to run with hadn't been used to immobilize and spread apart. They were quiet now, hands and fingers and knees, quiet and still. It was over. But inside my head there was noise, crashes and booms and clangs, like objects thrown too quickly to guard against. A white, white noise that I couldn't silence.

17

Those Specks of Dust

I remember the first time I considered just how fragile humans were. I don't mean in the head; I was only fifteen at the time and was unable to properly reason through anything. The only things I felt with any degree of certainty were my body and my wandering heartbeat. My head was a jumble of noise, static noise that kept getting louder and louder.

I had cut myself, for the first time, that weekend. That wasn't what made me think of fragility though; my body was a casing, and many things were done to it at that time.

I was holding Zaina's newborn brother. A tiny, poorly wrapped, wriggling mass of kicking legs and waving arms. His head was on my left forearm, pillowed by the gauze wrapped around my broken skin midway between wrist and elbow. *'What happened there?' 'Oh, I scraped myself on the corner of the dresser.'*

I was getting good at lies like that.

In any case, he wouldn't calm down, wiggling and wiggling.

I remember turning this way and that, casting around for help, terrified he was going to shimmy off my lap and faceplant on the floor. I lifted my knees, a sort of quasi-guardrail, straining to roll him back towards my belly. I held that position until my thighs screamed.

He did faceplant, ten years later, walking in the *zeffa* for Zaina's wedding. Behind Mish'al and the fathers, sandwiched between the brothers, his foot caught on the carpet as they walked down the wide aisle. From my vantage point, standing by Zaina's platform, he was there and then he wasn't. He flailed on the way down, making a grab for, but thankfully missing, his new brother-in-law's *bisht*. The procession ground to a halt, though, brothers pulling Moodi up by the arms. On his face was the bewildered, rage-infused embarrassment of a child who still has an instinct to act like it was intentional but is old enough to know it won't fly.

On that evening though, when he was new and smelled of powder and squirmed in my lap, Zaina's mother came, stooping and taking hold of him with practiced ease. I raised my arm as she lifted him and he skimmed my forearm, his tiny head catching on the buckle of my bulky watch as she pulled him away. He let out a pitiful-sounding protest.

'He doesn't want to leave you,' Zaina's mother laughed, rocking him a bit as she moved back to the sofa.

I didn't argue with her, but for the rest of the evening I hardly took my eyes off that baby. I thought I saw a red mark on the back of his head and panicked that it might be blood. It wasn't, but that didn't mean I hadn't hurt him. Nervous about him going to sleep and never waking up, I made as much noise as possible until Zaina's mother hissed at me to quiet down. I stayed in the den when Zaina and Mona, bored, went to her room. I watched him being fed, I tickled his feet while they changed him, I argued that it was too hot when they put a hat on him. I couldn't swallow down the fear that I'd done him some irreparable damage. He was so small – eyes like grapes, skin like a silk scarf, head like an uncooked egg.

I slept over that night. I lay awake in Zaina's bed, listening for sounds of distress from her parents' room. There were none; it was quiet all night.

When I woke in the morning, bleary-eyed and unrested, Baba was there, murmuring to Zaina's father in the downstairs foyer. He looked tired, my father did, as though he too had slept little or not well.

We drove to the hospital, and he tried to explain how my health nut of a sister was no longer pregnant. He spoke of stomach pains and then terrible bleeding and I stared out the window and thought about a baby that was suddenly no more.

It was the size of a pear, Nadia had said at a Friday lunch a few weeks back, plucking one from the fruit basket.

'Next appointment, they'll tell us the gender.'

'Don't find out,' Mama warned. 'Very bad luck; leave it to Allah.'

We snickered at this latest superstition, Baba kissing my mother on the forehead when she'd subsided in a huff. Later Nadia had been furious when I sliced into that pear, clear juice and white flesh glistening on the plate. She railed and raged about bad luck and my inexplicable thoughtlessness. She wouldn't listen to reason, not from Baba or her husband, and she was wide-eyed and fuming when I broke off a wedge of the fruit and ate it, chewing in her face. She screamed and stomped into the bathroom, cursing me throughout her ablutions and probably right through her prayers.

As we drove to the hospital I wondered if she would remember, if she would hate me, or would she be too preoccupied with her own guilt, knowing – as she did – that it had been a boy?

I didn't return to work; when they finally called, I told them I needed personal time. I did not, for one second, contemplate repercussions there. Part of me reveled in the instability. A voice in my head said to maximize the potential, use it as a catalyst for change. After spending my life keeping things steady, doing whatever it took to not rock the boat, suddenly all I wanted was drama. I imagined lining up Yousef and Bu Faisal side by side in front of my parents. '*On the left we have Yousef, very nice guy of thirty-two. Bit of a gym rat, follows fashion with a . . . let's say noteworthy dedication. There might be some unkind rumors about him floating around, but you know how people love to talk. On the right is Bu Faisal and, well . . . you could probably tell me more about him than I could ever tell you. Although I bet you don't know how much he hates peanuts and that he only pretends to care about the World Cup.*'

It occurred to me that if I were crazier, I might have been happier. They say ignorance is bliss, and I imagined insanity must be a kind of ignorance, and in it, perhaps, I could have coasted along in a haze. But I wasn't that crazy. I was capable of rationalizing, of remaining at the dining-room table when my mind had run upstairs to cower in the corner of my room. I could listen to my boss rabbit on about processes and due diligence when every part of my body insisted I was dying. I could sit at family functions, smiling away, when all I wanted to do was lie in the dark with my hands over my ears.

I was not crazy enough; was it bad that a part of me hoped I might be one day?

God knows he tried to get me there, with his litany of 'You're beautiful' and 'This is our secret' and 'Remember how I saved your life once' and 'Tell Mama or Baba and something very bad will happen'. Something very bad will happen. Full stop. There was never any way to know to *whom* exactly this very bad thing would happen. My parents? Just one of them? Me? Nadia? All or some of us? How was I to know with so vague and ambiguous a threat?

I said nothing. Nothing said I. For two years until the night I was sure I was bleeding to death, that he had finally succeeded, tearing me in half, and then in half again, and again, until I was ribbons, thin and shredded and barely holding together.

I had a good crack at crazy after that. There was an absence of tears (which everyone found troubling), of thought, of eye contact. A period of what I like to call cotton-for-brains. There were shouts and crying and murmurs behind half-closed doors. There were hastily administered pills to swallow down and Baba, smelling of dirt and air, quiet at my side. Mama banished – she was never in my recollections – and Nadia, with her fruity perfumes, only rarely. Never Mona or Zaina. The only constant was dirt and air.

I did not eat for the longest time. It's a wonder I didn't keel over from hunger. (I have no memory of how I was sustained: Nadia with spoons of flavored yoghurt? Baba with broths? Mama – no longer banished – wielding something pureed and smelling of cinnamon?) My first memory of eating by my own hand was a Coke-flavored lollipop Nadia brought me, which I propped into the hollow of my cheek as I stared at the wall, occasionally bestirring myself to swallow the soda syrup and saliva that pooled in my mouth.

No school for me. Mona and Zaina were told I had some very infectious disease (later Zaina would remember the lie). Nadia and her chatter were gone for hours – she was newly-married at the time and had a life with her husband to set up – Baba at work, and Mama puttering around the house, hardly ever cracking the door to my room. Only when my father came home was she constantly in and out. At the time I thought it was me, that she couldn't look at me after what had happened, that I was wearing it like a facial deformity. Later I realized it was her; she was ashamed, as if I – as if all of us – held her accountable for what he'd done.

After bringing in my breakfast and begging me for half an hour or so to eat, she would leave and I wouldn't see her again until three when Baba was due home. This gave me a very large window, which I eventually filled by taking that final step into crazy.

A fistful of painkillers. From the medicine cabinet. Easy to snatch. Swallowed down, two by dry and bitter two, with glasses of water from the pitcher the maid left by my bed each night.

There's a surrealism to this method. When you swallow the pills, even if it's the sixth or eighth one you've downed, your mind doesn't honestly believe you'll die. It doesn't panic the way it would with, say, hanging yourself or slitting your wrists. Those are acts that your mind immediately associates with pain and blood and death. But swallowing pills? It's so innocuous; something your brain has watched you do many, many times. And though it will partly realize that you're ingesting far too many of those little white things, the dominant part thinks that it will somehow be all right. That they're only pills after all.

I swallowed the pills down like a good patient; that's not where I went wrong. When I lay down to wait for them to work, I ended up on my stomach with my face to the wall. Vomiting, sobbing, Mama hearing, hospital, a pumping of a nearly empty stomach, back home, cot installed in my room, locks removed, not alone again for a very long time.

Weeks, or maybe months, later I started speaking in full sentences again. Speaking if only because my family was reaching so desperately for normalcy. First only to Baba, then to Nadia, then to Mama and the outside world. There was still a lack of eye contact. There was still the candle ritual, as though he remained a threat, liable to come bursting through the door at any moment.

That was my first brush with crazy, the kind they made movies about with wide-eyed bambis who managed to look glamorous hanging over a toilet bowl. Therapy was a no-no;

divulge our shame to a stranger? One who might know friends and family? A good dose of denial (apply liberally as needed) would do it. There was no other choice. Well, I suppose there was, but I've never been of the 'If at first you don't succeed' persuasion. So, I sailed the world's longest river; fake it till you make it, and all that. Normal behavior is a language you can learn. Humans are adaptable. It's one of our selling points. We can survive in most any situation. Blend in with the crowd. See the sheep, be the sheep.

It's not difficult to act like a normal person. It is, after all, a ritual like any other. You wake up, and dress for work. Do a caffeine run and complain about the traffic with colleagues. Go through the motions at the office – the filing of reports, phone calls to clients, meetings, and all the rest of it. Then home, and a quiet lunch with family. The evening is for television, friends, the gym (maybe; it depends on the anxiety levels). Dinner then shower then bed. Rinse and repeat, *ad nauseam*, forever and ever because that's all there is.

See? Easy.

I'd been doing it for fifteen years.

Was that it, then? My one and only shot at crazy? If I'd persisted, had another go, gone fully mad, been relegated to the loony bin, would I have felt liberated? No one, not even Mama, would expect the certifiable to marry. If something like that had happened, might it have been an attractive option to just let me shove off to some facsimile of a life elsewhere, somewhere I could be anonymous and free?

*　　*　　*

202

Mona and Zaina kept tabs on me with endless rounds of phone tag. It seemed if one wasn't on the line then it was the other. Our group chat was never silent, one of them constantly throwing out a suggestion to meet up or an invitation to come over. I dodged a lot of these propositions, telling the one that I was sick, or the other that I needed to stay home with Mama. This was patently untrue; I only saw my mother in passing, as she spent most of the time with her family. Nadia flitted in and out of the house. She didn't call much, but I did hear Baba on the phone sometimes, and it seemed he was talking to her. I overheard words like 'doctor' and 'coping' and 'flashbacks', all in Baba's monotonous grumble. He spent most of his time in the garden. His carefully tended trees and plants were bearing fruit: pinkish-yellow corn, bright green cucumbers, cherry tomatoes, and rows and rows of herbs. All of it segmented into neatly labeled plots that he visited daily, cutting a bit of mint for his afternoon tea or a few tomatoes for his salad at lunch.

Nature was the only thing thriving.

The flowers in my room had died. Only the lone white orchid Yousef had sent with a blank card survived. Occasionally I'd use a bottle of water on it, without a clue as to whether I was doing more harm than good. I played it music too: blaring tunes from my phone, or old CDs Rashid had dropped off. There had been a note in the bag, with his condolences to me. I didn't know why I was sure Mona would have told him the truth; it seemed like something she would do. But the note was too formal, the tone too genuine and sincere. I expected if he knew, he wouldn't have sent anything at all, or maybe just the

CDs without explanation. In any case, the music was on repeat, whether I was in the room or not, and the flower wasn't any more vibrant, but it wasn't dead either.

I didn't know why I was avoiding Zaina and Mona. They hadn't done anything to warrant it; they'd been supportive, kind . . . what they'd always been to me. In a creeping, subtle way I felt myself rejecting all that was familiar and safe, everything that I was accustomed to. Before, when I'd been a teenager and this restless, overwhelming anxiety took over, I would yearn for my bed in a way that was extreme and unhealthy. Hibernate is the only word for it. For days and weeks I would come out from under the covers only when I had to relieve myself or when threats and phone calls from officials forced me back to school. Even then, I was back in bed as soon as possible, so many blankets on me that my body was soaked with sweat and I felt permanently faint. Faint, but safe.

And here we all were, right back where we'd been fifteen years ago. I couldn't bear it. I couldn't bear the sameness of it all.

They cornered me though, the girls. They rolled up to the house, right into the driveway, and pulled me away – just like they'd done countless times before. I sat in the back, forehead against warm glass, while they tossed reprimands into the back seat. I was supposed to lean on them, they said. Why wasn't I letting them help? Why didn't I answer texts and phone calls?

'How are things with Rashid?'

Mona's eyes met mine in the rearview mirror, and I didn't need to see the rest of her face to know she was scowling.

'Things are fine,' she answered. Zaina looked at us, mouth open to ask a question, but I kept talking.

'Yeah? That's good to hear.'

'Why wouldn't things be good?' Zaina asked.

'We just had a little fight is all,' Mona said, and I could practically see the smoke coming out of her ears.

'About what?'

Mona shook her head, looking to her left before turning onto a main road. 'I can't remember. Something stupid.' I snorted at that, but they both ignored me. Zaina looked out her window while Mona turned the radio up.

I figured out where she was taking us and it softened my mood a bit. Years ago, before there was a fro-yo place on every corner, all we had was Mango World – these little refreshment stops scattered across the country. There was one in particular we used to go to; it was the furthest away from school, so we had to drive all the way up the Gulf Road to get there, thereby maximizing our outing. The place was no bigger than a highway rest-stop, too tiny to move in and with no chairs or tables. You ordered your ice-cream or milkshake or sundae from the car and they brought it out to you. I didn't think they even had a toilet, but the waiter nodded when Zaina asked him, and she jumped out of the car, calling out her order behind her as she headed for the shop.

'Have I done something to piss you off?' Mona asked once the man had left to take someone else's order.

I sighed, leaning back against the seat. 'No. I'm sorry about that.'

She was quiet for a moment, fiddling with the radio, keeping one eye on the shop. 'I ended it.'

'Good.'

'I did,' she repeated, meeting my eyes in the mirror.

'Good,' I said again.

She crossed her arms, tilting her head but not turning around to face me. 'So, no one has to know.'

'No one has to know,' I replied, thinking about Rashid and the old CDs and the way he always brought home a dessert whenever Zaina and I came over. He would stay out of the apartment, giving us our girl time, only returning when we were about to leave. And then, he would walk in with a box of cupcakes or slices of carrot cake or some disgusting marzipan thing he'd gotten because he thought the shape of it was interesting. We'd sit around the coffee table, gorging ourselves on the sweet stuff until we were about ready to pop, even though us girls had sworn we were going off sugar.

Could he tell, even then, that night in my yard, that there was something fundamentally wrong, some fracture or stain in me that no one could treat? Maybe there is such a thing as fate, and we were, all of us, destined to play these parts: Zaina, the optimist without doubt; Mona, the siren without fault; me, the coward without hope; and Rashid, the one who deserved better.

'You never said what happened with you two?'

She shook her head and looked out the window towards the ice-cream shop. 'You'll think it's stupid.'

Maybe, I thought, but all I said was, 'That's never stopped you from telling me things before.'

I saw her mouth in profile stretch into a brief smile. 'He wants kids.'

I twisted a hair tie around my fingers. 'But you said—'

'We didn't want kids. Yes, we did say that,' she said with a slow nod. 'It was one of the reasons I fell for him, that he didn't believe in that whole idea of it being our duty to have children, like how people think it's one of the goals of marriage. He didn't believe in that old-world crap. He agreed with me that the world was going to shit and we didn't need to add more people to it. He agreed that it wasn't selfish for us to want to focus on our careers and enjoy our lives. He agreed with me!' She hit her fists against the steering wheel.

'So, what happened?'

She sighed and leaned back against the headrest. 'He said he'd changed his mind, that he was young when he said those things and that now he thinks it's important to have kids. He started pressuring me, saying we could just have one, like that was some kind of compromise.' She scoffed out a laugh. 'I panicked, and then *he* came along.' Even now she would not name him. 'And he was so easy, so uncomplicated, and I could pretend I was single again, that I didn't have responsibilities, that I didn't have to think of anyone but myself.' She looked out the window again, and we could see Zaina coming out of the shop. 'I didn't mean to hurt him.'

I knew she meant Rashid, and it seemed to me she must have – on some level – meant to hurt him, but I didn't say anything more about it and neither did she.

Zaina cradled her bowl of ice-cream in both hands while the

waiter followed with the rest of our order. In the car she started to tell us how disgusting the bathroom was, but Mona wrinkled her nose and said, 'Not while we're eating.' So we sat in silence, listening to some Frenchwoman gurgle on the stereo. The day was warm, and Mona ended up turning the A/C on; she left the windows down, which probably wasn't good for the environment, but no one said anything about it. I focused on my ice-cream and fruit parfait, eating around the raspberries and digging out all the bananas to eat first. Zaina was making a mess, vanilla and chocolate leaking over the edges because the bowl was so full of cookies and cake slices. It was basically a bowl of diabetes. She had several napkins laid open like a patchwork blanket across her lap, but I knew that before she was halfway through, there'd be chocolate on her shirt. Mona was slurping at her smoothie. She could have kept driving, unencumbered as she was by a bowl or parfait, but she didn't. We stayed parked, there by the mosque, while we ate, just like when we were younger.

'I want to go away,' I said after a while.

Mona jumped on the idea. 'Girls' trip, yes.'

'I could do a weekend, I guess,' Zaina added with a tentative nod.

'I meant, go away permanently.' The girls turned around with such horrified looks that I couldn't help but laugh. 'As in leave the country, move.'

'Oh,' Zaina said, turning back around. 'You mean, go back to school?'

'Or something,' I murmured.

'"Permanently" implies more than school,' Mona pointed out.

'Yeah, it does.' I stirred the neglected raspberries in the soup of melted ice-cream until it turned pink and cream.

'Why don't you just go to school?' Zaina asked, digging at the remnants of her own dessert. 'If you go to the States, that's two, maybe three years abroad.' I made a humming noise of agreement, looking out the window at the cars pulling in to the parking lot and honking for service.

'Have you spoken to your parents?' Mona asked.

'Yeah.'

'And?' She tossed her empty cup out the window, managing to get it in the trash bin propped up against a lamp-post a few feet away.

'They weren't enthusiastic.'

'Shocker.'

'Well,' Zaina began, 'like I said, you can try again later.'

'Or I could just leave.'

The pause that followed stretched easily into a silence that I found uncomfortable yet welcome. Zaina reached into the back and I handed over my almost-empty parfait cup. She took it and her empty bowl and deposited them in the trash while Mona and I watched.

When she was back and the car was in motion again, she said, 'You're talking about running away.'

I laughed and shook my head. 'I'm too old to be a runaway.'

'You know what I mean.'

'If you're asking if I'm thinking of leaving without their . . .

permission . . .' I had to bite out that last word. 'Then the answer is yes, I am.'

She shook her head. 'That's insane.'

'Well, if the shoe fits . . .'

'This isn't funny,' she retorted, scowling at me.

I gave them the condensed version of the fight with my parents, about my suggestion of going away to school and how it was shot down, about Mama's insistence that it was a waste, about what a burden I'd become to them. I talked about how I was tired of playing by the rules, how futile it was, how I couldn't conform any longer and I desperately needed some control over something.

They didn't interrupt, letting me rant and rave, Mona driving and Zaina nodding along to the parts she'd already heard. I stopped mid-sentence, maybe even mid-word, just ran out of steam. I was so tired of talking.

'I think you should go,' Mona said. 'I think it would be really good for you.'

'Are you listening to yourself?' Zaina snapped. 'She can't just leave! Her parents would never forgive her for that.' She turned around to face me. 'Running away is permanent, Dahlia. You won't be able to take that back. They'll see it as a slap in the face.'

'Maybe they deserve a slap in the face,' Mona said under her breath, reminding me why I adored her.

'They don't deserve this,' Zaina said, crossing her arms and shaking her head. 'I know you think they've made mistakes, but forcing them to cut you off isn't the answer. And they will cut her off,' she insisted when Mona was about to interject. 'You know what her parents are like. This is a pride thing. If she leaves, they'll be forced to cut her off. Then what?' She turned back to me. 'How are you going to support yourself?'

'Oh, I don't know,' I said in a mocking tone, 'get a job maybe.'

'Do you know how hard it is to get a job abroad?' she shot back. 'Like a good job? Or do you just plan on waiting tables or something?'

'I'm not completely useless,' I muttered, looking out the window.

'I didn't say you were.'

'You might as well have.'

'Come on, guys,' Mona cut in. She fiddled with the stereo, turning the Frenchwoman up to the point where we couldn't comfortably talk over her. It was a clichéd song, full of accordions and Left Bank sounds; it made me think of mime artists in stripes, black berets, and ruby-red lips.

An imaginary me, in my head, went there, to Paris. She's terrified when she lands. Foreign country, unknown language, unfamiliar streets. For days she wanders up and down the *rues* and across the *arrondissements* and *jardins*, acclimating to this puzzling city with its light and people and quirks. Where will she find a home? St Germain and its *vie bohème*? Could she fit in with the art school students, find work in an English bookshop? Or would she end up in the crooked lanes of Montmartre, maybe in the sweaty kitchen of a kebab shop in the shadow of the basilica? Or perhaps she'd be taken in by the Eastern Europeans of the Marais and find work braiding challah bread?

'This is what Um Dawood was talking about,' Zaina said, pulling me from my thoughts.

'What?'

'The *fenjal* reader,' she replied, turning in her seat. 'She said you were planning something and that you should rethink it. This is what she meant.'

'Now, that's crazy.'

'It's just really extreme. You need to think hard about what you'd be doing.'

'I know.'

'You have other options,' she continued. 'Why do you act like you don't? Give it some time, maybe they'll come around to the school thing . . . or marry someone and move away with them.'

I shook my head then leaned it against the warm window. 'You make it sound so easy.'

'It could be,' she insisted.

'It really couldn't,' I argued.

She sighed. 'You know, sometimes I think your mother has a point, you do make things more difficult than they need to be.'

The silence in the wake of that comment rolled over us like dust in August. Mona turned the music up even louder, like she could drown out Zaina's words or chase them from our minds, or maybe shove them back down Zaina's throat. But what is said cannot be unsaid. It remained, documented in the log of everything we had ever said to one another – the snide remarks, the verbal jabs, and all those unintended words that resurrected old hurts.

The silence between us was unbearably loud and heavy, and it carried us all the way home.

18

When Day Breaks

I am a cloud stitched into the fabric of the sky. Shapeless, globular, and without substance. Poke me and your hand would slice right through.

I occasionally wonder what might have been. I don't wonder about silly things like whether or not I'd be married by now if it hadn't happened. I don't wonder whether Nadia's kids would have a cousin to play with, or how I'd have been invited when Mona and Zaina double-date (they were kind enough not to make me a fifth wheel). I don't wonder about those things. Ever.

I wonder about me. About the me that I am and the one that I might have been. When something traumatic happens at a formative age, it stops that development – not even stunting it, but sending it branching off in a whole other direction, making you someone you might never have otherwise been. Some of your traits might survive, some might evolve and adapt to your new circumstances, but some are sure to die away, to wither into indiscernible nothings.

Some (and here's the scary part) might never even be. Some traits might have been in the wings, waiting for the right time to assert themselves as fully fledged aspects of your personality. Confidence, say; or conviction; or inner strength. The kind of traits that need to flower and blossom in safety, like lion cubs roaring at their father, knowing they can bash him about and boast and get nothing more than a little slap. But put those cubs in front of a rival, let them roar and receive their wounds and scars, and they'll never roar again. Face the horror, the absolute ugliness of the world too soon, and there are parts of you that will just never be.

I cart these other selves around, these other 'me's yoked to the back of my mind. And they're heavy. They mature as I do, learn as I do, aspire and succumb to disappointments like I do; and we carry each other around, all these histories and possible lives.

If alternate realities exist, might there be a world with a whole Dahlia? One who laughs easily, who trusts, who doesn't shun attention? Might there be a *yathoom*-less Dahlia with no aches or hollows in her chest?

Is there a Dahlia who's happy . . . the kind of happy that requires no elaboration?

The days blended and the nights buckled, one into the next. I rarely slept and yet I didn't feel awake. I existed in an in-between state of agitated melancholy – aware of little, but feeling too much. I couldn't close my eyes without having those days and nights rush back to me. I tried to remember a fixed point, a time and date when the abuse started, but it was too much to ask of my mind. All I had was an endlessly looping slideshow of grins and lingering glances, hands too low on my body and fingers curling around the nape of my neck. I recalled the little escalations with chilling jolts of renewed panic: his hands on mine the first time he'd made me touch him; his rubber lips on my cheek when he tried to kiss my tears away; the blood throbbing in my face when he'd made me sit flush in his lap.

When the funeral I didn't attend was done and the ritual of mourning was over, I remained in a daze. It occurred to me that I was the only one who had ever suffered lasting effects; his emotions and reactions – if he'd had any – were transient and short-lived. It was always about immediate relief, temporary satisfaction. Even his death had been quick, when he should have gone in some drawn-out manner, covered in sores and boils, or his lungs drowning in some vile fluid. Not this expedient and merciful end that resolved nothing.

Bu Faisal's secretary was a Lebanese woman with poker-straight copper hair and too much makeup. She said he was busy, and when I asked her to tell him it was me, she gave me a look like I was wasting her time. But minutes later she hung up the phone and told me to go on through.

His office was modern and streamlined, all done in blacks and whites and glass. The desk was heavy and ornate, like an antique, espresso-colored and bare of the myriad items that tended to accumulate on desktops. All I saw was a day planner and a notepad with scribbles and doodles; these were bookended by his silver laptop at one end and a clear vase filled to the brim with white rocks at the other. Out of the wide mouth of the vase sprouted a squat tree or bush of some sort. Baba might know what it was called. It had thin branches, like mint green toothpicks, and white flowers the size of Q-tip heads.

The greeting I got that day was more muted than usual, no purple prose or profuse praise. Just a couple of 'Welcome's and an invitation to take one of the black leather chairs opposite the desk. I chose the one nearest to the vase, fingering a few of the delicate flowers.

'It's a gypsophila,' he said, picking up the phone and punching some numbers. When the call was answered, he asked for tea.

'It would be impossible to draw,' I said when he hung up.

'I'm sure you could manage it.'

I shook my head, feeling far too close to tears. 'Little flowers are impossible. There's too much detail; it's overwhelming.'

He hummed in agreement or understanding and tapped at his keyboard until the office boy came in with a tray of tea and sugar, glasses of water, and a plate of little butter cookies. He placed it on one end of Bu Faisal's desk without a word and left, closing the door behind him.

'Uncle Omar died.'

Bu Faisal paused from where he'd been about to place an *istikana* of tea before me. His eyes flitted across my face for a moment, then he put the tea saucer down and said, 'I know.'

I stared at the red-brown liquid, the flakes of saffron swirling, the steam rising. I was too agitated to plop in the sugar cube and stir. He returned to his seat, tending to his own *istikana* and avoiding my eyes.

'You're not going to offer your condolences?'

He chose the moment to take a long drink of tea, his gaze on the computer screen. When the silence grew uncomfortable, he said, 'No, I'm not.'

I didn't know what to do with that response, so I just let it hang in the air between us. I sipped at my water and looked out the wall of windows at the blue water and sky and the beige and gray-brown of the roads. I watched cranes lifting their loads at construction sites, long arms swinging left and right, making towers grow like concrete trees.

I was unaware of my tears until I tasted them, salty and wet on my lips. Lowering my face to hide them, I swiped a hand across my cheek.

'That's a bit rude,' I finally said.

He sighed and pushed the plate of cookies my way. 'I didn't care for him.'

'That's hardly a reason.' He shrugged, but I pressed him: 'Did you go to the funeral?' To that, he gave a shake of his head.

I looked down at my glass of water. It was trembling. No, my hand was trembling. And there was my knee, jiggling up and down. I was in blue sweatpants and a black hoodie. I had on the red flip-flops I wore in the bathroom so as not to slip. I couldn't remember the last time I'd looked at my hair. Bu Faisal had never seen me like this.

Why hadn't he gone to the funeral? Not liking someone was hardly a reason. It was a social custom. You showed up, offered condolences, and left. *Not* going was a statement. Baba hadn't gone. I hadn't. Neither Mona nor Zaina had gone.

I looked up at him. He was watching me closely, his hand on a box of tissues he'd pushed across the desk to me.

'What happened in London?'

There was a twitch at the outer corner of his left eye, and he pressed a hand to it. He seemed to be measuring his words, sighing again before he said, 'London . . . You were so young.'

I didn't like that, and I crossed my arms and legs, letting my gaze wander out the window. 'Not that young.'

'I knew Omar a long time,' he said, drawing my eyes back to his. 'He was, without a doubt, the worst man I've ever had the misfortune of knowing. The lowest of the low.'

My heart pounded in my head, bile crawled up my throat, and I forced down another sip of water to counter it. What did he know? He couldn't have known about me. I didn't want to contemplate a world where he'd known, all this time, what had happened to me, a world where we'd had meetings and gone to conferences and shared a black car in Berlin and all that time he'd known. I willed the possibility away.

'What happened?' I asked again.

He sighed, and I heard him crack his knuckles under the desk – the knuckles that had left bruises and cuts on Omar's face that didn't heal for weeks. 'He . . .' He hesitated, jerking his head to the side. 'He behaved inappropriately with my daughter, with Rulla. She came to me one morning, told me

219

what he'd said, how he'd put his hands on her.' He shook his head and his eyes sparked and I saw traces of the warrior he'd been that day. 'I ran all the way to Hyde Park, thought I'd have a heart attack before I even got there.'

Rulla was a few years younger than me. I turned away, watching birds sail across the window, such easy freedom. She had told her father, straight away. She'd told him and he'd dealt with it. I'd stayed quiet and been torn in half. More choices, more paths I could have taken, more 'me's spinning out in more possibilities. How much of what happened could have been avoided? How much of this had I brought on myself? I railed against the lack of control and the preordainment of my life, but was it my own doing? Was it not so much that society prevented me from making choices as much as it was that *I* refused to make them? Could a thirteen- or fourteen- or fifteen-year-old girl be expected to take control like that?

'Did my parents know?'

'They knew.'

I closed my eyes, though I sensed he was looking at me. My parents had known what he was. They'd known, all that time. It seemed to be a larger betrayal. I filed it away with all the other feelings I couldn't, at that moment, reason through.

'He was scum.'

'He was a monster,' I whispered.

His eyes went wide. 'Dahlia . . .'

I sprung up from my seat and moved to a side table against the wall, beside a black two-seater sofa. There was a trio of white candles on the table, never used. I ran my finger over the dry, grainy wax, itching to light it.

'Dahlia,' he said again, in a voice almost too low for me to hear.

I shook my head and sank into the sofa. The cushions were black and soft, and if I tried hard enough I imagined I could bury myself in them. I raked my fingers through my messy hair, and then I began to sob. Folded in half, chest to knees, I gave myself over to it. I heard the chair squeak again, then a rolling sound, and then a sinking in the cushion at my side.

A hand on my back, high and safe. The cooing of nonsense, low and unhelpful. Minutes passed like this, slow and likely torturous for him. I managed to get out that I didn't want to talk about it, and he just murmured some more of that soothing nonsense.

Sometime later, when I'd used half the box of tissues and forced down half a cup of tea because he insisted it would make me feel better, the words came. I didn't tell him what happened to me. My mouth wouldn't release those words, not even then. Instead out came a whole diatribe against my parents. At the first mention of them his eyes went dark and his lips curled in distaste, but I just carried on talking. I told him about the pressure, about the panic seeping from Mama's pores and infecting the whole family. I talked about feeling trapped and wanting to just leave. I said that I could marry Yousef, that it would be a way out, but that it would also be a lie, and I couldn't spend any more of my life parading around like I was normal.

'Let me help you. I can take you away from here.' He talked over my protests, just steamrolled over them. 'If that's what you want to do, then do it. You can't live your life for your parents, Dahlia. If you aren't happy here, leave. And if it's a question of money, I can help.'

I sat on the couch with puffy eyes and hitched breathing while he stood over me like some knight at a round table. There was a knock at the door. It was his secretary and she spoke to him in low tones; she could see me from the door and I looked down at my knees. I had a strange feeling that he'd opened it so far in order to show her that nothing inappropriate was happening. Certainly being talked about, but not actually happening.

He responded to whatever she said, but she argued, coming back at him with something else I couldn't hear. He ended it with a low reprimand, almost a growl, and shut the door. I was still studying my knees, shaking my head, and wondering if I ought to just leave. A quick 'Thanks, but no thanks,' and bolt.

'What are you suggesting?'

'You could go anywhere,' he said. I looked up to find him pacing the floor in front of his desk. 'London, New York, Paris . . . I'll set you up in a place. You'll have enough money to do whatever you want: go back to school, work, stay at home and draw all day. Whatever you want.'

'Why would you do that?' I asked with a frown. 'What do you get?' It was an indelicate question, but I was past caring.

He stopped short, frowned at me, then spread his hands in a gesture of concession. 'I'd have the knowledge that you were comfortable, safe, maybe even happy.' My face must have registered confusion as he continued, 'You'd be free to do as you like. I wouldn't bother you.'

I looked down at my knees, picking at a stray thread in my pants. Was he suggesting that I marry him instead of Yousef? How would that solve anything? It would have been moderately more honest; no one would have any illusions about what the marriage meant. An older man – perhaps his wife was neglecting him, perhaps he wanted to reclaim his youth – marries a much younger woman. It was a familiar story.

'I'd probably only see you whenever I flew in on business.'

'And you'd expect me to be with you then?' The question flew out of my mouth before I could catch it, landing with a plop at his feet.

He looked flustered. It was the first time I'd ever seen him like that, mouth opening and closing as he thought of and then aborted responses. His eyes darted around and his brows were wrinkled. It made the years fall away, and for a moment I could almost see the young man he must at one time have been.

'We get along well,' he finally said, eyes settling on the sky beyond the window. 'When I'm in town I could take you out. Dinner, theater, art shows, things like that.'

'You'd stay with me though,' I pressed. 'In the apartment or whatever.'

'Oh, hell,' he said, dropping into one of the seats in front of his desk. He ran a hand over his thin hair. 'I won't make you do anything, if that's what concerns you.' His eyes met mine, steady and calm. 'I wouldn't hurt you. Ever.'

I stood and moved to the window, looking out on busy highways. His promise discomfited me, mainly because I immediately recognized how unnecessary it was. Bu Faisal would never hurt me. He didn't have it in him. He was gentle and kind and much, much too generous.

'Who'd have thought that at the end of the day I'd end up a gold-digger?'

He sighed again. 'You're not a gold-digger.'

'People don't know that,' I replied, turning to him. 'People will say, "Oh, that Dahlia, little whore seduced a man her father's age—"'

'I'm a few years younger actually.'

'A family friend even—'

'I haven't been friendly with them in years.'

'And now she's living it up in wherever, like his own personal high-class escort.'

'Don't say that about yourself.'

'It's what people will think.'

'To hell with what people think!' he barked. 'Let them think whatever they want, Dahlia,' he added in a more measured tone. 'They'll think what they think and they'll gossip and talk and none of it means a damn thing. You and I will know what the true circumstances are – what does it matter what anyone else thinks?'

'You don't care what people think of you?'

'I'm too old to care,' he replied with a shrug. 'I probably did at one time, but not anymore.'

'Must be nice.'

He leveled his gaze at me. 'It is. And besides, you wouldn't be here to hear any of it.'

I turned back to the window, shaking my head as what we were discussing fell on me like a ton of bricks. 'This is crazy. My mother is friends with your wife. *I* know your wife. I still speak to her at weddings and gatherings. What would she think, or do you not care about that either?'

'What makes you think she has to know?'

I snapped back around to face him, eyes wide at the implication. 'You wouldn't marry me? What, you think you can just set me up somewhere like a kept mistress?' My voice was rising with my agitation, my feet carrying me back towards him. 'You can't treat me like that. I won't be that person. I don't need that from you.'

'Hey, hey,' he said, standing and putting his hands on my shoulders, circling his thumbs there like he was comforting a wild animal. 'Of course I'll marry you. I think too highly of you not to, but she doesn't have to know.'

I narrowed my eyes, studying him. 'Have you done this before?'

He threw his head back, laughing that eye-crinkling, belly laugh I was so familiar with. 'You think I have multiple wives set up on each continent?'

Wrinkling my nose, I replied, 'Can't be each. You only get four.'

He chuckled and let his hands drop to his sides. 'No, no others.'

'Why me, then?' I asked, shaking my head. 'Is it pity?'

He studied me for a moment, tilting his head. He always thinks before he speaks. It's one of his best qualities. 'Pity is not an ugly emotion,' he replied. 'It's an extension of sympathy, of empathy.' He searched for the right phrase. 'Of a desire to see someone else happy. Life has been unkind to you.' I lowered my eyes at that. 'I don't need a special reason to want to make things better. There is attraction.' My eyes darted back to his. 'I won't lie. But more than that there's affection, respect, an impulse to take care of you when so many have failed.'

My stomach somersaulted, panic catching like a flame, and I backed away. 'The attraction?' I asked, meeting his eye.

His eyes held mine, mouth set in a hard line, and he gave a sharp shake of his head. 'It's very new.'

I looked out the window, air rushing out of my lungs, thoughts tumbling too fast for me to catch them all.

Leave? Leave with Bu Faisal? Stay? Stay with Yousef? Had my life always been littered with choices that I was too blind or weak or ripped open to see? If I married him – that day, or the next, or the one after that – would it soften the blow? If I were a second wife, would Mama forgive me that? I saw these new paths laid out like gifts, and if I turned around, in my mind's eye, I saw all those other choices I could have, at one time, made, but which I'd ignored – out of cowardice or fear or complacency or some other useless emotion.

But running away with Bu Faisal, I had a sense the shame of it would eclipse, somehow, even that other unspeakable act. It would break them – my mother, my father, all of them. And in twenty years' time, when Nadia's little girl was ready to marry, the stain would still be there for society to hold up to the light, to hold against her. I was not the only one who would bear the consequences of such a path.

We, here, in this country, are taught to listen to others, to subjugate our desires to the wisdom of the collective, the tried and true of tradition. Seek the approval of the masses, of society. Heed, above all, your parents. Protect your reputation and the honor of the family. This is the way to lead a fulfilled life – a life with the respect of others and with respect for yourself.

It struck me then that there had to be a line, that my self-respect could not be so dependent on the approval of others, not even my parents. Bu Faisal was right. People would talk. It's what they do. They would call me a whore, a gold-digger, a disgrace to my family. They would call me all these things that no defense – from me or him or anyone – could undo. They would pass judgment with half a story, with the smallest kernels of truth, with nothing but speculation.

The thought struck me then, and I wondered: if a person were strong enough, brave enough, was reputation something they could do without?

19

There It Goes

'I'm too old to be doing shit like this,' Yousef said, groaning as he hit the ground.

I motioned him closer to the chain-link fence I was straddling. 'Well, I'm making up for lost time.' When he was below me, I let myself fall into his upraised arms.

Not as easy as it looked in movies.

I landed where I aimed, but Yousef's upper-body strength wasn't as advertised. He buckled like a paper fan and we ended up in a heap of tangled limbs in the dirt. An elbow to the ribs robbed him of breath, but still his hand clamped over my mouth to silence my laughter.

'I knew you would be the death of me,' he grumbled after a moment. He regained his feet and pulled me up to his side. 'Keep it down before someone hears us.'

He brushed dust and loose gravel from his jeans and groaned again when he saw a hole in the hem of his shirt. I brushed myself down as well and looked around. We were in a dirt lot, a dirt lot where, apparently, boats went to die. We were surrounded by all manner of once-seaworthy vessels: speedboats, dinghies, canoes, jet skis, and larger boats. All were caked in dust and grime, their bottoms dark and rusty. Tattered flags fluttered from railings, used-to-be-white T-shirts were still hooked to engines or wrapped around steering wheels. There was a tall beacon ahead, near the shore, blinking like a red eye. It was dark and windy and smelled of brine, and we could only see a few boats in any direction.

It had been a difficult couple of weeks. The memories kept coming, unbidden, whether I was asleep or wide awake. I saw things. His eyes appraising me, looking me up and down, taking note of how my body was developing. I could hear the deep smoker's rasp of his voice, complimenting me, asking me if I wanted him to buy me something. *'A new bag or shoes, maybe. Would that make you happy?'* And at night, when I was in bed, when I couldn't escape it, that night would return to me, and at that moment, he and the *yathoom* were one, pressing down on me, chest and shoulders and knees and pelvis, pressing down until I couldn't move, couldn't breathe. They tore at me, clawing until I was nothing.

And so that day, when work was over I asked Yousef if he wanted to go for a walk. We drove along the Gulf Road, all the way up the coast. We parked and walked, the sun setting at our backs. We didn't talk; I didn't want to talk. We just walked. Sometimes we took turns kicking a stone down the pavement; we detoured onto the beach, my heels dangling from my fingers as we strolled through wet sand like we were a couple; Yousef bought an ice-cream from a man parked in one of the lots we passed. The fourth *Azzan* rang out from a tiny mosque built almost on the beach, and still we didn't talk. I had said maybe ten words to him all day, but he didn't seem to care. I wanted to tell him about Bu Faisal and his outlandish suggestion, about my parents and their intransigence. I wanted to tell him everything. But as they so often did, words escaped me. And in any case, I didn't want to hear any more suggestions about how I should live my life.

We passed sandwich shops and buildings packed with lawyers' offices and dental clinics, and used car lots. And parking lot after parking lot after parking lot.

I'd seen the chain-link fence up ahead and knew what it was. I'd driven down that road countless times, and the sign always caught my eye: *Salmi Fishermen's Association.* There was something absurd about it; how big could the Salmi area be that their fishermen warranted their own association? There were only, maybe, a million Kuwaitis in the whole country; how many of them were fishermen *and* lived in Salmi? It made no sense.

I decided we should hop the fence.

Yousef had put up a token protest, but hadn't made us turn around. We peered into the dark lot, empty but for dead boats. Yousef mentioned that a guard might be on duty, and I made a crack about only the best for the SFA, but there was no one around. No lights in the lot, no voices on the other side of the fence, nothing but the traffic rolling steadily to our right and the water murmuring on our left. The latter made Yousef wonder if the beach area was open, if people could just keep walking down the beach until they were on the association's property, and I huffed that he was ruining it for me.

And so, up and over, and down in a tangle of limbs and dust and loose gravel.

We walked down the jumbled aisles, pausing to read the names of speedboats or spin the propeller on an engine. There was a mosque, no bigger than a shed, whitewashed with blue trim.

He hopped up into one of the bigger boats, snooping around, kicking up dust as he lifted tarps and coverings while I stayed on the ground wondering how much I could tell him about what was actually happening. I decided that it was nice, in a way, to have one person who didn't know the worst things about you.

He jumped back down, muttering that it was all crap, and we kept moving. There was a little room up by the gate, the size of two payphones stuck together. It was lit and the tinny sound of a radio spilled from its open windows. Yousef steered me away, back into the darker aisles at the far end of the shipyard.

'I need to get out of here,' I said.

He shushed me and whispered, 'Back over the fence, or should we try the beach?'

I shook my head. 'I meant I need to get out of the country.'
He shushed me again, turning back to the guard's station. 'He
can't hear us over the radio, Yousef.'

Nevertheless he pulled me deeper into the yard until the
traffic faded away and all we heard was the water. 'And go
where?' he asked.

I shrugged in the darkness. 'I don't know. London, maybe,
or the States.'

'Go back to school, you mean?'

'Maybe.'

'And leave me all alone with the boss?'

I let out a laugh. He looked so horrified by the prospect that
I wrapped my arms around his tiny torso and buried my face
in his chest. He didn't hesitate, hugging me close, his chin
resting at my temple.

'Is it to get your mother off your back?' he whispered.

'That's part of it.'

'We could still get married.'

I shook my head. 'No, we can't.'

He gave me a squeeze. 'No, I guess we can't.'

'You could leave too,' I murmured into his chest.

He sighed and it ruffled my hair. 'No, I need to have a son
to give my father's name to.'

At first, I thought the flashing white light was from cars on
the street. Only when the gruff voice barked out did I realize
we weren't alone. The guard, flashlight in hand, yelled at us in
a rapid-fire Egyptian dialect about police and indecency, and
Yousef and I were already running.

We separated. I went one way while he disappeared parallel to where the guard was approaching from.

The flashlight kept tracking back and forth, but I didn't turn to look. I heard the yelling, more threats and demands to come back, but I yanked off my heels and just ran. Deeper into the darkness, veering between boats and jet skis, trailing the fence in the direction of the water. I hoped he was right about the beach. I couldn't hear anything behind me anymore, but I didn't slow down. The soles of my feet were screaming, but I just kept aiming for the beach.

When I got there, when I crossed over from pavement and dirt to soft, cool sand, the fence came to an end. There was nothing but open beach and a succession of man-made cement ramps used to lower boats into the water. I clambered up the loose stones and cement blocks, slipping across wet ramps. One ramp, two, three – how many ramps did these fishermen need? Finally, I was up and over the last one, but I kept going. My heart was pounding, sweat pouring, feet probably bleeding, but I still didn't stop.

I hopscotched over wet seaweed and sharp shells, zig-zagging upward to smooth sand. I finally risked a glance behind me. There was no one there. He must have chosen to chase Yousef. I slowed to a jog down the stretch of beach, sighing as the cool sand relieved the pain in my soles, and up towards the restaurant that jutted out into the water. I paused in the half-empty parking lot, hands on knees to catch my breath, and wondered whether I should keep going or wait. Hands on knees wasn't working. I felt like I was going to pass out, so I put my shoes on my aching feet and kept walking, meandering over to the opposite end of the parking lot, eyes peeled for any sign of Yousef. The restaurant wasn't busy, only one group left while I was loitering and no cars entered the lot. Traffic was backed up on the road, horns honking, music blaring from windows.

A hand gripped my shoulder and I screamed.

'Shh,' Yousef hissed, clamping a hand over my mouth, but he couldn't control his laughter.

I pulled away and hit him. 'You piece of shit! You scared the crap out of me.'

He only laughed harder, guarding against my blows, doubling up and gripping his stomach – whether to try and stop laughing or to catch his breath, I didn't know. I kept hitting him all the same.

Even as he carried on laughing he pulled me along, setting a brisk pace as we started the long walk back to the car. He looked behind him every few minutes, but seemed satisfied that we weren't being followed. The guard had chased him, he said, but there was no way the fat dude would catch him. He said he'd run back to the fence, describing some parkour-like move as he clambered up and over.

'All he saw was the tailfeather,' he said with a smirk when I asked if the guy might be able to describe him. 'Anyway, he's not going to call anyone.'

His confidence eased my mind, and we dropped to a slower pace. I could no longer feel my feet, but it was a small price to pay. I could only imagine what Mama's reaction would have been, or Baba's even, if they'd had to come down to a police station because I'd broken into the Salmi fucking Fishermen's Association.

'Oh, hey,' Yousef said, pointing to a tall white building on our left. 'Remember how you said you wanted a tattoo.'

'Yeah,' I replied, glancing at the nondescript apartment complex.

'Well, there's a place in there apparently that does it. It's like a proper parlor or something.'

'Not licensed though.'

He looked at me like I was a moron. 'Of course it isn't licensed. But this guy I know got one there and said they were good. You know, clean and trained and everything.'

I stopped and tilted my head, staring at the building with its plain windows and boring exterior. 'Call your friend. See if they'll take me.'

Yousef turned back, coming to a stop before me. 'Dahlia, you're not serious.'

'I'm very serious.'

He was gaping at me, like he was seeing me for the first time. 'A tattoo is permanent.'

'I know.'

'Meaning it won't go away. It's forever.'

'I know what permanent means, Yousef. Call him.'

He stared at me for a long moment, a frown contorting his features. 'Why are you doing this?'

I pushed my hands through my hair, getting dirt and sand in the wind-knotted curls. 'Because it's my body. It's my body, and I want to.'

His eyes met mine and stayed there. I didn't know what he was looking for, but he seemed to find it because he took out his phone and made a call.

Several calls were made in the end. Yousef was on the phone the whole way back to the car, as we drove to the building, and as we waited out front. The tattoo place only took referrals from people they knew, so we had to park outside the building and wait for his friend to walk us in. While Yousef talked, I sketched designs on scraps of paper and the margins of newspapers I found in his car.

It had to be a dahlia – a Bishop of Llandaff, maybe. I drew rapidly, one after the other, in different mutations. A single dahlia, lonely and suspended. A cluster on a stem, crowded and confused. A trio in succession: horizontal, then vertical, then a trefoil. I returned to a single one on a little bough, added little shoots sprouting above and below it, but I hesitated to place flowers on them. I doodled around it – the same phrase over and over like a chant. I wrote it out in bold print, in cursive script, in swirls and sharp lines. Over and over, over and over.

The flimsy wooden door closed behind me. The apartment was dimly lit apart from the work area by the window with its strong spotlights. The entryway and the front of the living room were dark, illuminated only by lamps and weak candles. Framed designs lined the walls: blossoms and flowers, dragons with forked tongues, sharp-clawed tigers and orange koi fish, cobras and pythons, scrolls of calligraphy, in both Arabic and English.

The living room seemed to function as reception area, lounge, and studio simultaneously. A man sat at a small table near the door, hunched over a sketchbook; guys and girls were sprawled across the L-shaped sofa, smoking and laughing and watching one of those adult cartoons that I've never gotten the appeal of. One workstation by the window was empty, but a muscled man sat at the second one while the artist shaded his bicep in shimmering blues and whites.

Yousef turned to me with a half-smile, trying not to look nervous, while his friend walked up to the table with a swagger that clashed with his preppy look. Nevertheless, he had a pow-wow with Sketch Boy while Yousef and I stood and waited.

It was warm. I pulled at my shirt, feeling that awful small-of-the-back dampness; my trousers clung to my legs, and I wished I'd worn a dress. My feet were screaming in agony.

'This is Tariq,' Yousef's friend said to me.

Sketch Boy looked me up and down. 'My friends call me TQ.'

Sketch Boy did not fill me with confidence. He looked no older than eighteen, spotty chin, Heisenberg T-shirt, hair flopping across his forehead.

'So you want to get inked?'

The preppy friend gave me an encouraging nod forward. He didn't want me embarrassing him. 'Uh, yeah,' I said.

He put his pen down; the pad was filled with loopy designs, arrowheads, and sigils. He looked at me expectantly, spreading his ink-stained hands. 'Well?'

'Oh, right.' I moved forward to his table, pulling out a scrap of paper and smoothing it on the surface. 'I wanted this with this phrase somewhere around it.'

He scrutinized the blossom on the bough, turning it this way and that, asking if those little upside-down teardrops were meant to be buds that hadn't bloomed yet, and I said yes, somewhat offended that he had to ask. He turned to the words then, studying my small, cramped script – I'd tried to fit the phrase onto that specific drawing rather than make a new one. '*On the bat's back I do fly?*' he read out with a frown.

'It's Shakespeare.'

He seemed unimpressed, scowling at me as he read the words again. 'Are you sure?'

'I want it inked on my body, so, yeah, I'm pretty sure.' I looked over to Yousef and his friend. The preppy boy was eyeing a girl on the sofa.

My-Friends-Call-Me-TQ scratched at his cheek and frowned some more. 'I don't know, dude.'

'Are you offering an opinion or a disclaimer about your abilities?'

'What?'

I looked over at the artist tattooing the blue sea creature. 'Can I speak to someone else?'

Sketch Boy followed my gaze, then turned back to me. 'Hey, I've been doing this as long as he has, all right? And I'm just as good.'

'Then I don't understand what the problem is,' I replied with a huff.

'Right,' he said, picking up the scrap of paper. 'Any particular font?'

I shrugged. 'Something elegant, classy. Something I won't get bored of.'

'Fine.' He nodded. 'Give me a few minutes to sketch something out.'

I wandered over to the calligraphy scrolls, my eyes scanning the letters and words, but not taking any in. There were interesting fonts with sharp brushstrokes and precise angles, and there were patently ridiculous fonts, all bubbly and cartoonish. There was a poster of symbols and zodiac signs and runes that looked like semaphore.

I had a moment of clarity, a crystal-clear vision of what this act would say to my parents. A tattoo is a statement, an expression. It would say, for me, all the things I couldn't say. And if actions speak louder than words, they also speak harder, and this act would perhaps ring harshest of all.

'Where did you want it?'

I turned to Sketch Boy and bared my right shoulder. He nodded and got back to work. Yousef and his friend had been accepted onto the sofa, separated by two girls and a sleeping guy. Turning back to the calligraphy on the wall, I picked out the letters of Baba's name and wondered if I was going too far.

When I was twenty-five I felt like I was losing my best friends forever.

It was two weeks since Mona had fulfilled her end of the marriage pact, announcing her and Rashid's engagement to us in a three-way call. Not much of a shock as they'd been together for a couple of years. I had taken it well, not so much as an intake of breath at the news. Zaina was very upset though, talking some nonsense about it being too fast – in a world where marrying someone you've known less than six months is normal.

What she meant was it was too early in the year. Twenty-five. The year we were supposed to marry as per a later iteration of the pact. Mona didn't take it seriously either, laughing out loud when I'd mentioned it as a reason for Zaina's lack of enthusiasm. All the same, I wasn't surprised when, three weeks later, she announced her own engagement to Mish'al – a prospect arranged through friends of her mother.

Mona was furious, charging Zaina with stealing her thunder and instigating a passionate, if short-lived feud, which I stayed out of.

A part of me wasn't sure she'd go through with it. I recoiled from the thought of an arranged marriage – though I knew most, if not all, of us were destined for one. But I couldn't imagine her marrying him just for the pact. Not even Zaina, with her bizarre devotion to destiny, could do that. '*Kismet wa naseeb*', that's what we were told. Our lives, all the gains and losses, were apportioned ahead of time, written in some cosmic book by a guiding hand.

I never thought about God much. I observed the pillars of the faith like anyone else, praying and fasting out of habit, but I never thought about God, about a plan, about the idea of faith that Zaina was always on about. There was the problem of pain, of gains without merit and unjust worlds, of sins unpunished and the blood of the innocent. I wasn't smart enough to ponder such things, so I left the question alone, nodding along and echoing Zaina's '*Allah kareem.*'

As the day of Zaina's *milcha* approached, the day for men to gather and sign her over to the care of her husband, I panicked. She'd known him less than three months, and even though it happens all the time, I panicked. There was an immediacy to it, a concreteness that made it more real than when it was a second cousin or friend of the family. It wasn't abstract; they would share a bathroom and a bed. She would be living with him, waking with him, expected to sleep with him.

I felt a desperate need to warn her about something I couldn't find words for.

I accosted her at the end of a last-minute dress fitting. She was in a good mood driving me home, not even moaning about Mona missing this fitting (along with all the others). She was bubbly, excited, going on about the dress and jewels and hair and makeup, and I felt bad for bringing her down, I did, but I couldn't contain my worries anymore.

I started slow, agreeing that yes, it was all terribly exciting, yes, it was a whole new life, and no, things would never be quite the same. But it wasn't long before my anxieties bubbled over.

'But can you imagine spending your life with him?'

She turned to me. 'You don't think I've imagined that? I'm getting married in a week.'

I nodded and looked out the window on my side. 'And you're sure he's the one?'

She shrugged, sighed, then shrugged again, and in that moment she seemed incredibly wise. 'Love comes later; all you need at first is respect and affection, *maybe* even attraction. Later, when you nurse him through an illness for the first time or the first time he holds you when you're crying, that's when love comes.'

She was reciting someone else's words. How many times had she repeated them to herself? How many times before she started to believe it? Or was she still working on belief?

'And if it doesn't come? If it doesn't work?'

She frowned at me like that was an impossibility, and perhaps, to her, it was. Fiddling with the radio, she said, 'That's not an option. We'll make it work.'

'You're still young, Zaina. You don't have to do this now.' She stopped the radio at a station spitting something fast and heavy. She didn't look at me, but I continued regardless, 'If it's to do with Mona—'

'Mona!'

I picked at imaginary lint on my pants. 'Yeah, I mean none of us is taking the pact seriously.' She snorted and shook her head. 'We don't have to get married this year.'

'I want to,' she said, turning to me. She repeated it. 'Do you honestly think I'd go through with this if it were just about the pact? If I didn't really want to marry him?'

That was exactly what I thought, but I only mumbled, 'You don't even know him.'

'So?' There were sparks of defensiveness now, bursting from her skin, from the gold flecks in her eyes, pushing against me. 'Your parents, my parents, Mona's, none of them knew each other, and they're still together, still happy.'

'That was a different time.'

She shook her head. 'Time has nothing to do with it. People are people and marriage is what it's always been. It's like now everyone wants a love match because it's cool or whatever.' I looked away from her dig at our friend. 'How many of those marriages end in divorce?' She counted them off on her fingers. 'Jenan, Rana, your cousin Hana, Fajer from university, that girl we went to high school with – oh, what was her name?'

'Lulu.'

'Yeah.' She slammed on the brakes as some guy on a motorbike screamed through the junction. The expletives she reserved for road rage spilled from her mouth with a vehemence I found unwarranted and made me think the rant was at least partly directed at me, or Mona, or some weighted average of the two.

Like conversations past and those yet to come, my best points were made in my head. There I extracted from her confessions of doubt and jealousy and a rivalry with Mona she never voiced. There she fought valiantly but ultimately conceded that none of it was worth a slapdash marriage. I hacked away at the pact, that tree that would never fall, delivering glancing blows and reopening wounds.

'*Allah kareem.*'

'Hmm?'

'God willing, it'll all work out.'

This was a terribly optimistic remark, but one that I was used to hearing from her. She had far too much faith that life was just, too much belief that if she played by the rules, God would reward her. I knew better; there was no cause and effect relation to what you got in life. No karma, no good things to those who wait, no tabs kept on such things. It was a crapshoot. The entire enterprise was like some cosmic lottery you hadn't bought a ticket for.

20

You Will Not Escape

My actions were deliberate.

For a week I'd kept silent. Silent and covered while the tattoo healed. Silent when the skin around it itched. Silent when it turned red. Silent when it hurt; I could deal with the pain. Pain is real.

It was late afternoon and faint breezes blew off the Gulf; there was a churn to the blue waters, I could see it from the picnic table we'd set up in front of the chalet, by the edge of the plateau and the eighty or so steps down to the beach. The sun hung placid and uninterested in the sky, its rays barely touching the ground.

The top I wore was loose and sheer. I knew at some point it would slip off my shoulder and my parents would see what I had done. But still, I'd fidgeted with it all morning and all through our lunch preparation, jerking the wide neck into a tighter fold when I lost my nerve and draping a scarf it was too warm to wear across my shoulders while I helped Baba squeeze lemons and oranges for juice. I pulled the scarf even tighter when Rashid, Mona, and her parents came in, having called with a last-minute acceptance of Mama's standing lunch invitation.

I could have backed out then, it would have been understandable, on the grounds that the confrontation should be a family affair. I could have run upstairs and put on a different shirt, one that fully covered my shoulders.

But I didn't. Like I said, my actions were deliberate.

For a moment, just the one, I considered dragging Mona to my room to show it to her, so that I could have at least one friendly, unsurprised face at the table. But I didn't do that either. A part of me wanted to see that look on her face – the one that said to everyone that I hadn't told her first.

I raked my hair into a bun high on my head and put the scarf in my lap halfway through lunch, when Nadia's kids had wolfed theirs down and run off to the beach with three or four maids in tow. Baba was on my right, exactly where I needed him to be, Mama across the table by Mona's mother. Mona was by me, but spent most of her time catching up with my sister.

I waited for it to happen naturally, for the neck of my top to slip off my shoulder as per its design. I stretched for bread, leaned across the table to refill my juice, passed salads and chicken and hummus and olive oil. And nothing. The thing stayed in place throughout.

The tea was being served, mini-cupcakes and coffee cake

slices springing up across the table, and I knew I'd have to force it.

I pulled my sleeves down so my hands retreated into the cuffs. A breeze whispered against my bare shoulder.

And I waited.

He looked at me three times and still missed it. The fourth time he glanced my way it was to ask about something he and Rashid were talking about. His black eyes flicked down to the inked petals. They shuttered once, twice. Something passed over his features, and he said, 'You had henna done.'

'I hate the smell of henna.' My voice was weak, almost a whisper. I could barely hear it over my heart.

'What then? One of those stickers?'

Rashid knew it was real then and his eyes caught Mona's. She fell silent beside me. It seemed even the Gulf was holding its breath for us.

I didn't trust my voice, so I shook my head.

Baba blinked rapidly, like a computer trying to process too much data at once. Buffering and buffering. He leaned over. His breath was hot on my shoulder and his fingers smelled of garlic. 'What are you saying, Dahlia?'

Mama's attention had been captured, but she couldn't see what he was looking at from her seat. His thumb pressed hard into me, rubbing, rubbing, dragging the skin as he muttered the impossibility of it under his breath.

'What did you do?' Mona asked. It seemed she and Nadia and our mothers moved as one being to my side of the table.

And then, there was a lot of yelling.

'Have you lost your mind?!'

'Why didn't you tell me?'

'It isn't real. It can't be!'

Baba's thumb was burrowing a hole into me, his eyes never meeting mine. It was painful. Mama's hand gripped the bun of my hair, wrenching my head back so I was forced to look at her. My heart beat so loud and hard I feared it might explode.

'Answer me! Say it isn't real.'

'It's real. Look at it!' Baba yelled in a panic. He tossed water at my shoulder, drenching me in the cold liquid, and supplemented his thumb with a napkin. Rubbing and rubbing. 'It won't go.'

'You're insane. You've lost your mind.' Mama was still gripping my hair so hard my scalp screamed, jerking me around as she yelled. 'Why would you do this? Why ruin yourself like this?'

I was a rubber band snapping. 'I'm already ruined!' I broke free of both their hands and rose to my feet, knocking the chair over with a loud crack. I glanced at Mona. She was wearing that look I wanted, shaking her little pixie head from side to side.

'It's okay,' Nadia said, holding our mother's arm back when it looked like she might strike me. 'It's okay. They're removable now. I've seen it. They take them off with lasers.' Mona nodded like a bobblehead.

My skin throbbed. 'I'm not getting it removed.'

'Yes, you are!' Mama was seething, spitting her rage. Mona nudged Rashid, gesturing for him to lead her parents into the chalet.

'Dahlia, listen to me,' Baba said, approaching me with one garlicky finger in my face. 'You will get it removed. You will get it removed as soon as possible.'

'No.' My lips trembled, my body trembled, my heart trembled.

'What do you mean, "No"?' he barked. 'You think you're just going to walk around like that? *My daughter* walking around with that on her shoulder!'

'You're going to hell,' Mama chimed in, and I didn't feel I was in a position to argue with that. 'It's *haram*. Tattoos are *haram*, you know this.'

'Mama—' Nadia began.

'It's true. What, are you not praying as well? Do you plan to stop praying? How are you going to pray to Allah with that abomination on your body? How many other sins are you committing?'

'Oh, spare me, *Yumma*,' I sneered. 'You're not worried about my soul. You're worried what people will say, what your friends and society will say when they find out.'

'They won't find out,' Baba interjected, 'because you're getting it removed even if I have to hold you down myself.'

'You'll never get married now,' Mama said over him.

'Good!'

She recoiled, mouth clamping shut as though I'd slapped her. But we're stoic creatures, my mother and I. We don't cry in front of people, not if we can help it, and she wouldn't cry then.

In the quiet that followed, as my father rubbed his hands

over his graying hair and I passed a hand over my wet and aching skin, Mona tried to mend what we were shredding.

'Don't think like that, *Khalti*,' she said to Mama. 'Things are different now. I know a lot of girls, and Rashid knows men, who have tattoos. It's not like it was before.'

'Mona,' Baba snapped, his voice like a hard, cracking whip. She was shocked, as was I; he hadn't scolded her since we were children. 'Apologize to your parents, but I think our family needs to be alone.'

I would have preferred witnesses, but I could see she was at least half-relieved by the dismissal. She squeezed my arm as she moved past, but my eyes stayed locked on my parents as though expecting them to launch at me.

'I don't know what more to do,' Mama moaned, sinking into a chair and dumping her head in her hands. '*Khalas*, I wash my hands of you.'

'Mama!' Nadia gasped, dropping a hand on her shoulder to quiet her.

I won't lie: there was a definite relief, a crackling joy, that shuddered through me at her words. It tasted like freedom, wet and sweet on my tongue. I was indecisive; should I push them harder, get them to sever the bonds now? Or should I measure my response, see if they'd bend before it was torn forever?

'Shh,' Baba hissed at her before turning to me. 'Let's sit and talk about this like adults.' He took his advice, sitting ungracefully in the seat by Mama, a strained expression on his face as he waited for me to follow. 'What's this about?'

'I've told you what it's about,' I said with a sigh, refusing to return to my seat. 'Over and over I've told you, but you don't listen to me.'

'You did this because you're bored at your job?' He looked at me like I might have a head injury.

'No.'

'What then? Because of your mother pushing you to marry? To hell with it! Don't get married, I don't care.' Mama gasped, but he placed a hand on her arm to prevent her from speaking. 'If she doesn't want it, you can't force her!'

'It's not just that. I need to be away from here. I need to leave. Go back to school, be somewhere else, *something else.*' I hated the whining quality of my voice but was unable to control it. I felt faint and very close to collapsing.

'No.' Here his voice had a ring of conviction, of finality, that I was not used to hearing. It was so sudden and abrupt that I flinched as though he'd struck me, and, in some ways, I would rather he had. 'No. You want to change jobs, fine. You want to put off marriage, fine.' He shook his head, like this was some mighty concession on their part. 'But you cannot leave. To go, to live abroad on your own? Forget that, Dahlia. Remove it from your mind.' He met my eye. 'It will not happen.'

He stood up then. He stood and walked away. Mama stood and with one last disgusted look at me, she scurried after him. Nadia, shaking her head, approached the steps to the beach, looking down at the little lives she could still hold in the palm of her hand.

Panic thundered through me, numbing my fingers and lifting

my head. My *yathoom* did a jig of glee on my lungs. He cackled and sing-songed in my ear.

'*Never, never, never. You'll never, ever be free . . .*'

21

It Is Time

The air was charged and hostile, the three of us avoiding one another like magnets whose polarities had reversed. We'd created – I'd created – sharp, heated spaces between us that no one would come forward to fill. There was a frustration, a defeat of sorts, that slithered across cold marble and down silent walls. It was as though something had died there.

I was convinced the only reason I hadn't been dragged forcibly to a laser clinic yet was that my parents were worried I might make a very public spectacle of myself – and also they hadn't the foggiest idea where a clinic offering such a service might be, nor how to discreetly inquire after one.

So they said nothing, and I said nothing, and the house remained harsh and silent and toxic.

My concerns were warranted. I seemed to have gone a step too far, to a place to which my father's forgiveness would not stretch. He didn't talk to me, hardly even looked at me. And in those rare moments when his face turned my way, I nearly crumbled under the disappointment I saw there.

He'd forgiven many missteps of mine: at fourteen when I'd stolen the car because I was running away to Zaina's house; or two years later when he'd caught me smoking on the roof; when I was nineteen and he'd had to pick me up from the police station. He forgave it all, calming Mama's histrionics and assuring me that he still loved me and all was well.

All was not well. This seemed beyond him. Who knew he harbored such religious tendencies, or that he cared so much what others thought? Or maybe it was none of the above, maybe it was just straightforward disappointment, disconnected from any other considerations.

I found a perverse delight in it though – or perhaps delight is the wrong word; it was more of a quiet satisfaction with the idea that finally they'd stopped to notice, finally they saw that I needed some modicum of control over something. More importantly, they could now see that if I did not have it, I was willing to wrench it from their grasp.

Word of what I'd done reached Zaina, who called me full of screeching recriminations and confused pauses. She was as bewildered by me as she had perhaps ever been. She reached back into our past, deep into my history, turning it over and combing it through for signs that something like this had been coming. Even someone as close to me as Zaina struggled to reconcile this action with the creature she was used to, the one that had always danced just inside the line. And I thought how easily she would have fit in our family, how with just a few minute twists of fate she might have been their daughter. And then, everyone would have been happier . . . or at least more at ease.

I texted Bu Faisal and asked him to meet me at the *memsha*. I'd been running for an hour and I was tired and sweaty, with aching muscles and bubbly blisters on the balls of my feet. A knee-jiggling, jittery energy had not left me. I didn't know what else to do, how to keep the panic at bay. I had considered calling Yousef, seeing if he had anything to calm my mood, but I'd never done that and he'd want to know why and what was wrong and I didn't want to talk anymore. I was so tired of talking, all these infinite loops that went nowhere and resolved nothing.

It was past nine and the footpath was deserted and dark. It was just me and tunnels of thick trees sprouting from desert sand, interspersed with tall white streetlamps. The moon was high overhead, shrouded in a mist that translated to humidity on the ground. Aside from the moon the night was empty, empty and dead. There was no sound around me, not an insect buzzing or a cat mewing or a cricket chirping. No night orchestra or constellations to name. Nothing. Even the air was dead, no breeze to stir the branches or rustle the leaves.

Death is a kind of nature. I pulled my feet up onto the bench, propped my chin in the dip between my knees and waited.

He found me there. He found me, rocking too lightly to be seen, with the roar of the highway far behind me. He sat at my side, quietly at first, then with soft words and hesitant questions. So hesitant, like I was some fragile thing liable to go to pieces at any moment. And perhaps I was exactly that. I didn't look at him. My eyes were on the gravel pathway, and I let his questions chase themselves.

He didn't touch me, just sat at my side. I felt his eyes on me; what must he have been thinking? That I might be too much of a handful? That perhaps he should renege on his offer? He asked me what was wrong in about five variations. And I was torn between a mad desire to rope him into a commitment and an even madder compulsion to push him away.

I pulled my sleeve up, baring my right shoulder to him, eyes still glued to the ground.

There was silence again, but it was not quite as bad as the dead night surrounding us. It was a contemplative silence, one I recognized as him thinking about his response rather than reacting. I waited for disappointment to win out. He's from my parents' generation, where getting a tattoo is a horrible transgression, where it's equated with intentionally scarring your body, where it's tantamount to turning your back on religion and renouncing your family. I'd known this on some level, known it when I'd been getting it done. And though I couldn't honestly say I'd thought about it at the time, was it possible this whole thing was an act of subconscious self-sabotage?

He touched me then, just the back of his index finger lightly brushing the skin of my shoulder. I watched it move over the smooth black ink, and then it was the calloused pad of that finger, gentle as it traced the lines and curves and lettering. It lulled me, caused a feeling of safety and calm to rise in me. It

256

almost didn't matter whether he approved of it or not; I just didn't want the feeling to go away.

'Let me get you out of here.' His voice was so low I thought I'd imagined the words.

There are moments in our lives that feel epic, even if we don't know what will come next; perhaps they feel that way *because* we don't know what will come next. When you drove a car alone for the first time and it was the sweetest freedom you'd ever known; when you graduated college and the world seemed limitless and full; when you said no to a choice made for you and came out the other side. These moments are so fleeting, and yet they hold within them entire galaxies spinning with possibilities. One word, one action could alter your entire life.

My eyes flicked up and Bu Faisal's lips were moving. He repeated himself, stronger and louder, as though willing me to believe him.

My *yathoom* rested, and I breathed a little easier.

At home, I stood dripping wet – wrapped in a towel, my skin hot from a long shower – and stared at the wall of Goyas. I had them in a grid, seven rows and more columns than I cared to count. They were printed out in different sizes and with differing clarity, but it didn't matter. There was a story there, I was sure; a story of entrapment, dissolution, and veneers. From the illusions of courtship to the squatting asses, the flying beasts and yawning maws, there was a story there if only I could puzzle it out. Every time I thought I was close to getting it, like just then in the shower, I'd face the gallery and grow befuddled once more. The meaning faded, the string of a loose balloon floating away. And then, this flash of something ugly, a resentment would rise up in me so fast I was dizzy with it. If I'd gone away to school before, if I'd really pushed for an art degree straight off the bat, would I have been able to really see his Caprices? Would it have made sense to me? Would I have seen more than his brief explanations allow?

Was it too late to be who I might have been?

I began taking them down one by one in a haphazard way, paying no mind to the order of the grid. Down came *Love and Death,* all the hunters and the shameful ones. I peeled them off the wall with careful fingers, mindful of tape and paint and not to rip the paper, though I could have always just printed out others. I laid them face down on the bed, a neat little pile of what Goya called the 'foibles and follies of civilized society'.

There was a knock, and then Mama opened the door. I was momentarily stunned, my hands freezing against the wall. Aside from the occasional sound of acknowledgment, we'd said nothing to one another since that day at the chalet. That old shame had washed up on her shore again, or perhaps she really was done with me. In any case, she was behaving as she had when I was fifteen and cotton-brained and unable to understand why she wouldn't look at me. She moved around the house like a ghost – a shadow against the wall, a rustling on the stairs, a dark outline before her bedroom door closed. If there had ever been a chance for us to be close, for me to seek out her comfort, it had long since passed.

'You're finally taking those down,' she said, nodding to the half-empty wall. '*Hamdilla.*'

I felt a childish urge to pretend I was just rearranging the grid, but I quashed it and resumed peeling off the pieces of paper. She watched me from the doorway, quiet as I removed print after print, laying them down on the growing pile.

'There's a wedding next month,' she said. My hands froze again, although the paper they held trembled slightly. 'We'll go.'

'It's not proper.'

'Why not?' she asked.

'He just died.' I rearranged the pile on the bed, refusing to look at her.

'It will have been long enough by then.'

I didn't say anything. She held herself tense, one thin hand gripping the door jamb, but I didn't argue. Let her make her plans; they were all just words.

'And remind me to ask Nadia where we can get that abomination removed,' she added, pointing at my bare shoulder before turning and shutting the door behind her.

When she was gone, I turned the Goyas over and spread them across the duvet, my hand moving in widening circles until it looked like a grayscale hurricane on an ocean of blue. A few fell off the edge and fluttered to the floor. There was a cyclone in my mind, thoughts whirling and spinning, loop-the-loops of sour words and bitter contention. It felt like all the arguments, all the hurts, all the doubts were speeding across my mind like a movie. I didn't hate my parents; there was resentment, and perhaps there always would be, but I didn't hate them.

Maybe the Goyas aren't a story, but a series of nightmares and worst-case scenarios.

And this final print, number 80, I picked it up from where it had drifted to the floor. The four men, each with an expression more grotesque than the last. Outstretched arms, biting thumbs, screaming mouths. *It is time*, the print declared, and the men appeared eager for it. It is time.

One thought crashed through all the others in my head, demanding to be heard.

My life here is over.

I said the words out loud because thinking is passive whereas speaking would make it so. I had to believe as much.

Have you ever seen an orchid flower die? It happens in less time than you'd think. The flower is there, in bloom and fine, and then suddenly one day, it falls, just plops straight off the stem to the pot below. You pick it up with gentle fingers, though you know it's dead. It doesn't look dead, that's the problem. The petals are white, veiny and dry, but still white, no indication that entropy has won.

And the plant is fine. It may be no more than a bare stalk, but it's erect and proud, confident that another flower will bloom.

The sameness of my routine was vomit-inducing. The nausea assaulted me at the coffee shop I stopped at on my way to work; it settled in when the barista called out my order without asking me what I wanted. I had a 'usual'. The traffic was backed up on the 40, like always, cars inching along and weaving through lanes, looking for the one moving the fastest. I had visions of speeding up on overpasses, of crashing through barriers, launching myself onto the roads below. Bile flirted with my esophagus when the same awful songs came on the radio.

The air outside my window was warm and damp, like a sauna or one of those hot yoga classes people say are so good for you. Our long trek through another summer had begun. Soon there would be blistering winds and gritty sandstorms, suffocating days and humid nights. The dust would invade our homes, our bodies, our everything, scratching away at us as though trying to erode our very existence. It would continue for months on end until you were certain the sky would never be clear again.

'Hey.'

I turned from the window and smiled at Yousef, who had an elbow propped up on my cubicle wall. 'Hey.'

'All good?'

'Can't complain,' I replied, doodling on the desk calendar before me.

'Are you feeling better?'

'Yeah, loads.'

'What about . . . ?'

I looked up to find him nodding towards his shoulder. I waved away his concern with a smile. 'I forget it's there.'

'Have your parents seen it?'

I gave him an abbreviated version of the goings-on at my

house: the fight with my parents, the words we'd flung at one another, the threats and pleas. He nodded along, unsurprised by any of it.

'You can't really be upset,' he said when I was done. 'You knew that's how they would take it.'

'I know,' I agreed. My doodle had morphed into a bird, some alarming creature that looked like a cross between a crow and an owl.

Despite the inhospitality of the weather, I wished I were outside. I yearned for every kind of freedom possible. I wished that I were a bird, a bulbul or zarzour, soaring from branch to branch, alighting maybe here, maybe there. To be a child again, blissfully ignorant of everything to come, or a man, able to get in a car and drive to Istanbul – thirty-odd hours and you're there.

I wondered where I could be in thirty-odd hours if I really put my mind to it.

I took a long coffee break, going to a café a few blocks from my office. The weather had shifted, the wind kicking up, hostile and sharp with dust. It didn't deter me, and as I walked I pretended it was a glorious spring day. I imagined the sky was blue and not flat beige, that those shapes on the horizon weren't dust clouds, but the fluffier sort. I skipped across busy intersections, skirting honking cars and past construction workers milling about work sites with nothing to do.

There was a ticking time bomb in my breast. I could feel it, thumping against the *yathoom*, just begging me to do something.

To just, for the love of God, *do* something. I felt restless, reckless, as though, given the opportunity, I could walk forever, to the edge of my life and straight off the side perhaps.

Walking back to work, I noticed a black car keeping pace with me. At first I thought it was just someone who was lost or maybe looking for a place to park, but it stayed on my heel as I approached my building and I eventually turned to look. An Indian driver was in the front, and in the back seat, behind a dark window and even darker sunglasses, I made out the precise features of Bu Faisal's wife.

The car stopped, the engine rumbling with a heavy purr, and she lowered the window to greet me. There was an awkward moment, and I hesitated before discarding the idea of leaning into the car to kiss her cheeks. Her face was made up to the fullest: caked foundation and bronzer too dark for her tone; rosy cheeks; and a bright peach gloss on her lips.

'How's your mother doing?' she asked when we'd exchanged greetings.

'*Hamdilla.*' It was the standard reply, and she accepted it with a frown of sympathy.

'I didn't see you at the funeral.' She lowered her massive sunglasses, revealing heavily drawn brows two shades darker than her walnut hair and eyes loaded with green shadow and spider-black lashes.

'I was sick,' I replied, my lie smooth and rehearsed.

She pursed her lips. '*Salamat.* Not too sick, I hope.'

Sick enough, I thought, but I said, 'Just a stomach bug.'

She nodded, and her dark eyes looked me up and down.

'You look like you've put on some weight, so maybe it's not such a bad thing.' Such comments were commonplace. A woman's body or face were fair game for anyone to comment on, and it was best not to respond to such things. She smiled wide to soften the insult. 'Bu Faisal's secretary says you stopped by the other day.'

'I did,' I replied, my eyes wandering to the office building up ahead like I had somewhere to be. 'It was about some work thing.'

'Work thing?' she repeated with a nod and a secret sort of smile. 'Nancy said it didn't look like you had come from work.'

What had I been thinking, showing up at his office looking like that? How could I have thought it would go unnoticed? I struggled to keep my voice even. 'I hadn't, but I had papers to drop off.'

She nodded again and tapped her sunglasses against her lips. 'A company like yours must have messengers for that sort of thing. Surely you don't need to go so out of your way?'

'Of course,' I replied.

She tilted her head, looked at me like she knew something I didn't, like her eyes not only saw through me, but into the future, like she could see into my head and knew what I was considering.

There was a part of me that, when faced with his flesh-and-blood wife, recoiled from the idea. The scandal would be horrendous, and with me not there, it would fall squarely on my mother's shoulders. And my father's. They didn't deserve it, but we were, all of us, accustomed to getting what we didn't deserve. I didn't deserve what had happened to me, Mama didn't deserve such a cousin, and Baba didn't deserve all these lives that made no sense and that he couldn't keep in line.

But life was intolerable, and I could not, would not, stomach it any longer. The panic flapped above my head like the wings of a thousand insects.

Later, after I'd swallowed several cups of coffee and shuffled the pending documents on my desk into a multitude of configurations, after I'd given the hybrid bird wings and sent him soaring across the calendar, I found myself on the internet pulling up plane tickets. I searched for flights leaving that night, leaving in the early hours of the morning, leaving in the next hour. I listed, in big bold letters, all the possible destinations. Capitals and travel hubs marched down and across my notepad like little soldiers telling me not to be afraid: Paris (did the Marais fit after all?), London (my parents would immediately suspect it), New York (infrequent flights; I would have to transit somewhere). There were destinations less desirable – Moscow in April hardly seemed like a sensible idea. There were patently ridiculous destinations, but that didn't stop me from click-click-clicking away at images of the Maldives or Mykonos or Tenerife.

I put my head in my hands and cloned myself a dozen times over, sending each little feeler-me out on a hypothetical journey. These simulacrums scampered off, reporting back on how easy it was to get on in Paris, even if you didn't speak the language – the French are much friendlier than people think. London was quite expensive, they concurred, but then again, the dinar was awfully strong. New York was no better, but my savings would stretch even further there. I picked up my pen again, filling my desk calendar with crude doodles of monuments: leaning Big Bens and Eiffel Towers, indistinct Statues of Liberty and cartoonish Kremlins.

A beep sounded from the computer, and I looked over to see a new email notification. I ignored it and as my eyes returned to the pen, they swept across the Japanese fan Bu Faisal had given me all those weeks before. It had been folded up and tucked into the mug I used as a pen holder. Yousef must have done it, not wanting to risk it being stolen or lost while I was out of the office. I plucked it up and unfolded it, fanning it all the way open, and ran my fingers lightly over the delicate silk and etched bamboo. I traced the scene, my fingertip following the lines of trees and sky and the ladies trapped in that forever-winter.

22

I Have Chosen

The little plane is hovering over Newfoundland, about to cross into the US. We've been on this plane for ten hours, and still when we land our journey won't be complete. Bu Faisal – he's asked me to call him Nasser, but I don't think of him that way yet – won't say where the next plane will take us; he insists on treating this like a vacation rather than what it is – a brutal tearing of the fabric of my life.

It was a perverse and manic spontaneity that gripped me as I held that Japanese fan, the one that is tucked into my bag under the seat in front of me. There is a part of me that's quite sure I've lost my mind. No rational person would behave as I have in the last few hours. What sane person waltzes into their boss's office and quits? Without preamble or explanation? Who then renounces the balance of their salary and paid vacation time in lieu of providing notice? Just so they can leave, free and clear, that day?

You'd have to be at least a little crazy to then go home and try to pack up your life as quickly as possible while arousing as little suspicion as you can. My parents weren't home, but the maids were, and all it would take was one phone call from them to bring the whole thing crashing down.

It's amazing how little the junk you accumulate matters. When you're forced to squeeze your life into two suitcases and a carry-on, you learn what items you can and can't live without. Aside from clothing and shoes, in went books on art, and posters unframed and carefully rolled back into their tubes, pictures of my family and Mona and Zaina, my sketchbooks and illustrations.

One illustration – a Waterhouse girl, her veil whipping in the wind – I'd had mounted and framed a couple of weeks back. I sent it off with the driver, wrapped up with a note in an envelope with Rashid's name on it, to Mona's house.

I considered leaving a letter for Mama; all while packing, I drafted and redrafted it in my head, but no words seemed sufficient for the enormity of what I was doing to her. I thought of calling Baba, pulled up his contact in my phone log a few times, but I never hit 'dial'. For a moment I considered calling my sister, but Nadia was sure to panic and drive over to intercept me. I would contact them later, I decided, which is when I did something that, if not a crazy person then certainly a stupid person would do.

I sent three texts – to Yousef, Mona, and Zaina. All variations on the same message, variations of the same reason for what I was doing.

It was one of the girls who called Baba.

*   *   *

He found me sucking down a coffee while I waited for Bu Faisal to return from the currency exchange. I was thinking about the calls I'd have to make when we got to wherever we ended up – calls to the girls, to Nadia, to Yousef, Mama and Baba. I was thinking about repercussions, about tearing things asunder, about actions you can't ever take back.

When our eyes met, I had a childish impulse to turn and run to the bathroom. My stomach leapt into my throat and the coffee burned like acid in my gut.

He looked sad, almost as sad as when I was fifteen. He looked older, too, as though our lives and all our choices had finally caught up with him. Or maybe I was seeing him through new eyes. I don't know.

Lies were told.

'I'm travelling on my own,' I said, while my eyes darted around the departure hall to see if I could spot Bu Faisal.

'Everything will be fine, if you just come home,' Baba said, his voice strange and pleading.

A blatant lie, one I didn't even bother disputing. Much of what was said were regurgitated lines, but we recited them as faithfully as actors in a play.

He was angry, his eyes flashing as he said, 'Come home now.'

I shook my head. 'What are you going to do,' I whispered, 'drag me kicking and screaming through the airport?' His eyes darted this way and that, taking in the travelers hustling around us. 'Because there will be kicking, Baba.' His eyes returned to mine. 'Screaming, too.'

'Why are you doing this?' he asked, his voice as low as mine.

I looked to the ceiling; anything to keep the tears from falling. I wouldn't cry there. 'I can't breathe here. I can't breathe.'

He glanced down at the blue passport clutched in my hand, with the boarding pass sticking out of it, and I had a wild notion of him ripping it away from me and taking off down the escalator. His eyes moved to the bag at my feet, stuffed and bulging with last minute things I'd decided I couldn't part with: photos of my family and the girls, from back when things were simpler; a dull blue and white *nazar* pendant from a night long ago in California; a little ceramic shaggy cow Yousef had brought me from a trip to Scotland; that pink soup bowl of a candle.

'I already failed you once.'

I looked up, but he wouldn't meet my eye; his gaze hovered somewhere over my shoulder, on the neon of a store sign or the muted brown and green of the coffee shop.

'If you go . . .' He shook his head, looked down at our feet. 'I couldn't protect you there. I'd be failing you all over again.'

I was filled with a curious combination of warmth and shame. I glanced down at his hands, his right one fisted and impotent. I saw the knuckles as they'd been, purple and swollen. He'd hit Omar so hard that he'd sprained the wrist and broken the thumb. Somehow, in my head, that physical assault had absolved him of any blame over what had happened. I'd always directed that at Mama, at her pleading for his ultimate silence on the matter, but perhaps there was fault to be laid at his feet. Or perhaps none of it mattered, and we'd all passed the point where it might have been salvaged. In any case, I had no desire to point fingers.

Baba's countenance was alive with emotion: shock, sadness, relief (perhaps?), maybe pride – I couldn't tell. His face was a symphony, and I couldn't pick out the strings. Underneath it all was defeat, I think. He had the look of a man finally, finally, buckling under a world he could not control. How long had he labored, an Atlas on bended knee, desperate to hold up these lives that just wouldn't work out the way he'd planned?

I wished I could snatch that look away, replace it with something benign or comforting, but it was too late for that.

I tucked myself into his chest. His arms wrapped around me and he pressed 'Shhs' against my hair, like he had when I was a child and I'd fallen down. Reassurances spilled from my lips: 'It wasn't your fault', 'It was a long time ago', 'You don't have to protect me anymore'.

I'm not sure if we believed it; the words sounded hollow to my ears, but they managed to fill the space between us.

I don't think my mother and I will ever reconcile. I don't think our future holds a big heart-to-heart where she listens and I understand. I don't know what she will think of the choices I've made; I don't even know whether she *knows* what I've decided yet. If she doesn't, she will soon enough. Word travels fast, and it won't be long before the whole country knows.

At least I'm no longer her burden . . . Her shame, perhaps, but no longer a burden.

There is no longer the question of what to do with me; whether she likes it or not, the answer has been provided. She can insist that she tried to give me a 'normal' life, a life that I should have wanted, a life as close to her safe and predictable one as she could get. She can tell people how I rejected it, time and again I rejected what she had sought so tirelessly to provide me with. She can talk about how she tried her best, but what do you do with so obstinate a daughter? She's free to shake her head along with the other aunties, lamenting my wasted youth.

'She's someone else's problem now.' That's what the nods from all the aunties will wish to convey. There will be those who will chuckle, and then pass along rumors and say what a gold-digger I am and how this seems like something I would do. They won't know why I've been such trouble; they won't know the history and that my actions, if not justifiable, are certainly reasonable. And maybe Mama, in her heart of hearts, where my father cannot see, will be just a little bit glad.

I've been waiting for the panic, for the can't-breathe, malfunctioning, make-it-stop sense of impending doom. I keep expecting the anxiety to metastasize, to mushroom into a nuclear cloud of blinding terror.

I expected it on the plane when the cabin crew went through their safety spiel. The signs were there – jumpy knees, tingly fingers, that fainting sensation not far away. But they went through their adopt-the-brace-position and help-yourself-before-helping-others routine, and I was still all there.

I was calm as we flew over Iran, the peaks of Zagros snowy and jagged outside my window. I dozed as we crossed into Turkey, waking every once in a while as the magnitude of it all pressed me deeper into my seat – or were we still gaining altitude? The night was black and heavy over the continent. Below us were tiny villages lit up in orange and white, twisting and arching against the Rhine like koi fish.

The moving plane on the map was crossing into that great blue expanse when Bu Faisal fell asleep. Just as it does when I stump him with an indelicate question, his face looked youthful in slumber. The generous mouth was slack under a mustache that twitched every now and then. His thick brows were relaxed, not pinched like I felt mine to be. I lifted my hand to his face, placing the pads of two fingers to the skin between his brows. It was cool, slightly dry, the hair coarse against my fingers. He didn't stir, not even his breathing changed. I brought my hand to my own face, smoothing the skin between my brows, trying to relax the knot there. I saw movement beneath his eyelids, a sign of deep sleep, and I wondered how he could be so untroubled. The panic nearly lit me up like flash paper then; it came on so strong I gripped my armrest to stay grounded – no small feat when you're 40,000-plus feet in the heavens. Did his calm stem from a lack of commitment? A knowledge that if I got to be too much, he could just leave? What would I do then?

We're flying over land now, and still he sleeps. On the inside of my left wrist, I draw yet another Ariel. In miniature, in India ink, he balances on the bough of a vein. Upraised arms, elated mouth, stars like fireworks bursting at his side.

I remind myself that I'm not entirely useless. I have skills, marketable ones even. I will not be dependent on him. I'm accepting his help; I'll accept what will no doubt be his excessive generosity, but I will also stand on my own. If I'm leaning on him now, I won't be forever . . . But then what – do I throw him over when I feel steady on my feet? Looking at him now – his calm face, his shoulders filling the seat beside me – I can't imagine it.

I have chosen him. I can't say why, or what I want him to be, but I have chosen him.

His breathing changes, a hitch and a puff, and then his eyes open, one at a time. He scans my features; for what, I don't know. Then he makes a silly face, and I smile for the first time in a long time. He doesn't touch me. He's so wary of touching me, so careful of where his hands land, where his body is in relation to mine. It makes me feel delicate, important, like what I might want matters to him.

I am thirty, and I have made my first decision. I have chosen this; I have chosen him.

I have chosen.

ACKNOWLEDGMENTS

There are many people responsible for the book in your hands. Certainly more than I could ever hope to name . . . but I'll try.

My eternal gratitude goes to my fantastic agent, Melissa Edwards of Stonesong Literary Agency, for believing in me and in this story. You are my champion. Many, many thanks also go to Ben Fowler at Abner Stein for being so encouraging and supportive and for bringing the next person I'm going to thank into my life – Ann Bissell! Ann, I could not have hoped for a better editor. From the first meeting your enthusiasm and feel for Dahlia and her story moved me more than you can ever know. I'm so honoured to have partnered with you on this book. I also owe a huge debt of gratitude to the Borough Press family – Suzie Dooré, Emilie Chambeyron, Amber Burlinson, Ore Agbaje-Williams, and everyone else who made me feel so valued and who put so much time and thoughtful effort into this book.

A quick thank you to my professors and fellow writers at the University of Edinburgh for pushing me to write a story about Kuwait when I really didn't want to. This book began in the cold basements of George Square, and I'm so thankful for all your notes. Special thanks to Catherine Cronenberg, Jenny Gray, and Christina Neuwirth for their support and friendship.

I'd like to thank my friends for the constant encouragement, especially Deena AlShatti, Dana Zubaid, Nilufar Khaja, Badria AlHumaidhi, Bodour Behbehani, and Waleed Jarjouhi. A special thank you to Fawaz AlFares for coming up with the perfect title at the eleventh hour! And a super-special thank you to Fatima AlJassim whose Twitter habit makes all things possible. Thank you for watching the hashtags and pushing me when I wanted to stop pushing myself, for reading every draft of this book, and for giving such helpful notes. This book honestly wouldn't have happened without you.

I must thank my parents and the rest of my extended family for their boundless support, especially Anwar AlAmmar for being such a great sounding board for ideas, and my mother, Linda, for never telling me I couldn't read what I wanted to read.